Breck's Quandary

mark mitten

MILFORD HOUSE

an imprint of Sunbury Press, Inc.
Mechanicsburg, PA USA

MILFORD
HOUSE

an imprint of Sunbury Press, Inc.
Mechanicsburg, PA USA

NOTE: This is a work of fiction. Names, characters, places and incidents are the product of the author's imagination or are used fictitiously, and any resemblance to actual persons, living or dead, business establishments, events or locales is entirely coincidental.

For information about special discounts for bulk purchases, please contact Sunbury Press Orders Dept. at (855) 338-8359 or orders@sunburypress.com.

To request one of our authors for speaking engagements or book signings, please contact Sunbury Press Publicity Dept. at publicity@sunburypress.com.

ISBN: 978-1-62006-019-3 (Trade paperback)

Library of Congress Control Number: Application in Process

FIRST MILFORD HOUSE PRESS EDITION: May 2019

Product of the United States of America
0 1 1 2 3 5 8 13 21 34 55

Set in Bookman Old Style
Designed by Crystal Devine
Cover by Mark Mitten
Edited by Lawrence Knorr

Continue the Enlightenment!

CHAPTER 1

Black Ice

The headlights were dull. They barely did anything. It was obvious Breck was driving on black ice. He knew there was a drop-off on the right. A rocky cliff towered on his left, gritty and overhung, he could feel it, but so many snowflakes were swirling from the sky all he could see was the hood of his old beater Jeep. The speedometer needle bounced around the number ten. What did they make these headlights out of? A flashlight could do better. A candle could do better. All those fancy SUVs back in town, with their diamond white beams. He wanted headlights like that.

Breck kept both hands on the steering wheel.

Until the lighter knob clicked in the dashboard.

He reached down without taking his eyes off the road and pulled it out. The tiny red coils gave off a soft glow. He had a cigarette in his mouth but stopped short of lighting it. He wasn't going to light it. He wanted to. If for no other reason than some hot smoke in his lungs.

"I thought you quit."

Breck was talking to himself. He pushed the lighter back into the dash, crumpled the cigarette and stuck it in his coat pocket.

The Jeep was an icebox. The heater barely worked. It was a 1977 CJ7 with the original soft top and old rusty snaps that held it in place. Every winter Breck wedged a big piece of cardboard in front of the radiator grill to keep the bitter winds from cooling off the engine. It didn't do much. The air coming from the vents at his feet was lukewarm.

Red Mountain Pass and its death drop ravine. When were they going to send a road crew and fix the guardrails? Year after year, snow slides broke loose and raked them off, casting the twisted steel into thin air, and down, down onto the river rocks far below and every summer a road crew had to replace them with new ones. Backhoes and orange cones. Those boys had steady work and steady pay. Not a bad gig.

All this fresh snow. It was late in the spring for a snowstorm this bad. Down in Denver, it was typical May weather. Sunny and seventies. But this was the high country, and the rules didn't apply at this altitude.

Driving under that cliffside was nerve-racking. Breck grit his teeth and double checked his lap belt was clipped tight, although if anything broke loose the Jeep would get swept over the edge in the blink of an eye and there wouldn't be a thing he could do about it.

He kept it in low gear and went slow. Four-wheel drive or not, black ice didn't discriminate.

Finally, the road curved out of the canyon and the danger was over. With trees on both sides, Breck's breathing came easier. The road was still slick as glass but what was the worst-case scenario? Slide into a tree trunk? At least the road crew wouldn't be winching him out of a 300-foot ravine.

The windshield wipers swished back and forth, leaving wet streaks. Breck leaned forward, pressing against the steering wheel to see better, and wiped the fog off the glass. There it was. A little green street sign—Timber Ridge Road. Wheel tracks wound into the woods, but the fresh powder was filling them in quick.

The CB was on. Mounted behind the stick shift, it had an orange digital display. Blocky channel numerals that flickered. It was hard to read and harder to reach, and it was also useless. Ever since the snow started falling it was nothing but static. And of course, his cell phone never got a signal outside of town. He didn't even bother checking to see if it was working.

Breck shifted into first gear and angled up Timber Ridge Road. Getting off the icy pavement made him feel better. Side roads never got plowed, but driving through the snow was much better than driving over exposed ice. The tires had something to grip.

A quarter mile in, Breck cut the headlights and eased to a stop. He knew where he was. He knew all these roads and back-roads. This one in particular. Not the first time he'd been there.

Nestled in a stand of bare gray aspen, just a dark shape in the night, was an old cabin with a green tin roof. Of course, almost all the cabins had a green tin roof. But this address he knew, from a spin cycle of small-time drug busts.

Breck frowned.

He did not know who owned the black Range Rover parked out front.

Rotating the cylinder on his .44 Special, Breck checked to make sure all five chambers contained a live round.

The cabin was dark.

A flashlight was lying in the passenger seat. Taking it, Breck clicked it on and off. Batteries worked. He checked the CB one last time, fiddling with the squelch dial just for kicks. Nothing. So he turned the radio off, in case it squawked at the wrong moment, got outside, and stepped into the darkness.

"Alright," he mumbled, zipping up his coat. "Good times."

CHAPTER 2

Burn, Little Man

The Quandary County Sheriff's Office wasn't in a regular office building. It was in an old stone church built in the 1800s. Peaked roof. Stained glass. Pretty much what anyone would expect. As long as they weren't expecting ductwork or proper heating. A big potbelly stove took up one whole corner of the room.

Deputy Jenny O'Hara cupped her hands and blew air inside to warm up. She had on a bright green marshmallow coat with a Quandary County Sheriff's logo. Men's size XL and way too big. Trying to see outside, she caught her reflection in the front window. She cringed. The standard issue stocking cap had a giant fluffy matching-green tassel that wobbled. Turn to the left, wobble. Turn to the right, wobble. Her badge might as well say Deputy of Whoville.

Even wearing her warmies, Jenny felt chilled to the bone. She glanced over at the stove. Why not shove in another chunk of split wood? The thing was blistering hot. But her desk was about as far away from the stove as logistically possible. As a bonus, it was planted by the front door. Every time it opened, a fresh blast of cold air swirled right in. Not that anyone was coming or going.

But first, she picked up the CB mic and pressed the button.

"Come in, Breck. Come in. This is Jenny, can you hear me? Please respond."

Static.

The channel number flickered on the tiny screen like it was about to go out for good. She hated these CBs. Breck bought them off eBay last summer. *Vintage.* That was the word choice used in the listing. Like it was a good thing. One for the station, one for the Jeep, and one for the snowmobile but the snowmobile was parked out front with a bad solenoid or something. Did snowmobiles even have solenoids? It hadn't worked all winter, and they didn't have the money to fix it. And neither of them were good at fixing snowmobiles, it turned out.

"Some trucker is missing this thing right about now." She scratched at an old Confederate flag sticker. "Piece of crap."

Jenny pulled off the stocking cap and ran her fingers through her red hair. Then she took a pair of scissors and snipped off the tassel.

"You're going to burn, little man."

She went to the stove and flicked it into the flames. Then she loaded it with as much wood as she could cram in there. Breck was always telling her to go easy with the wood pile, wood wasn't cheap, yadda yadda.

Going back to the front window, Jenny pressed her face to the glass. The snow was really coming down and it was getting worse every minute. She could barely make out anything besides the dumpster and the snowmobile. A couple of amber street lamps on Main Street, twinkling in the snowy haze like stars. No one was out in this mess. Breck shouldn't be either.

The phone had rung earlier before the weather turned bad. An anonymous tip.

Somebody got a peek through a neighbor's window and spotted a room full of marijuana plants. Heat lamps and water hoses. An illegal grow room. 1355 Timber Ridge Road. Yeah, that made sense. Jenny knew who lived there. Freddy Bolton, local stoner. It would be no surprise if he was growing his own product now.

She tried talking Breck out of going since he had to drive up the canyon to get there, but he thought it was better that way. The element of surprise. Freddy would be holed up inside, watching TV or playing video games. The plants in plain sight. What was he going to do, lie about it? It would be an easy bust.

"That's a pretty nosy neighbor—peeping through windows in these conditions. Kind of pervy, too." A good reminder to pull the blinds at night.

Her laptop was on the desk, open. A weather radar filled the screen. A big storm inching its way across the map. *Winter Storm Warning* was flashing.

She picked up her cell phone and stared at it. Nope. Zero bars. She skidded it across the desktop, then grabbed the CB mic one more time.

"Pick up, Breck. It's not worth it. You should just come on back. You copy?"

Static.

"Hey. The storm is getting really bad. It's not safe. Backup can't get there with the roads this bad . . . Breck? The storm is messing up the cell signal, by the way. My phone is useless. All we got is CB. Copy that?"

He didn't copy that. She wasn't getting through. Maybe he was fine. And maybe he was at the bottom of the ravine.

Jenny sighed and looked out the window again. That junky snowmobile. Buried in its own little tomb of snow and ice, handlebars sticking out like frozen arms, forever grasping for help that never arrived. She gave it a new name every day. Glacier Neanderthal. Frosty The Broke Mobile. Donner Pass Meat Wagon. Crime Scene Santa.

"Even if that thing worked, I'm not driving up these roads in a frickin' blizzard. You better be safe and sound, Breck. Cuz I'm the only backup you got."

CHAPTER 3

Bad Reception

B reck jumped when he heard a snap. It came from the trees. He shined the flashlight into the forest, back and forth, and there it was—a mule deer. Cage of antlers and two glassy black eyes, staring right back at him.

Each snowflake that dropped through the beam twinkled, sharp and distinct. Little crystals.

Breck lowered his revolver.

"Don't worry. I'm not after you."

Breck cut the flashlight. Let his eyes adjust to the darkness. It was basically pitch black. The low clouds cut off any stars or moonlight. Even the glow of the town in the distance was gone in this weather.

Through the boles and branches, a neighbor had his living room lit up. An orange rectangle floating in the blackness.

His eyes went back to the cabin. The Range Rover parked out front. Brushing the snow from his face, Breck moved through the fresh powder, cautious. He brought his gun up again.

He waited. Watching. Nothing moved.

Something was off here.

Clicking on his light, Breck tried to get a look inside the vehicle, shining it in the windows. The glass had a heavy tint but in the beam, he could see through. The front seats were empty. But the back was jammed full of potted plants, each in a small plastic bucket. Breck knew marijuana when he saw it. Couple more months and these would be ready for harvest.

He headed for the cabin. It was an older construction, maybe from the '70s. Thick Ponderosa pine logs with white chinking that looked like cement. The front door had an old-timey look, too, with a big oval window, flowers etched in the glass.

Breck shined his light through the large living room window. A couch, TV, bookcase. Fireplace. Coffee table speckled with old cigarettes and roach butts. No one was in there, but not too long ago someone had been. A pizza box was laying on the coffee table, and a half-drunk bottle of Coke.

Breck checked the door handle. It clicked. Unlocked. Slowly, he pushed it open and lit up the entry. Shadows danced all the way down a narrow hallway, carpeted in ratty, stained Berber.

"Sheriff's Office!" Breck stepped inside. "Freddy, it's me. I'm coming in."

The light switch didn't work. He flicked it up and down a couple of times.

"Still a little stony, bro? Turn on the lights. This isn't a joke."

Breck had been in there before and knew the basic layout. The living room was on the right, through the archway. Bathroom door on the left. Straight ahead, down the hall, was the kitchen.

A strong waft of weed. No mistaking that heavy, earthy smell, was there?

A little further up the hall, past the bathroom, was a second door. It was cracked open, emanating a soft warm glow. Breck gave it a push and peered inside. A bedroom, but no bed. Glowing heat lamps dangled from ceiling hooks, with those big chicken shack light bulbs. A half dozen circular fans. Clumps of dirt were stomped in the carpet and someone had snaked a water hose through a hole in the wall. A grow room. Round impressions in the carpet—that was where the plants had been. Now they were in the SUV parked out front.

"Too late, Freddy. You're busted."

Up ahead, in the kitchen, around the corner, Breck heard the raspy flick of a lighter. A faint yellow light shined for just a moment and he saw the refrigerator and stove but it was all he could see from where he was standing before the flame went out.

Breck moved down the hallway with soft, cautious steps. Leaning around the corner, he swept his flashlight around the room, gun up.

Seated in a chair, with a Glock laying on the dining table in plain sight, was a well-dressed man with dark hair and eyes, and a trimmed mustache. He drew on a cigarette and exhaled gray smoke. It wasn't Freddy.

"You are trespassing, amigo."

Breck tensed up. This was it. What was off?

"Who are you?"

"You don't wanna know."

He had a thick Mexican accent. Breck felt a tingle in his stomach. This was not what he was expecting. The town of Quandary was in the middle of the Colorado mountains. It was a ski town. Tourists and art dealers. College kids on winter break.

Squinting in the flashlight, the stranger took another drag.

Breck didn't like this.

"Get down on the floor! Now!"

The strange man smiled.

"I don't think I will do that."

Someone hit Breck over the head.

CHAPTER 4

Bad Council

The Denver meteorologist kept pointing at a giant green screen map and making gestures like he was waving in a Boeing 747 for a landing.

"Yeah, I'm not blind," Jenny muttered.

The storm had shifted. The worst part was angling over Quandary even then. It was supposed to curve out over the plains, according to the forecast earlier in the day, but here it was, spinning out over the Continental Divide instead. Ramping up into a full-blown blizzard.

"How come these weather guys always get it wrong? That's your job, dude. Get it right."

Jenny clicked the mouse to shut him up, then closed the laptop. The WIFI was getting glitchy anyway. She was surprised it was still working, actually. The internet service in Quandary sucked on a good day, let alone in bad weather.

It was Time for plan B. As much as she didn't want to. Jenny scrolled through her cell for the City Hall number, picked up the landline receiver and dialed. It rang a couple of times.

"City Hall."

Jenny cleared her throat.

"This is Deputy Jenny O'Hara. Is the mayor available?"

"One moment please."

The receptionist was a young blonde intern named . . . Brittany maybe? That sounded right. Some snowboardy college name. Jenny could hear her snap her gum.

"This is Mayor Matthews. I was just heading home. How can I help you, deputy?"

Jenny sat up in her chair. That was quick. She thought for sure it was going straight to voicemail.

"Sorry to bother you, sir, but I can't get through to Breck, and I'm concerned for his safety. He went out on a call, he hasn't radioed in, and this blizzard . . ."

"Deputy, is this really something to bother the Mayor of Quandary with? It's after hours, the roads are bad and I'm . . . Just because he didn't radio in doesn't mean anything. Maybe he stopped for a burger and a doughnut, took a nap in the driver's seat, who the hell knows. Have you tried *looking* for him?"

The fellow sounded irritated. He wasn't exactly the cheery type, anyhow. Jenny clenched the edge of the desk with her free hand.

"Well, no sir. But this wasn't a regular call. Breck is investigating an illegal grow house, he hasn't responded to the radio and it's been way too long. You see, we had an anonymous tip."

"What's the problem, deputy? Go. Drive out there. That's your job. That's why I pay you."

Jenny turned red. She hated this guy. Didn't take much to remember why.

"No patrol car, remember? You and the city council have busted our budget. All I got is the department snowmobile and it's a flaming piece of junk. I can't take that thing up the pass."

"You're a big girl. Figure it out. Call me if there really *is* a problem."

He hung up.

The dial tone hummed.

"Nice."

Jenny put the receiver down, a little too hard, making the whole desk shake. Mayor Matthews. What a douche. Typical politician. Everything backward and nothing ever gets done. And the special icing? He had it out for them, for no good reason.

She tried the firehouse but got nothing. Not a complete surprise. The fire chief was in Cheyenne at a conference and the only other firefighters were volunteers on call. And no one was on call, apparently. That was messed up. Good thing it was a blizzard and not a forest fire.

Just for a moment, Jenny considered calling Breck's younger brother, Danny. He ran the Quandary Brewery, just up the street.

He had a heavy duty pickup truck with four-wheel drive. But Breck wouldn't like that. Relying on Danny, for police business. Or at all, for any reason. They lived in the same tiny mountain town, but Jenny knew those two barely saw each other. Good old-fashioned family tension.

She stared at the CB radio again, as if just by staring at it she could get a response. And it worked.

"Jenny . . ." It was Breck. "You there?"

CHAPTER 5

In the Wind

Sitting in the driver seat, Breck shivered. He tried to start the engine. It cranked and cranked, but didn't turn over. He leaned his head against the steering wheel.

The CB crackled and Jenny's voice made it through the static.

"Breck. What's going on out there? Been trying . . . radio . . . for hours."

He fumbled for the CB. The rubber spiral cord was knotted around the stick shift. He yanked and twisted and somehow managed to unwrap it in the dark.

"They got away."

"Who got away? What hap . . . you . . . alright?"

Her voice sounded a thousand miles away. It was hard to make out what she was saying. The throbbing in his temples didn't help any, either. His head hurt.

Breck felt around behind his ear and winced. Fresh blood on his fingertips.

The Jeep rocked in a gust of wind. Blizzard wind. When did this move in? How long had he been out?

"Who called in that tip?"

"What?" Jenny's voice kept crackling. "Say again?"

Breck turned the key, but on this try, the starter buzzed an angry metal whir. Like a chainsaw chewing up the engine block. Not good. He shut it off immediately and took a few deep breaths. He needed to get this thing looked at. Breck wiped the condensation off the window with his sleeve and eyed Freddy's cabin. The black Range Rover was gone. Worst case scenario, he knew there were some nice warm heat lamps in there.

"Breck? I tried calling . . . dumbass. You copy?"

He tried the ignition one more time. No more metal whir, just a regular coughing starter death choke. It cranked for a few long seconds and then the engine started to chug, and chug some more, and he kept the key turned and tapped the gas pedal and hoped it caught before the battery died.

"Come on, come on."

The CJ7 roared to life.

"Oh, thank God."

He pulled a knob on the dashboard, the headlights came on and the interior gauges lit up. Heater on high. He held his hands over the vent for a few seconds but it was just cold air.

Hard to see in the faint glow of the gauge lights, but the little clock on the dash read 9:15. What time did he go in there? It hurt to think. That was pretty sloppy, not to watch his six. Someone had snuck up behind him. That took some skill. No one snuck up on Breck. Must have been hiding in a closet or the shadows somewhere. He should have gone in there first thing and cleared each room before he ever went into that kitchen.

Freddy's cabin. Breck had been in there a dozen times before. The guy was just a local stoner and a small-time pot dealer whose biggest accomplishment in life was delivering pizza to the right address. But now? A grow room? With heat lamps, a water line and fans. Freddy must have stepped up his game. Growing cannabis in a cabin in the middle of winter took effort and planning, forethought and prep. Maybe he got in over his head, in the process. Because those were cartel men.

"Breck? You there? Talk to me."

The CB cord had wound around the stick shift again like it had a mind of its own. Instead of fighting it, he leaned low to speak into the mic.

"Tell you when I see you."

CHAPTER 6

Heavy Is the Crown

Outside City Hall, the receptionist Brittany scraped the snow off her windshield, got inside and slowly inched out of the parking lot. The snow was deep but she made it into the street.

Mayor Matthews watched her tail lights, two bright red blips in the darkness.

"Stop riding your brake or you're going to spin out."

But of course, the girl couldn't hear him. No one could. He was all by himself. Everyone had gone home. Everyone—meaning Brittany and Mrs. Long, the librarian. City Hall wasn't exactly a big building, and certainly nothing ornate. A couple of offices, conference room, and a council chamber. The public library took up the rest of the place. Could have been worse. One of the jokers on the city council wanted to lease out an empty corner and put in a Subway. It was that fat freak, Mike Jameson. He always had a meatball sandwich at every single council meeting. How he got fat eating Subway was a mystery. The closest one was in Frisco, ten miles away!

Pulling out his car keys, the mayor pushed the auto-start. Time to get those seat warmers going. The running lights on his new BMW X3 SUV flashed and carbon monoxide puffed from the tailpipe. Seeing snow all over his nice car ticked him off. He was the mayor of Quandary. He shouldn't have to scrape snow. There should be a garage. Or a carport at least. Something. He made a mental note for the next council meeting. Bring it up formally. He could get Jameson to second the motion. Mention a Subway might be in the cards, maybe next fiscal year. That's all it would take to get him to bite.

His phone vibrated. A text.

Got the green.

The mayor hefted the phone in his hand like he was weighing the words.

He looked outside again, past the parking lot. The snow was flying. Straight ahead, somewhere in the darkness, was the ski resort. Ski runs stretching up to the peaks. No one was on the slopes in this weather, but they would be in the days to come. The fresh powder would keep it open a few more weeks. Till the end of May if they were lucky. It was good for business. And business was what Mayor Matthews cared about. It was up to him. To keep things running. Progressing. Thinking big.

He smirked.

"Heavy is the crown."

Outside, there was a little metal USGS elevation marker set into the concrete landing by the front door. A small bronze disk, inscribed: *State of Colorado – City of Quandary – 9600 feet.*

He glanced down, through the glass door. The landing and the stairs leading down to the parking lot were buried. He told Brittany to keep it shoveled, and she had gone out there a dozen times. But now that she was gone it was already piling up again. That little marker was under there somewhere.

It was a good reminder. This was not some hick village on the plains. Some yawn town in the Midwest. It was the top of the world. And the top of the world didn't have room for small thinkers. And Mayor Matthews was always thinking big.

You got it all out? he texted.

His phone buzzed again.

Sí.

CHAPTER 7

Rambo Crap

There were two jail cells in the Sheriff's Office. Old school iron rods. Big skeleton style keyholes. Breck liked to say it was full-on Clint Eastwood. An Old West fear factor. Make the baddies sweat a little. Maybe. Jenny thought it looked more like Andy Griffith.

One cell was heaped with shanks of split pine. The woodpile. A pine beetle infestation a few years back had killed off a bunch of trees in the national forest, up along Boreal Pass Road. One of the locals had gone out and chopped a ton of firewood, sold it at the fairgrounds and must have walked away rich. That was smart. Jenny knelt and grabbed a couple of pieces. She did like the smell of burning wood. But she always went home smelling like a campfire.

Headlights flashed through the front window.

Jenny dropped the wood and went over to see. It was the Jeep. Finally. It was almost one o'clock in the morning. Took him long enough. All she could think about was the canyon road above the town, with that steep drop off. No guard rail for a long, long way, and with those twists and turns it was nothing but a free fall if you took your eyes off the pavement for even a second. It was easy to imagine anyone driving off the edge in a midnight whiteout. Was it still called a whiteout at midnight?

Even someone like Breck. What if his cell phone slipped onto the floorboards and he reached down for it at the wrong moment? Or, trying to sneak a cigarette, he reached down for that push-in lighter knob and, zing, went over the edge. Bye-bye. *I'm going to steal that dash lighter. Just take it.*

When the door opened, Breck didn't bother to close it but leaned on the doorjamb, letting in all the cold air.

"Hey. Do you know what time it is? I thought you rolled the Jeep or something." Jenny waited for a reply but didn't get one. "Shut that thing, it's freezing."

Breck pulled the door closed behind him and took a clumsy step but then stopped again. He started to take off his coat but arched his shoulders funny.

"Ow."

Frowning, Jenny checked him over.

"You're hurt."

"Yeah."

"What happened out there?"

"Something's going on. Something . . . big. Bigger than we thought."

She helped him ease off the coat. Wobbling the whole way, Breck hustled for his desk so he could sit down before gravity dropped him first. He sat and sighed. Pointed to the back of his head and Jenny leaned close to see.

"You're bleeding, buddy." Jenny walked over to the bathroom. Tore off some paper towels. "So what's going on with Freddy? The guy is a walking caricature. Delivers pizzas, sells joints. What, now he's got his own greenhouse?"

She turned on the faucet, running some cold tap water over the towels.

"He wasn't there. But I think the cartel was."

"What? You mean, like Mexico?"

Jenny shut off the faucet. She squeezed out the excess in the big washtub sink. If they ever got any funds to fix this place up, she would start right there. Felt like a gas station bathroom. And not one of those nice gas stations. The gross kind.

Breck reached up and touched his hair, and jerked.

"Quit messing with it," she said, coming over. "Here, let me."

The cut on his head had clotted, and she was careful not to make it bleed again.

"How's that?"

"I need an aspirin or something."

"Hold this here for a while."

He reached up and took the cold paper towel wad, and pressed it in place. Jenny sat on the edge of the desk. She looked out the window, thinking. Trying to make sense of it all. How long had she been a deputy in Quandary? Three years now? Long enough to know who was who and Freddy was small time, for sure. Everyone and everything in Quandary was small time.

"This town is like a hundred people. Speeding tickets. Drunk and disorderly. That's about the extent of it. Why would a Mexican cartel be here?" She drummed her fingers on the desktop. "The skiers maybe? Buying weed?"

Breck nodded.

"Lots of rich spoiled Hollywood kids come through here."

Jenny leaned forward, concerned.

"You could have been killed, Breck."

"I wasn't."

That ticked her off.

"Oh, that's a good attitude."

Breck glanced up at her with a wry smile.

"I like to think positive."

But Jenny wasn't impressed.

"Enough with the John Wayne, John McClane, Rambo crap."

"Aw. You're worried about me."

She went back to the woodpile, and scooped up the pieces she had dropped.

"I'm worried about me. If you get murdered by some drug cartel, then I'm going to be sheriff. And I don't wanna be the one who deals with that city council."

She loaded the potbelly and slammed the iron door shut.

Breck's expression was serious. She didn't see that look very often. Did he really just have a run in with a drug cartel? Here?

"The CB. It was pretty choppy," Breck said. "But I think you said you called the mayor?"

"He's such a douche."

"Not much help, then?"

"Mayor McCheese would have been more help." She held her cold hands against the hot stove, hunching close to warm up. "Now I want a cheeseburger."

Breck examined the wet paper towel wad. There was some blood on it, but not much.

"Where's that aspirin?"

CHAPTER 8

Willows

Like every Friday night, Danny Dyer kept the Quandary Brewery open late. Well into the early hours. People always hung out in the tap room until the sun came up. With this surprise spring storm, though, everyone left as soon as the snow began to fly. But Danny kept the doors unlocked and the lights on. What if someone decided to ride it out over a pint of Ten Mile Milk Stout? That was his top seller. Named after the Ten Mile Range, the mountain ridge rising above town. It was dark and not too bitter. He used nitro to give it an extra smooth creamy carbonation.

Growing up, Danny was a straight D student in high school. But as soon as he was out on his own, in his first apartment, he learned how to brew. It started in a bathtub. Old Coors bottles. He graduated to a five-gallon bucket system, then glass carboys and hydrometers. It only got better from there. Now here he was, in his own place. Big stainless-steel mash tuns and fermenting vats lined the back wall.

But Danny wasn't completely alone. There was someone else there. Freddy. He had walked in earlier just as the sun was setting. Spooked. He holed up in Danny's office. Even after the place cleared out, Freddy stayed back there. Blinds were drawn.

Better check on him.

Pulling a pint glass from the stack, Danny went over to the taps and poured a glass of Ten Mile. He rapped on the office door.

"Yo man."

The knob didn't turn. It was locked.

Two little pink fingertips parted the blinds. Freddy, eyes darting.

"Yo man," Danny repeated.

Click. The door eased open a crack.

"It's all good, partner." He handed Freddy the pint. "Come on outta there. Relax."

They went out and sat on stools at the bar. The hum of refrigeration and boiling wort was calming.

"It's over," Freddy muttered. He was hunched over his glass, cradling it like a kitten.

Danny clapped him on the back. "Yeah, it is."

"Naw, I mean the game. The jig. My grow house just got raided."

Raided? Danny slid off his stool and went around to get himself a beer. He grabbed another glass from the stack.

"So what went down exactly?"

Freddy exhaled and took a slow sip.

"Those tamale cats I was telling you about. They showed up again. On my doorstep this time. Only they didn't knock. I had to rabbit out the back door, man."

"Not good." Danny came back around and sat next to him. "They steal it all?"

Freddy shrugged.

"Had to drive all the way down the canyon before my cell worked." He sneered. "I narced on my own grow."

"Well, in that case, Breck's collared them by now and they won't be messing with us from behind bars. No worries. We can start over."

The smell of boiling grain and yeast filled the air. Like a bakery. Danny loved that smell. It reminded him of the homemade wheat bread his mom used to make. When it was fresh from the oven, Breck and Danny would fight over who got the first piece. Danny would knife a pat of butter on his and watch as it melted on the hot bread.

"Gotta do what you gotta do, man."

Freddy didn't reply.

On the wall next to the taps, there were a bunch of framed photos. Most of them were locals taken at the brewery. Laughing faces. Thumbs up. Bare dude butts. But there were also several old Dyer family shots in the mix. Mountain picnics. Trail hikes when they were kids. Danny's eyes always went to a certain one.

Breck holding Danny's hand as they waded up a creek. They were just kids. Striped shirts. Bowl haircuts. With his other hand, Breck was clinging to the willow branches.

"Monterrey." Freddy rubbed his fingers. They were trembling. He was getting jittery again. "Them cats said they were from Monterrey. Back then. First time I saw 'em when they were playing nice. Acted all pro."

Danny nodded. He remembered that day. Freddy told him all about it. They were offering them a business opportunity. Step it up. Get rich. It was sometime in the autumn, before the river iced up. The leaves were yellow. Must have been late September. Early October.

"Who were these guys again? I forget what you said."

Another quick quaky sip.

"Two of 'em. Main cat called himself Zorrero. 'And meet my business partner, El Sangrador.' I looked that one up, man. *The blood-letter.* It was a bad vibe from the get-go."

Danny was always shorter than Breck. As kids and adults. That day, the one in the photo, Danny had been the first one in the creek, drawn in by that foaming ice cold water. Raking his fingers down into the fine sand beneath the surface. Gold. He was always looking for flakes of glittery gold in those mountain creeks. Their dad used to drive the whole family up to see old mines. The kind with thick timber frames. Yellow mounds of gravel. Tailings, they were called. Their dad even brought along a couple of metal plates and taught them to pan for gold in the streams.

"What did you say to them, back then?" Danny asked. "You remember?"

"Yeah, I told them to suck it. They take off and I thought that was it. End of story. Now here I am, how many months later, sitting on the couch, I see 'em pull up in my *driveway,* man. Packing some big ass pistolas. I ain't waiting to see if they knock, so I jet out the back and get the hell out of Dodge."

He gulped the last of his beer until it was gone.

"They were just sizing us up the first time." Danny itched his yellow beard, thinking it through. "That's what they were doing. Now they're moving in, and pushing us out."

"I gotta toss a whiz." Freddy got up and went into the bathroom.

That cold clear creek water. The flecks of gold in the sand. Breck. One hand clenching Danny's, keeping him safe. The other gripping the willow branches. Keeping them both safe.

The front door latch was rusty and it always made a loud metallic clunk when it opened. Danny turned around. Went pale. This had to be them. The Mexican man, Zorrero, and his "business partner," El Sangrador. Stepping inside the brewery. And they were carrying some big ass pistolas.

CHAPTER 9

Magic Potion

Jenny poured two cups of coffee. Dropped a few aspirins into Breck's.

"Magic potion. Drink up."

They were *Ski Quandary!* mugs from the ski resort gift shop.

"The one I saw was the top dog. He had poise." Breck closed his eyes, replaying the kitchen showdown in his mind. "There were two of them. Could have been more, but I doubt it. If they had numbers, they wouldn't hide in the shadows. Jump me like that."

"What was a Mexican cartel doing in Freddy's cabin?" Jenny couldn't believe it. "This is freaking America."

Breck blew the steam from the surface of his coffee. "Good times."

"Were you wearing your vest?"

Jenny frowned. She knew the answer.

"Local sheriff shot?" He shrugged. "That would bring the feds and they know it."

"Lucky you."

Setting her *Ski Quandary!* mug down, Jenny pulled out her sidearm. Checked the loads. Somebody snuck up on Breck and knocked him out. That was insane. And a game changer.

"Okay. Let me get this straight," she said. "Freddy is working with real drug runners now? Our Freddy? Rinky dink Freddy? He's like a walking talking Cabbage Patch doll."

From the corner of her eye, Jenny looked Breck over. She had never seen him shaken up before, even a little bit. He was acting as if nothing happened but she could see something in his eyes. Self-reproach at being dry-gulched? Or the realization that he could have got off worse than just a pistol-whip? Those men could have shot him dead just as easy.

"Those cartels in Mexico are uber violent, you know?" Jenny said. "I've been keeping up with headlines and they've spread all over that country like cancer. It's a cartel freak show down there. The border towns, too. It's sick what they do. Acid. Incinerators. Hell, they chop people up in Cancún these days. You got off easy. You should really wear that vest."

"Preaching to the choir."

"The choir would have been wearing their vests."

"Choirs wear robes."

"You see the State Department posted a travel advisory on their website now?" Jenny flipped open her laptop. "Here, let me read it to you. *Violent crime, such as homicide, kidnapping, carjacking, and robbery, is widespread in Mexico. Do not travel to Colima, Guerrero, Michoacán, Sinaloa, Tamaulipas, due to crime.* And the list goes on. No wonder all those poor people are swimming the Rio Grande."

Breck started to take a sip of coffee but stopped to yawn. Maybe he wasn't being macho. Maybe he was just flat out tired.

With the roads like they were, Jenny knew Breck wasn't going to drive back to his house. Not with his head oozing blood. It wouldn't be the first time he had slept on the jail cell cot. It was his home away from home. He even kept a mummy-style sleeping bag at the office, just for that reason.

"Tell you what. I'll get out of here and let you catch some sleep."

Jenny lived in a small rental cottage a couple of doors down, so she always made it home no matter what the weather was doing, or how long the day lasted.

"To nosey neighbors." She held up her coffee. "And the pervy ones."

Breck raised his mug, too, in a sarcastic toast.

"Yeah."

"Freddy's going to prison for this. And so are his new buddy pals." Jenny tried a big smile to brighten things up. "Hey, don't sweat it. We'll track those crap weasels down, whatever hole they're hiding in."

Breck glanced at the telephone on her desk. He sat up.

"We recorded that, right? The anonymous tip?"

"Hell yeah, we did."

Jenny opened the laptop again. A USB cable connected it to the phone. They always recorded calls to the station. She clicked the mouse until she found the right audio file and hit the play button.

Sheriff's Office. Deputy O'Hara speaking.

Yeah man. There are some big marijuana plants in my, uh, neighbor's cabin. 1355 Timber Ridge Road. Saw it through the window. Got a whole room full of 'em and heat lamps and water hoses and all that. If you get up there quick you can toss these cats in jail. Better hurry, though, before they get away.

And your name, sir?

It's . . . uhh . . . Jack. Jill. Jones. Vin Diesel.

The call ended.

Breck crossed his arms.

"That's Freddy."

They listened to the message again. Breck shook his head.

"He's pinching his nose or something, but that's him."

Jenny was confused.

"Wait, what? Why would he rat on his own gig? With his cartel pals there? That doesn't make sense."

The landline rang. Since she was sitting right there, Jenny grabbed it.

"Sheriff's Office?" She gave Breck a worried look. "We'll be right there."

She hung up the phone, and set her *Ski Quandary!* mug on the desk too hard, spilling coffee in the process, but she didn't care. No time to waste.

"Breck . . ."

"What happened?"

"It's your brother. He's been shot."

CHAPTER 10

Stay Sharp

B reck's Jeep had the original soft top. The old canvas was faded and cracked. Some of the snaps were broken. Jenny wore her stocking cap and zipped her coat for the chilly ride. The wind whistled in from all over the place.

"We need a patrol car." Jenny jammed her hands in her pockets. In the rush out the door, she forgot her winter gloves.

Breck ignored her.

It was true. For a lot of reasons. It may be loud and leaky, but at least he never had to worry about getting stuck in deep snow or summer mud. The Jeep had some big all-terrain tires. BF Goodrich. Big fatties. And a lift kit that jacked up the suspension. High ground clearance was a must. His gas mileage had been bad before that, now it was worse. It got like ten miles per gallon and the worst part was the fuel gauge was broken. Every time he filled up, he did the math. Wrote down the odometer so he knew exactly when he needed to hit the pumps. More than once, he'd sputtered to a stop on some back road. Had to hike out.

At least they didn't have far to go.

The Quandary Brewery was right there on Main Street, only a few blocks from the Sheriff's Office. It was on the edge of town, the last building before the road started winding up the canyon. Breck had just driven past it when he came back into town.

Besides an ambulance with its lights flashing, and Danny's Dodge Ram, there was an old Honda Civic parked out front. It had a triangular light-up sign stuck on top: *High Country Pizza—We Deliver.*

"Hey." Jenny glanced at Breck. "That's Freddy's beater."

Of course, they both knew that. There was only one pizza joint in town. It had become a habit to order pizza at least once a week, usually on Wednesdays. A little midweek boost.

Danny. Shot? Without thinking, Breck reached down and pushed in the dashboard lighter. He suddenly wanted a cigarette. Jenny reached down and pushed it again, turning it off. Self-appointed lung guardian.

"No," she said.

Breck exhaled sharply, his stomach tight. "Yeah, yeah, yeah." He felt that same feeling. Like back at the cabin. He patted his belt holster to make sure his .44 was where it should be.

Those red and blue flashing lights lit up the snowbanks in the parking lot. *Quandary County Medical Center* was written on the doors. The local hospital was barely bigger than a reception desk and an ER, and an ambulance. The nurses took turns going out on calls. Breck mashed the brakes and flung open his door. He started to get out, but paused and glanced over at Jenny.

"He's probably fine." She ginned up a thin, hopeful smile. "He's fine, Breck."

"Stay sharp. Watch our six."

Inside the brewery, Danny was lying on the floor in front of the bar. Two paramedics were kneeling over him. Women, nurses from the hospital. Danny groaned as they lifted him onto a stretcher. He was conscious. They were pressing bandages over his chest. Red blood was all over his shirt, hands, the floor.

Breck leaned over him. "You alright?"

Danny's big yellow beard. Flecked with blood and spit. Eyes fluttering. "Yeah. Just some random robbery gone bad."

"Robbery?"

"Just some college kids. Snowboarders, I think."

"You sure?"

"Yeah, no big deal. No big deal. They didn't get nothing."

The paramedics wheeled him through the front door. He was in serious pain, moaning the whole way out. And like that, he was gone.

Jenny was looking around. Behind the bar, the vats. Fermentation tanks. Steel gauges. She went and opened the office door, her gun drawn.

"All clear in here."

The place was deserted. Breck realized he was breathing heavily. He took a couple of deep ones to steady himself. It had been a long day already, before all this. He suddenly felt overheated and a little shaky. He needed to eat something. He hadn't eaten anything except a bowl of oatmeal, and that was for breakfast. A million years ago.

Jenny started for the restroom and noticed the door was cracked. A face, eyes darting.

"Freddy! I see you."

She kicked open the door, hard, and they heard him hit the floor.

CHAPTER 11

Cashbox

Jenny dragged Freddy out of the restroom by his shoes. Ankle-high, powder blue, Converse brand.

"Where are you going?"

"Nowhere, man. You gotta save me, man."

Freddy had stringy hair on a regular day. Stress sweat made him look like a swim champ. It also produced a gold medal decomp onion reek. Jenny pulled him all the way down the hallway and flopped him like a wet fish.

"You're gross." She grabbed a napkin from the bar to wipe her hands. "And I am not a man. I am a lady."

Breck towered over him, eyes dark, clearly unhappy. Freddy started to sit up but Breck put his boot on his chest.

"Save you? From what. College kids?"

"What college kids?" He clung onto Breck's leg, like a drowning man on a life raft.

Jenny didn't buy it. "I just found you crouching in the bathroom with the fear of God in your eyes. Let's not play that game."

Eyes blinking, Freddy struggled to compute.

"Just tell me they're gone, man."

"Who are we talking about?" Breck gave Freddy's chest a quick pump with his boot heel.

Squirming, he gripped Breck's leg even tighter. "I'm so freaked, man!"

"Are you baked?"

Breck gave him another chest pump.

"Naw, I ain't burned one all day. But I sure could use a hit right now." He looked hurt that Breck was treating him this way. "Some crazy cats just tried to snuff my pipe. Chipotle drug lords . . . What kids?"

Danny was the one lying. There were no college kids. It wasn't a robbery. Why would he say that? Sighing, Breck took his foot off and walked over to the bar. Sat on a stool. There was a bowl of peanuts and he ate a handful.

Jenny gave him a headshake. "Need a snack, do we?"

"Sorry. I haven't eaten all day. I'm starting to crash."

Sitting up on his elbows, Freddy stared at the door.

"They're not coming back," Jenny told him.

"They showed up at my place. Stole my grow. Then they showed up here. Shot your bro, bro. Poor Danny. Is he gonna be okay?" He looked up at her, like a lost puppy. "Can I get up, please?"

She shrugged. "Fine."

Freddy scrambled up and took the stool next to Breck.

"Can I have some?"

Breck pushed the peanut bowl towards him.

Freddy ate some, still eyeing the door as if a grizzly might bust in any minute.

"I tried. I called. You all need to check your messages."

Breck knew that. He knew a lot more than Freddy realized. "So tell me something. Why didn't those two cartel men shoot *you?*"

The weed dealer sat up a little taller, obviously trying to gauge the situation. How much to say. How much not to say. Breck was the sheriff, after all.

"Well, you know."

"No, I don't know."

"Danny and me . . ." Freddy cleared his throat. "We keep this town green."

Eyebrows shooting up, Jenny came a step closer.

"What are you talking about? Are you saying Breck's *brother* is in on this? Distribution?" Her eyes narrowed. "Naw, I don't buy it. You gotta get up pretty early in the A.M. to fool me."

Freddy started to reach for another nut, but Breck took the bowl of peanuts away.

"Talk."

"Danny? He's the cashbox, baby. The Kickstarter. Runs the funds. He's the brains and I'm the brawn. We grow it all in my cabin. Or did." He studied Breck's face in disbelief. "You gotta know. Right?"

Breck did not know. But it all made sense now. Freddy was a high school dropout behind-the-gym kind of dealer. He didn't have the know how to go it alone. Not something this big. Throwing the bowl of peanuts across the room, he headed out the door.

"I'm going to the hospital."

He rammed open the door and disappeared in the swirling snow.

"Hey! You drove me here!" Jenny flapped her arms in frustration. "How am I getting home? It's ten degrees out there."

But he was already gone. She heard the Jeep fire up and drive off. What a night. She looked around. The empty tables. The tall silver brewing equipment. The scattered peanuts, Danny's blood on the floor—Jenny's eyes finally landed on Freddy. Like a sage grand master of all things true and false, he nodded serenely.

"We can take my wheels." He gave her a wink. "Back to your place?"

Disgusted, she held out her hand. "Give me your keys."

CHAPTER 12

Pretty Sneaky

It was now two in the morning. Pulling into the Sheriff's Office parking lot, Jenny parked Freddy's Honda Civic next to the snowmobile. Two lamentable rides. Side by side. Right next to the dumpster. So fitting.

"Inside." She put it in park. The dome light kicked on when she opened the door. But Freddy didn't move.

"I never sat on this side before."

He was in the passenger seat. Looking around like it was all new. He flapped the sun visor up and down a couple of times. Opened the glove box and pulled out a wad of McDonald's napkins.

"Still smell like McNugs."

Jenny reached over the console and unlatched his seatbelt.

"Get out."

She jingled the keys in front of his face to remind him he wasn't going anywhere. Then she went for it. Into the freezing night air, hands in her coat pockets, Jenny hustled for the front door and unlocked it as quick as she could. Standing in the doorway, she waved frantically. Finally, Freddy got out and began to follow. For no good reason, he decided to walk in her footprints in the snow, step by step. Ever so slowly.

"You got small feet."

She snapped her fingers. "Yeah? You got a small brain. Let's go!"

He chuckled like it was a joke.

"You're pretty snarky. I can dig it."

Finally, inside the building, Jenny took off her stocking cap. Her red hair was damp. She marched straight over to the potbelly stove and opened the iron door. She blew on the coals and loaded it with split pine.

"You want my official statement or something?" Freddy asked. He pushed around some papers on her desk. Clicked a ballpoint pen.

But Jenny wanted him in the jail cell. She guided him by the elbow across the room and locked him inside. Freddy gripped the iron bars and heaved and pulled like he thought he could make the whole cage sway. He couldn't.

"Hey, man. This ain't right."

"Your Civic stinks like pepperoni." Jenny took off her big coat and sniffed it. "Now I stink like pepperoni."

"Foxy lady with a badge. Want to see a movie Friday?"

"How about no. And gross." Jenny glared at him. It was late. She was exhausted. She should be in her own bed, eyes closed, dreaming the night away. Time to shut this down. "I like my men clean and responsible. And drug-free. Whatever happened to *Just Say No*, anyway? I guess that went out with Nancy Reagan. Now, it's like, 'Look at me. I smoke weed. I think it's cool, but really, I'm just a pizza-stank emo.'"

The wood in the stove popped and sizzled. Freddy's face fell.

That was a little harsh. Suddenly feeling bad, Jenny rubbed her eyes with her knuckles. She shouldn't have said all that. Necessarily. Well, not all in one breath anyhow.

"Freddy . . . Breck's brother was just shot. This is pretty serious." She looked at him, a little softer this time. "Okay?"

"Aw, dude. A lady lecture."

He sat down on the cot. Breck's dark blue sleeping bag was spread out. Zero-degree mummy bag. Marmot—name brand. "Well, looky here." Breck's nice fluffy pillow was there, too, laying on top of the flat pancake prisoner pillow. Freddy laid down and wiggled around. Got comfy. "It's like I'm on vacay. Better than Airbnb. Cheaper, too."

"Hey, zip it. I need to hear this."

The sound of a low voice was coming from the CB. Jenny walked over to her desk and turned up the volume.

"That better not be country." Freddy watched her with his puppy dog eyes. "I bet Breck listens to country, doesn't he? Put it on top forty. Maybe JT is bringing sexy back."

"Not kidding. Shut your pie hole."

"White male. Gunshot wound to the upper torso. Three minutes out."

It was one of the nurses in the ambulance. Melinda. The hospital wasn't all that big. Not like the ones in Denver. There were just a couple of doctors. Maybe a dozen staff. All familiar faces and as many times as Jenny had been in there, they all knew her, too.

"Hospital personnel have been alerted. Go directly to the south-side emergency entrance."

That was the woman at the front desk, Michelle. Every time they had to contact the hospital, Michelle was usually the one who they talked to. She was Jenny's age. Mid-thirties. Breck even asked her out on a date once. Dinner at the Subway in Frisco. Jenny shook her head as she thought about it. Smooth move, Breck. Never got that second date, did ya?

The door opened. Two men walked inside the Sheriff's Office. One had slick dark brown hair and a well-trimmed mustache. Dress pants and a black coat. The other had sunglasses, a buzz cut, and an AR-15.

Zorrero and El Sangrador.

"What the frick?" Jenny grabbed her sidearm and slid into a firing stance. "Do not move!"

Behind her, Freddy rolled off the cot and crab-crawled underneath, out of sight.

"Ah, here you are." Zorrero was addressing Freddy's blue Converse tennis shoes, sticking out. He ignored Jenny completely. "You pretty sneaky. But I find you."

He walked over to the cell and leaned down to see beneath the cot. His footsteps seemed loud, clopping across the old oak floorboards. Jenny swung her gun from man to man, not sure who to cover. Caught between them. Who was more dangerous?

"Freeze! Turn around, put your hands behind your head."

Jenny decided to cover El Sangrador since he had an AR-15 trained on her. She only had a 9mm Luger. Better than nothing. Barely. His was a semi-automatic rifle. One shot per trigger pull, just like hers. At least it wasn't full auto. But it would leave a much bigger hole than her pipsqueak pistol. If it came to pulling triggers, she would only get one shot. It would have to count.

Turning towards Jenny, like he just noticed her for the first time, Zorrero smiled and cocked his head a little. He was measuring her up. Then he began to walk towards her.

"I said freeze." Jenny flipped around and pointed her gun at his chest. "Do not move."

The man was wearing black leather driving gloves. He waved his hand at her like he was swatting away a fly.

"Oh, put that away. You won't get hurt. Not today."

Jenny took a step backward and bumped into Breck's desk. "Last warning. I will shoot to kill."

But Zorrero kept coming. Slowly. Step by step. Uncomfortably close. He reached out and gently pushed the gun barrel down. For some reason, Jenny let him. A feeling washed over her. A feeling of helplessness. Her skin tingled. Ice cold and red hot at the same time. There was nothing she could do.

"Shhh, shh, shh." He shushed her like it was bedtime.

Jenny trembled.

"What cartel are you with?"

Zorrero smiled.

"The kind you don't mess with."

CHAPTER 13

Grit and Insubordination

Given the facts of the moment, Breck's usual clunky hellos were left by the wayside. On every other occasion, when he walked into the lobby at Quandary County Medical Center, Michelle at the front desk, normal conversation was somehow subconsciously jettisoned for awkward crash and burn chit chat.

Holding one hand over the phone receiver, Michelle gave him a compassionate wave.

"He's in pre-op."

While she finished up with the caller, Breck rested his hands on the reception counter. His eyes drifted. The lobby was painted a serene cream. Wood trim. Big screen TV on a brick facade. Soft sconce lights on the walls. An oil painting of a grassy mountain lake. He never really noticed any of it before. He still didn't. Seemed like a hazy dream.

Concern and anger were roiling around in his head the whole drive over. But now. It all seemed to deflate for some reason. There was a decent sofa near the Coke machine. Sitting sounded good. His brain was fried. He started to walk over but Michelle put the caller on hold.

"Sorry about your brother, Breck," Michelle spoke kindly. Straightforward. "It's a through and through. That's the good news. But it was pretty close to his heart. As soon as they're out of surgery, we'll know more. I'm really sorry."

Breck nodded.

"Okay."

"It may be a while, but . . . you want to wait till he's out?"

"Yeah. I'll be over there."

The phone beeped and line two flashed. She glanced down at it.

"Busy night. I better get this."

"No problem."

Breck wandered over to the Coke machine and pulled out his wallet. He looked back at the front desk. Michelle was typing and talking on the phone. Her voice was all business with whoever she was talking to. Probably the Colorado State Patrol. Crash on the interstate, from what he could tell. The lobby was pretty much empty. It was after hours. The night shift.

Breck got a Coke and sank onto the sofa. He put the can down on the end table and pulled out the crumpled cigarette from his coat pocket. The one he had stuffed in there on the way up the canyon. It was leaking dried bits of tobacco, but he tried to straighten it out. Maybe it was worth saving.

"You know you can't light that thing in here."

Jarred, Breck looked up to see who it was. Mayor Matthews. Standing over him like a statue. Where did he come from? Thin air?

"I thought you gave up those cancer sticks anyhow. They'll kill you, Breck."

"Something will."

The mayor was wearing a gray overcoat with wet globs of snow on the shoulders. He must have just come inside. Breck hadn't even heard the swish of the automatic doors. Or his footsteps on the tile. He was pretty distracted, though.

Breck leaned back on the little couch and bumped the back of his head. He winced. Forgot about that. He sat up, sore, and checked to see if it was bleeding again. It wasn't.

With a dramatic sigh, the mayor took a seat across from him. He removed his gloves and set them carefully on the seat cushion. Loosened his knit neck scarf.

"Sorry to hear what happened. Your brother was a good man."

"Still is. Ain't dead yet."

Breck opened the can of Coke. But he just held it in his hand.

"A lot of serious things have been going wrong in this town." The mayor paused to choose his next words. "Maybe it's time you stepped down. Pass the badge on to someone else."

There it was. Breck smiled and took a sip. Never a missed opportunity with this guy.

"You got here almost as quick as I did," Breck said.

The mayor shrugged.

"I know everything that happens in this town."

"Everything?"

That irritated him. Breck could see it in his face.

"Listen. I only want what's best." Matthews pointed a finger. "Just like you. We're on the same team."

"Just like me."

But Breck's tone said otherwise.

The Mayor clenched his teeth. His eyes blazed. That set him off.

"Your brother's been shot. And you blew that drug bust in Freddy's cabin. Yeah, I heard about that. And your little deputy girl, calling me. 'Help I don't know what to do.' Being Sheriff of Quandary is a big job. It takes elephant balls. But you miss more than you catch, these days. How about a leave of absence, Breck? At the very least. Get your head on straight. Arizona is nice this time of year. But you need more than just a weekend getaway, don't you? Maybe something more . . . permanent."

Breck took another sip of Coke.

"Maybe I should run for mayor."

Matthews leaned forward, his voice ugly.

"I can take your badge. Give it to someone who knows how to keep crime out of Quandary. Keep our innocent citizens safe. From getting shot."

That was pretty low. Now it was Breck's turn to clench his teeth.

A voice on the intercom:

Code eight in OR one. Doctor Heller to OR one, immediately.

Breck turned. A couple of nurses were calling at each other in the far end of the main hallway. Rushing around. Pushing a crash cart. At the front desk, Michelle was on the phone again. Hearing the commotion, she stood and leaned over the counter to see, phone cord stretched tight.

Breck turned back to Matthews.

"You better pray to God you're not sitting here in two seconds."

Grabbing his gloves, the mayor got to his feet and started for the front entrance. He paused.

"Grit is one thing. Insubordination is another. Don't forget that, Breck."

The automatic glass doors parted, and the mayor of Quandary walked out into the night.

Cold air. Snowflakes hovering in the parking lot lights. Swish. The doors closed.

Doctor Heller to OR one.

Breck stood up, anxious, but didn't know where to go or what to do. He opened his hand. The cigarette was completely crumpled now. Must have squeezed the hell out of it while he was talking to Matthews. He walked to a wastebasket and dropped it in, along with the can of Coke. He didn't feel like drinking or smoking or eating or thinking or feeling or anything at all.

CHAPTER 14

X Marks the Spot

Turning his back on Jenny, Zorrero surveilled the Sheriff's Office. His eyes roved around. From the cell to the stove, the desks to the CB and laptop. He spotted the tac closet and opened the door. Rifles, extra handguns, and ammunition. Bulletproof vests with SHERIFF in big block letters. He let out a soft chuckle and closed it up again.

Jenny, pale, still had her pistol in her hand. Drooping down by her side.

"What do you want?" she asked.

Strolling back to the cell, the cartel man pointed at Freddy.

"Open it up."

"I can't. Breck has the key with him."

"Is that right?" He smiled knowingly. Zorrero was wearing a shoulder holster beneath his overcoat and pulled out his Glock. He stuck it in between the bars. "I just wanna say hi."

Freddy risked a peek from under the cot. When he saw the gun, he waved his hands frantically.

"No, no, nooo!"

"Don't!" Jenny shouted, but stayed still. The blood-letter never moved, spoke, or lowered his weapon. Every time she looked at him, all she saw was that rifle barrel. Like staring at the sun.

"Just one easy, easy question." Zorrero addressed Freddy. "You got any more we don't know about?"

"No, man. You got it all. All of it."

The CB was sitting on her desk. Jenny knew it was too far away. If she even looked at it wrong, she knew the man with the rifle would fire. She could sense his eyes, behind those silver aviator sunglasses. Staring at her. Watching. Waiting.

"You no longer sell cannabis. Not even a *mota*," Zorrero said. "No ganja. No dime bags. No dabs. No hash. No nothing to nobody. You understand?"

Freddy crawled back out of sight.

"I promise, man."

"Gonna hold you to that, amigo." Glancing over at his henchman, Zorrero smiled. "I think this little hamster wet himself."

Tucking the Glock back in its holster, he crossed the room, pausing to button up his coat. He glanced back at Jenny, and the Luger in her hand.

"Don't hurt yourself."

Then they left.

Jenny stood there for a moment, not sure what just happened. Her cheeks were colorless, her breath coming in short gasps. Were they playing games? Would they come right back in and shoot up the place? She hustled to the front door and locked the deadbolt, her fingers shaking.

What could she have done differently?

"They gone, man?" Freddy had indeed wet himself. His jeans were damp. "Let me outta here."

The CB. Jenny ran to her desk and grabbed the mic.

"Breck. Sheriff Breckenridge Dyer. Where are you? Copy?"

The radio hissed static.

"Please, Breck. Pick up, please."

"Jenny?" It was Michelle from the hospital. "He's right here. Hold for the sheriff."

"Roger that."

She took a couple of steps toward the window, stretching the CB cord as far as it would go. The weather had died down. There was still snow in the air, but not much. In the light of the streetlamps, she spotted the black Range Rover heading slowly up the street. It left a pair of tire tracks in the wet snow. The brake lights flashed for a second, and she felt her stomach lurch. But they kept driving.

"Jen?" Breck was on the radio. "I'm here. My brother. He's . . . he's in surgery."

Jenny lost sight of the Range Rover.

"Hey. We've got trouble here. I hate to ask . . ." Her mind reeled. "No, I'm sorry. Forget it. It's leveled out. For now. Just come back when you can."

"What's going on?" His voice sounded weird. Jenny knew Breck was going through some heavy stuff. So was she, but it was over now. For her. But Danny wasn't out of the woods yet. She could tell Breck was worried. She had never seen him worried before. This was new ground.

"Just a very close call. Tell you when I see you. Thoughts and prayers for Danny. Okay? Jenny out."

She set the mic back on the desk. What was going on? She wanted answers.

"I need to go home and change. Open up."

Freddy. She swiveled around and gave him a withering glare. He wilted a little, but he looked pretty wilty as a rule, so it wasn't much of a change.

"What the hell's going on?" Jenny demanded. "Who were those men? Why were they here?"

Backing down, he took a seat on the cot. On Breck's nice sleeping bag.

"Yeah, uh . . ."

"Yeah, uh . . . look at me. I'm a dummy-stink who huffs weed all day. Duh doy." Jenny was done with the kid gloves. "Get smart, Freddy. Can't you see what's going on?"

He hung his head. "Sorry. This is all crazy, man. Not my fault."

"Not your fault?" She clapped to get his attention. "Look at me. Is this what you want your life to be? Shot to death by some cartel hit men who drove all the way up here from Mexico? Crap, Freddy. And for what? So people can get stoned stupid? Where there's drugs, there's violence. End of story. Get it?"

But if Freddy got it, he wasn't letting on.

"Another lady lecture. This sucks."

"Shut up. I'm going out for some air."

"Wait, what?" He jumped up, alarmed. "But what if they come back? You can't leave me alone. You can't!"

Jenny went to her desk, grabbing a ballpoint pen and a piece of blank paper. She started scrawling something.

"I'm gonna draw you a map, and you can tell them where to go. Here's the jail. And here's your butthole. X marks the spot."

Crumpling the paper into a wad, she tossed it at him like a baseball. It hit the bars and bounced onto the floor. Unlocking the deadbolt, Jenny stepped outside and slammed the door behind her.

The street was empty.

The only tire tracks were from the Range Rover. Stretching off. It was over.

Things could have gone very badly. She could be dead. Freddy, too. Leaning against the old manky Civic, Jenny felt weak again. Whatever adrenaline was pumping through her just wore off. Her stomach went sour, too. She wasn't going to hurl. She refused.

"Don't freak, Jenny. Don't freak out. Not now. You are a strong, bad momma woman."

She took a deep breath but coughed. Her mouth was really dry. Then she broke down and cried a little.

CHAPTER 15

Honest Abe

When Mayor Matthews saw the Range Rover idling in front of his house, he didn't pull into the garage like usual. He drove past and kept going. The headlights on the Range Rover flicked on, and they trailed him up the winding icy street.

Matthews lived in a 5,000-square-foot mountainside home. Same road as all the fancy ski condos, but at the top of the final switchback.

Six beds, seven baths. Rustic modern. Big yellow wood beams. Walk-out stone patio with a hot tub and fire pit. It was beyond nice. Avant-garde mine style chandeliers. River stone fireplace two stories high. It would have been wrong not to hang that giant elk head trophy above the mantle, so he did. Picked it up on a backcountry expedition the first year he was elected mayor.

One of the council members was Johnny Tibbs. He owned a big dude ranch on the edge of town. Part of the gig was outfitting. Taking hunters out for a week or two at a time. Matthews had never hunted before. Or slept in a big canvas tent with a woodstove, piped up through the roof in the middle of the wilderness. Dutch oven ribs and beans at night. Beer and booze in a tin cup. It was a blast. And Tibbs knew how to track elk. Quarter the carcass and pack out the meat. The head, too. He made sure his clients got the kill shot they paid for.

But that was the first and last positive experience Matthews had with Tibbs. Turned out, they were on opposite ends of almost every issue the city council debated. Tibbs liked his second amendment. He even wanted the school teachers armed. That was a big one they fought over that first meeting, and it went downhill after that.

Eyrie Road. That was a good street name to live on. Regal. Unassailable. And if his house was the eagle's nest, the road stopped there. Dead-end in a cul de sac. Matthews hooked the steering wheel and pulled his BMW around in a tight circle. The Range Rover was right behind him. It circled, too, and sidled up real close.

The tinted passenger window scrolled down. Zorrero.

Ignoring him, Matthews watched the street for a moment. Was anyone else following him? Any strange cars parked in the shadows? Pine trees lined both sides of the road. That heavy wet spring snow coated everything. He could see his house easily. Dark, except the porch lights that lined his driveway. Lit it up like a landing strip.

His daughter was in there. Asleep to the world. Aspen was nineteen years old. Taking a year off before college to ski all winter long. They were supposed to get up early for breakfast. Meet his ex at the Blue Moose for an espresso and french toast.

"I told you. Never show up at my place," Matthews said, lowering his window to talk.

Zorrero leaned out. Handed him a hot pink sticky note.

"Go buy a GPS and plug those numbers in. But don't Google it. If the feds ever poke around, they'll start with your hard drive."

Coordinates.

"Where is it?"

"Off Boreal Pass." Zorrero looked around. "This snow will melt pretty quick, then we'll get it all planted up good."

Matthews cranked his car heater on full blast. The seat warmer on high. With the window down, he was getting chilly.

"You shot Breck's brother. No one gets hurt. Remember? No one dies. Otherwise, the feds *will* start poking around."

"*Accidente.*" A small smile spread across Zorrero's face.

"Well, that can't happen again." Matthews placed the sticky note in the center console compartment, closing it tight. "Progressive. Businessmen. Those were your words."

"*Sí.* Not your grandfather's cartel." Sounded like a joke, but Zorrero seemed serious. "We don't do things like they do in Guerrero. Trust me. Honest Abe."

"We can only be business partners if we *have* a business." Matthews frowned. "Don't come to my house again."

Zorrero rolled his window up halfway and stopped.

"Make sure that sheriff don't cause no more trouble. And we won't have no more *accidentes*."

The black Range Rover pulled forward and drove away. Right past Matthews' driveway and on down Eyrie Road and disappeared in the night.

Zorrero was right about one thing. The snow would melt quickly. Once the sun came out. That's how spring worked in Colorado. It wouldn't be long. Summer was right around the corner. The pressure was on. To get things in order before the next city council meeting. First Tuesday of every month. Matthews needed a majority vote. He knew he could talk Jameson into voting his way. A moonbeam Subway shop. Tibbs was going to be a much harder sell. But he needed Tibbs to get that majority. Besides those two, there were two women on the council and he knew they wouldn't vote to legalize weed, that was for sure.

Marijuana was legal for people to possess in the state, for private use. But each city and county had to decide whether or not to play along. At the moment, recreational and medical were both illegal to sell in Quandary. No business permits. Matthews planned on changing that. And he planned on opening his own dispensary. Big house, sleek car, frosty ex-wife, and a daughter looking into college. The paycheck he got as mayor was barely a lifeline. And Matthews wanted more than to just survive.

CHAPTER 16

I'll Quit

In the jaundice gleam of the Jeep's headlights, Breck saw Jenny leaning against Freddy's Honda. He could tell she was out of sorts. Maybe more than he was. He cut the engine and got out.

Eyes red, Jenny sniffed and held her chin up.

"Under control." Before he could even ask. "All good here."

But Breck was out of steam. Instead of a barrage of questions, he leaned up against the Honda, too, and looked up at the stars. The low storm clouds were gone now. The air was chilly but absolutely still. After all the high winds and blowing snow, it felt strangely serene. He pulled out a package of new cigarettes he got from the 7-Eleven by the hospital. American Spirit brand. He tore off the plastic wrapping. She didn't say anything this time. In fact, Jenny held out her hand.

"Gimme."

Breck gave her a side look. "*You* want one?"

He tapped the bottom of the package until one slid halfway out.

"Here you go."

Snatching the whole package, Jenny slam-dunked it in the dumpster. Then she screamed, a little primal, and kicked the big metal thing. It rang like a gong.

"Alright, I'll quit."

He pulled out a second package from the 7-Eleven and tossed it in, too. And a couple of cheapy Bic lighters. Jenny sniffed again. Breck tried to remember what she had said over the CB.

Something had gone wrong. But it was foggy in his mind. Was her nose dribbling from the cold, or had she been crying?

Jenny came and stood directly in front of him, looking right into his eyes.

"You're not . . . *quitting* . . . are you?"

He shrugged.

"No. I'm not quitting."

"Good. Cuz then I'd be sheriff, and I don't want to be the one who answers to that city council."

"Yeah, you said that earlier."

"Hate those clowns."

"You and me both."

A tear leaked out of her eye but Jenny laughed, a little awkwardly. It was more cathartic than anything. But Breck smiled. Good sign. They loved to hate on the council. Once a month, Breck went to City Hall, sat in the council chambers, listened for a couple of hours while the council members droned on about parking meters or loading zones. Or how the Safeway parking lot was too bright at night and they should reduce light pollution. Motion to amend the Parking Lot Light Requirements Policy. Motion seconded. Motion passed. Pursuant to due call and notice thereof, parking lot lights are now required to use low wattage eco-bulbs. Then they'd finally get around to calling for the Sheriff's Report. He'd rattle off the monthly crime statistics. Thirty-seven calls. Three thefts. Twelve parking violations. Six traffic citations. Mailbox damage. Couple dog complaints. Thank you, good night. Three hours wasted. He could have been home watching TV.

"Hey, how's your brother?"

Breck leaned against the Civic again, arms crossed. He looked back up at the stars. Exhaled slowly. His breath floated up, like a puff of cigarette smoke. Those American Spirits in the dumpster. Maybe he'd dig them out later.

"Cardiac event on the table. But they got him back."

"Oh, Breck. I'm so sorry."

"It's okay. He's okay. Or will be."

Orion was in the southern sky. Just above the long black ridge. That was always Breck's favorite constellation. Ever since he was a kid. Danny was a Big Dipper fan. Or had been, back then. Maybe he still was.

"So what happened? Here? With you?" Breck studied her, feeling like he was missing something. "You got Freddy locked up?"

Jenny raked her fingers through her damp hair. Her stocking cap was still inside, on the desk. Her brow furrowed.

"Yeah, he's in there. You're gonna want to throw your mummy bag away. Or in the wash machine, at least."

"What happened?" Breck asked again. He saw her eyes water. She shifted feet and gave him a pained look.

"Two cartel men. They walked right in here. They . . . they scared me, Breck."

A cold streak shot down his spine. Breck pulled his .44 Special. Eyed the street, twisting around. How many times can he draw his weapon in one night?

"It's like I woke up yesterday, and the world went wonky." Jenny rubbed her eyes. Bloodshot. They stung. Then she pushed her hands deep in her warm pockets. "This coat makes me feel like a giant marshmallow."

"Same guys that jumped me." The street was empty. The buildings dark. Breck holstered his gun again. "Sorry, Jen. I should have been here."

"Don't sweat it." Now that the shock was wearing off, and the gut wrench of being cornered, she was feeling ticked. Mad at the bad guys. Mad at herself. For letting them get the best of her. "I can take care of myself."

Breck felt awful. Getting clocked on the head was the least of it. Danny got shot in the chest. Heart attack in surgery. He almost forgot about the mayor's buddy talk. But it was forgettable. The whole time he was at the hospital, Jenny was going through her own private hell. Right here. In the Sheriff's Office. Those cartel men. They had no fear. He needed to keep that in mind.

"You got my back, I got yours." Breck squeezed her marshmallow sleeve. "That's how we roll."

Down the street, a car drove up to the Blue Moose Deli.

"What time is it?"

"I don't know," Jenny said. "My phone's inside."

"They're opening up. Buy you breakfast?"

"Large coffee, no cream." She headed for the front door. "Freddy's in there, scared to death I'm going to abandon him. I better stay here. And a breakfast burrito. Chorizo and scrambled egg. Get me one of those."

CHAPTER 17

Wakey, Wakey

Easing into a booth while they fired up the grill, Breck nodded off. The Blue Moose was empty. It didn't really open for another half hour, but the cook let him inside anyhow.

His cell phone buzzed. Yawning, he sat up and stretched. The hospital. Michelle sent him a text. Danny was out of surgery. Stable condition. Smiley face.

The cook came out of the kitchen with a plastic to-go bag. Breck took out his wallet and thumbed out some greenbacks.

"How many times I gotta tell ya?" The cook wore an apron flecked with flour. "Blue lives matter. Your money's no good here."

Regardless, Breck tucked the cash in the man's apron pocket. "Appreciate it, my friend." And he did appreciate it. Support for law enforcement. But he didn't want to be a burden. "Blue Moose matters."

Taking the food and coffees, Breck stepped out the door. The sky was showing some color. Sun would come up over the ridge, but it would still be awhile. Since the eatery was just a short walk from the Sheriff's Office, Breck didn't bother driving.

He paused as the city plow driver went up the street. Orange light bar on the roof flickering. The big truck had a plow blade as tall as he was. Breck watched him go by and then stepped out into the street. No one had gotten up to shovel the sidewalks yet. Now that there was somewhere to land that was dry, a robin swooped down onto the asphalt and danced around. Looking confused. What was all this white stuff? Where was the green grass?

"Me too, bud. I'm done with all this."

Main Street. It was the main street in Quandary. Historic brick buildings. Most of them were built in the 1800s. A lot of Victorian charm. Refurbished. The old and the new. The Starbucks was even in an old yellow house with a couple of big cedar trees out front and a wrought iron sign.

The town was starting to wake up. Breck heard a car door behind him and turned to see. Silver BMW all-wheel drive. Hackles went up. It was Mayor Matthews. Enough was enough. That guy was turning up everywhere. Breck kept walking. Maybe Matthews wouldn't see him.

The mayor went straight inside the Blue Moose, staring at his phone the whole way. Breck relaxed again. Close call.

The Sheriff's Office parking lot was buried with big drifts. He kicked through the snow. He would have to shovel this. Later. After he ate.

As he walked up, Jenny opened the door. "Java." She must have been watching through the window.

"Two cream." Breck handed her a cardboard cup. "How is sleeping beauty?"

"Stinking up the place. Smells like a pepperoni died in here. After whizzing on your sleeping bag."

"Delightful."

Breck set the food on his desk and took off his coat. In the jail cell, Freddy was buried in the sleeping bag. Snoring. Zipped up tight like a butterfly in a cocoon.

"How's Danny?" she asked.

"He'll make it." Breck pulled out a foil-wrapped breakfast burrito and gave it to her. He had biscuits and gravy. It was in a Styrofoam tray with a lid. Smelled good. He was overdue for a decent meal. "I'll probably head over to the hospital later. See what he has to say for himself."

Jenny took a bite and closed her eyes, savoring it.

"So I put out a BOLO on that Range Rover," she said. "I spoke to the boys up in Alma and the State Patrol down in Frisco. How can those cartel freaks just disappear?"

They heard rustling. Freddy sat up on the cot. All they could see was his face. Nose twitching.

Jenny went over to the cell. "Wakey, wakey." She took out her keys and fished around for the right one.

"Hey, lady cop." Freddy unzipped the bag a little. Stuck his head out. "I love waking up to your eyes."

"You wish."

Unlocking the cell, Jenny swung it wide open and went back to her breakfast.

"Get up."

Climbing all the way out, Freddy looked bad. His hair was matted. Clothes creased all over the place. His jeans were damp with urine. He took a few steps, moseying like a cowboy off a long trail ride.

He looked to see what they were eating. "Dang, man."

Freddy started to come closer, but Jenny held up her hand.

"Have you seen those things? Big white scoopy things. You crawl in. It's got hot water in there. Soap."

"A bath?"

"Yeah, you should get one of those."

Breck scraped up some gravy with his fork and ate it. He looked the guy over. Overgrown kid. Stuck in time. It was kind of sad. Except for the fact that he was somehow caught up with a professional drug cartel. How did that happen? What was the story there?

"I can go?" Freddy was surprised. He glanced out the front window, nervous about what was out there. He clearly didn't want to go. He pointed at Jenny's burrito. "Did you get me anything?"

Jenny looked at him in disbelief.

"You were growing marijuana plants. Dozens. A room full. In your house. That's full-on illegal."

"Those cartel cats stole it all, man."

"And that's why I'm not going to charge you," Breck said. "No evidence."

"Look what they did to Breck's brother. And what they could have done to us. Remember? That wasn't just a bad dream, buddy. And the stakes are high." Jenny was starting to get mad again. Trying to communicate the obvious. How much clearer did it need to be? "Higher than any bomb weed will get you."

Freddy looked offended.

"It's called *recreational.* No big deal."

"All fun and games. Till somebody gets hurt."

She took another bite of burrito, and Freddy's stomach growled.

Breck pulled the badge off his belt clip and set it on the desk for dramatic effect. "Do me a favor, Freddy. Stay out of the biz."

"You know what?" Freddy zipped up his wrinkly jacket. "I'm outta here."

He punched open the door and strolled out into the morning sunlight. They heard his footsteps slosh in the soft wet snow. Breck went over to the doorway and watched. Freddy got in his Honda Civic and tried to back up. The tires spun. Breck went out and pushed while he reversed it. A couple tries and he made it into the street, fan belt whining.

"Screw you, man!" Freddy shouted and drove off.

If the State Patrol hadn't seen their vehicle on the interstate, or the Alma police up past the canyon, then the cartel men were still around. Holed up nearby. There were a hundred cabins dotting the woods.

"You think it's all over now?" Jenny asked.

Breck did not.

"I think it's just getting started."

CHAPTER 18

The Boss

L ooking up when the door opened, Mayor Matthews brightened when his teenage daughter Aspen appeared. Then he frowned when he saw his ex-wife Valerie materialize right behind her.

"Oh. You made it." He didn't try to hide his disappointment.

Valerie Matthews lived in Frisco, ten miles away. It wasn't far, but with the surprise blizzard, he was hoping the county had shut down the highway. Apparently not.

"Daddy, be nice to mom." Aspen hooked her arm through Valerie's. "I haven't seen her all week."

"You text her ten times a day."

"She likes me better, Seneca." Valerie looked victorious for a moment. Then got pouty. "But now she's a grown girl and can live where she chooses. Even if it's here with her loudmouth father when her own bedroom is just down the road. With me."

"You know I love you, but the ski slopes are in my backyard." Aspen smiled at them both and patted her father on the hand. "At daddy's house."

Mayor Matthews hated his given name. Seneca. It was clunky. Sounded like a gas station. It was the name of a Roman philosopher. One of the Stoics who flushed away their lives trying to be ethical and unfettered by all the good things in life.

His phone vibrated. It was a text.

"See?" Aspen said. "You get texts all day, too."

La policía got an APB. Fix it.

The mayor slid the phone off the table and into his pocket. "You're right. I do. But see, I'm putting it away." A quick glance out the window. No Range Rover.

Even though she was staying with him, Matthews talked his daughter into driving separately to the Blue Moose for breakfast. After they ate, Aspen could head off to the slopes. Besides, he said, he had to drive straight to City Hall for an important appointment. A bit of a fudge.

He did have an appointment. But it was with the loan agent at the Blue River Bank. He was going to get a second mortgage. On his ex-wife's house. He had bought it for her as part of the divorce but it was still in his name.

And he needed the cash to invest. In a Clear Span arena. Fabric walls stretched tight over a big steel frame. Like a gigantic white speed bump.

He would tell the bank it was for horseback riding. His daughter rode. Dressage. That was true. And a good story to get the funding. He had adorable photos printed up in full color, in the business plan packet. Horse shows. Ribbons. Trophies. But this arena was not just for fun. Quandary could use a therapeutic horseback riding program. Handicapped kids needed to ride, too, didn't they? How could they say no to that?

There was no time to waste on the truth. Matthews needed the building up immediately. Once he got the city council to approve cannabis, he would turn it into a gigantic climate-controlled marijuana greenhouse. The thing cost $150,000. And that was just the structure itself, not considering offices, water and electricity and a paved parking lot. A big investment. But it would come back a thousand times inside a year.

The future was looking bright. Business plan. Business partners. Competition? Out of the way. Freddy and Danny were sidelined. And the plants Zorrero stole from them would give him a good head start on product. He didn't have to buy seeds and start from scratch. The cartel knew the ins and outs of cultivation and Zorrero had ties to investors down south, too.

The time was right. The time was now. Matthews was ready to roll. All puns aside.

"I'm getting french toast and a hazelnut caramel cappuccino." Aspen passed him the menu. "Mom lives off mimosas. What are you getting, daddy?"

He studied the options. One item caught his eye.

"Here we go. Buttermilk pancakes, eggs, and sirloin steak." He tapped it with his fingertip. "It's called *The Boss.*"

Valerie snorted. "You don't need to be an ass, Seneca."

He gave her a thin smile. "Maybe I do."

CHAPTER 19

Que Hora Es?

Scraping the sleep out of his eyes, El Sangrador knocked his knees on the steering wheel trying to get comfortable. He looked over at the passenger seat, jealous. Zorrero had much more leg room, plus a warm fleece blanket pulled over his head to block out the sunlight. El Sangrador wanted a blanket. And more leg room. But such was life.

There were all kinds of dirt roads that trailed off into the National Forest. There was one, in particular, they were interested in. Boreal Pass Road. They were parked at the turn-off, a few miles behind the Quandary Brewery, hidden among some snowy blue spruce.

They had a good view of several A-frame rental cabins.

"Nobody in that one." El Sangrador glanced at Zorrero, who didn't move. "No tire track or footprint. No porchlight or smoke from the chimney. Is empty."

In the rearview mirror, all he could see were green marijuana buds.

"We gotta get all this flower some warm light and water. Quick before they die."

From beneath the blanket, Zorrero gave a groan. "*Que hora es?* I ain't done sleeping. Shut up."

Off beyond the cabins, the blood-letter watched some men with cowboy hats drive into a fenced pasture in a flatbed pickup stacked with hay. A couple of them were standing on the stack, cutting open the twine and chucking flakes of hay left and right. A herd of horses rushed out of the trees. They nipped and pinned their ears at each other. It was obvious who the dominant ones were. They got to eat first.

El Sangrador chuckled as one big brown horse chased a little gray pony all over the place, kicking up snow.

"Heh, heh. I like that one."

But Zorrero ignored him.

There was a sign near the pasture gate, hung on two tall wooden posts. The Tibbs Ranch. Beneath it, a big old wagon wheel was propped up to mark a private driveway leading to the main lodge.

"See? They got smoke in *their* chimneys. People moving around."

The blood-letter was determined to make his point. There had to be soft beds in those rental cabins. The sooner they broke in, the sooner he got to lie on one.

Checking his cell phone, El Sangrador was pleased to see there were a couple of bars. There was a cell tower up on the tall hill above the ranch. It was supposed to look like a pine tree, but it looked fake.

"The gringo who owns this outfit must be very rich. They put that tower right above his place."

His phone worked in Quandary. But everywhere else, he had nothing. Until they parked there. Which was why they were eyeing the rental cabins. They needed to stay out of sight for a while. But Zorrero and El Sangrador were part of a food chain. They had to report in faithfully. If a day went by without a specific phone call at a specific time to a specific person, it would set off some red flags.

The blood-letter reached around behind the driver's seat. The AR-15 rifle was back there, and so was a Colt .45. He pulled it out and admired it. White pearl grips. Just like in all the Old West movies. Seeing those cowboys feed their horses made him feel like he was in an Old West movie.

Putting on his mirror sunglasses, he took the key out of the ignition and set it on the dashboard. He didn't want to annoy Zorrero with that electronic beeping sound when he opened his door. The blood-letter made sure not to slam it shut, either.

Walking through the wet slushy snow, he crossed the quiet street and made his way over to the A-frame. He went up the front steps onto the deck and boldly peered in through the windows. It was as he suspected. No one was inside.

The door was locked, naturally. But that did not matter. Going around to the back door, the blood-letter used his Colt .45 to knock out a pane of glass. He reached through and undid the lock. All of three seconds. It was that easy.

The kitchen was narrow and all the appliances were small versions. The fridge was waist-high. The stove only had two burners. No dishwasher. Wash rack next to the sink. At least there was a microwave. The blood-letter liked to eat popcorn.

The kitchen was roofed in by an upper loft and he climbed the ladder to see what was up there. A couple of small bare mattresses and an old trunk in between. Like the Goldilocks story, El Sangrador laid down on each. Both mattresses were thin as pancakes and hard as rocks.

Through the triangular windows, he had a bird's eye of the road. And the Tibbs Ranch and those cowboys in their pickup. He could see quite a ways.

Climbing back down, El Sangrador roamed the living room area. There was an old wood stove with a sooty smokestack poking through the sloped ceiling, but also some electric baseboard heaters. He found the thermostat and turned the dial on high. He heard them buzz.

That would take the chill off.

He checked the faucet, but no water came out. It had probably been shut off for the winter so the pipes wouldn't freeze. He would need to get it going so they could get those plants watered.

There were instructions printed out on a piece of white paper, for the rental guests. Do this. Don't do that. Rules, rules, rules. There were a contact name and number. This place belonged to the Tibbs Ranch. Probably for their summer clients and the hunters in the fall.

Well, it wasn't summer yet. For now, it would serve as a hothouse to keep that cannabis alive and well. Until they could get it planted in the ground with some proper sunshine.

The blood-letter tried out the couch. It had rust-red cushions and a throw blanket stitched with a kitschy doodle of a black bear eating honey. And it was very soft. He set his revolver on the coffee table, put his feet up, and pulled the blanket over his head to block the sunlight.

CHAPTER 20

Just for a Second

The mountains all around Quandary were white and bright, but the city plow driver had done his job. The streets that crisscrossed town were clear. Wet pavement glistened in the morning sun.

Breck pulled the Jeep up to the hospital entrance, got out and left the driver door open so Jenny could take the wheel.

"Sure you don't want to come in?"

"Nope. Going hunting." She slid out and walked around to the driver's side door. "Tell Danny I say hi and heal up."

"You need a boost?"

Breck laced his fingers together, as a joke.

"No, I don't need a *boost.*"

But Jenny was short and getting in the driver's seat took some gymnastics. She gripped the frame and hopped a couple of times to get in.

Breck started for the hospital entrance. The automatic sliding doors at the front entrance swished apart. He paused and looked back.

"Armed and dangerous. That's a thing." He had to shout because the Jeep was loud. It had a transplanted Corvette engine under the hood and grumbled at an idle. "If you spot them, call me."

"Yeah, well. If I do find them, how you gonna get there?"

"Just call me." Breck headed inside, talking over his shoulder. "If the cells don't work, radio Michelle."

Oh yeah. It was a stick shift. Jenny stared at it for a moment. "Crap."

When was the last time she'd driven a manual transmission? Breck was inside the lobby now. Out of sight. She hoped the walls were thick enough the sound of grinding gears couldn't reach him. Putting it in first, she eased off the clutch and the Jeep jerked forward. Jenny wrestled the wheel. Didn't this thing have power steering? Parked cars ahead! She braked and it chugged, almost stalling. Somehow, she made it out of there without scraping paint.

"You go, girl."

With a metallic protest, she found second gear, and third was even smoother. It was all coming back. She started to relax. To own it. Until she saw a stop light in the distance. *Stay green. Stay green.* But it did not. Blazing yellow, devil red. Jenny stomped on the brake but forgot about the clutch. The Jeep lurched, sputtered and died. Now she'd have to get it going again. With traffic stacking up behind her.

The light went green and she froze and some idiot started honking his horn.

"Off to the races."

Pop the clutch. Peel the tires. But she was moving again.

Now, where did those baddies go? She passed the 7-Eleven, then the fire station, and then City Hall. She frowned as she drove by, but there was only one vehicle there. The librarian's Subaru Outback. The mayor's BMW wasn't there but Jenny spotted it at the Blue River Bank. What was that guy up to? It didn't matter. As long as he wasn't in her hair.

"If I was a cartel freak, where would I hide?"

Winding through town, she checked every side road, alleyway, and driveway. Risking a clutchy recon through the Safeway parking lot, she managed to emerge on the far side without raking off anybody's side-mirror. She flushed with pride.

"It's the simple things."

The CB was silent. Her phone was, too, but that was alright. With these clear skies, Jenny knew the cell signal was fine and Breck was having a heart to heart with his drug-pimp little brother. Freddy, okay. But Danny? Really? She could barely believe it. But getting gunned down by cartel hitmen was pretty hard to deny.

The ski resort. Another parking lot to navigate. Jenny was feeling better about starts and stops, but downshifting was stressful. So she didn't try. She kicked the Jeep out of gear and coasted in between the rows of parked vehicles until she ran out of momentum.

Jenny didn't see the black Range Rover, but she did see the mayor's daughter Aspen, and the mayor's receptionist Brittany. The girls had parked side by side and were taking skis off their roof racks, chatting the whole time.

"Skiing on a weekday," Jenny muttered. "I want to be twenty again."

She cruised past High Country Pizza, turned on Main Street, and drove down to check out Danny's brewery. The doors were locked. She pulled up alongside the curb and watched it for a while. What if the perps returned to the scene of the crime? Anything was possible, apparently.

Come noon, several hungry souls rattled the door handle. Stared in the windows. Looked around, confused. A lot of them were obviously skiers and mountain climbers, the way they were dressed, just looking for a burger. Lunch options were limited in Quandary. The Blue Moose only served coffee and breakfast. Besides a burrito and Slurpee at 7-Eleven, the only other option was a greasy hemp-baked pizza or a ten-minute drive to the Subway in Frisco.

Jenny unbuckled her seat belt and relaxed.

Her eyelids were heavy. She fought to keep them open but it was a losing battle. Leaning back, Jenny closed her eyes.

"Just for a second."

CHAPTER 21

Witty

Classic hospital smell. Disinfectant? Probably. And a classic hospital room chair in the corner. Not exactly comfortable for long periods of time. Breck sat up and rubbed his back. Danny was out of it. Juiced up on post-op drugs. Why did he even expect his brother to be awake so soon? Let alone coherent enough for a talk? Maybe it was for the best. Spending some time mentally replaying the past twenty-four hours in a quiet hospital room wasn't the worst idea.

"He wake up yet?"

It was Michelle. She was leaning against the door jamb. She was the office manager, so she didn't have to wear scrubs like the nursing staff. A Quandary County Medical Center name badge hung from her neck.

"Dead to the world." Breck squinted as soon as he said it. "You know what I mean."

"It was a dicey operation. Doctor Heller was here, so there's that. He used to do combat surgery in Iraq."

"Ah, good." Breck was starting to feel tongue-tied, trying to think of something to say that wasn't stupid.

"So what happened?" she asked.

Breck caught the scent of her hair. It somehow made it through the disinfectant. What did she say?

"Sorry. I'm sure you can't talk about it." Michelle mistook his bumbling for professionalism.

"Yeah, not really. Ongoing investigation. You know the drill."

Giving up on the chair, Breck stood up. He glanced at his younger brother. That big yellow beard. Mouth open and breathing deep—just like when they were kids, sharing a bedroom.

"He got caught up in something." Breck went over next to her. "You still got a security guard around here, right?"

"Is there anything to worry about?"

They were speaking in low voices so they wouldn't disturb Danny. Michelle's eyes were dark brown. They made her seem solemn. Attractive. But unreadable. Talking with her, up close like this, made him feel the same way he had felt on their Subway date, once upon a time.

"Yeah, it's just that the suspects are still out there. Looks like they split town, but it's good to play it safe. You know."

A phone started ringing. Michelle leaned out in the hallway to check the front desk. None of the nurses were anywhere near it.

"Check in with you later, Breck."

She went to get it and Breck watched her go. Nothing witty came to mind. Why was he trying to think of something witty? He went back over to the corner chair. Before he could sit down, he heard Michelle's voice on the intercom.

Sheriff Dyer, come to the front desk immedia . . . Breck, get down here. Quick!

Bolting down the hallway was like skating on ice. The floor tiles were slick. The maintenance guy had been mopping when he first arrived. Breck almost knocked a vase of flowers off the front desk skidding to a stop.

"You guys must get half your business from this hallway alone."

Now that was stupid. Subway stupid. Certainly not witty. And even if it was, the look on Michelle's face made it fall even flatter.

"The ski resort, Breck. There's been an avalanche." She never got rattled. But she was rattled. "Two skiers are missing. They think it's Aspen Matthews and Brittany Chisholm, the girl from City Hall."

The blizzard. It must have loaded the slopes overnight. Let loose when the sun came out.

"Can I borrow your car?" Breck asked.

Michelle grabbed her car keys out of her bag and ran around the desk.

"Gonna need all the help you can find. I'm coming with."

CHAPTER 22

Hawaii Vacation

The hospital wasn't too far away from the ski resort and while Michelle drove, Breck got Jenny on his cell phone. All the 9-1-1 calls were forwarded to her phone, so she already knew about the avalanche. And she was there already, too. They pulled in and parked behind the Jeep at the resort entrance.

"Every second counts." Jenny turned and pointed at the ridge. "The debris field is on the south side of Peak Three. They've got snowmobiles, ready to go. The manager's waiting for us by the chairlift. He pulled the staff together for a search crew."

The shortest path to the lift was directly through the resort. Breck, Jenny, and Michelle ran through the main corridor, past the gift shop and food court, and out the slope side entry. Sure enough, a group of employees was there, near the chairlift, pulling on coats and passing around probe poles and shovels to dig with. Snowmobiles were parked nearby, engines idling.

The resort manager was there, a young guy named Cash. It wasn't his real name. And it wasn't a nod to Johnny Cash, either. Breck made the mistake to ask once. Cash explained that if you visualize something it will come true. And if you name things after things you want, those things will actualize. Eventually. Send out positive vibes and the Universe will hear. He even had a cat named Hawaii Vacation.

"Hey. You. Did the girls have avalanche beacons?" Breck felt weird calling him Cash. So he avoided calling him anything.

"I don't know, but we have a bunch of transceivers in case they do." Cash held up a nylon sack. "There's like a dozen in here."

Breck looked around, counting heads.

"That's enough. One for everybody."

He climbed onto the lead machine and revved it up. Checked the fuel gauge out of habit. Too many times on the side of the road.

"Even though it slid already, that slope may be unstable," Breck said. "One person in the danger zone, that's me. I go first and check it out. Once we know it's safe, spread out and do a grid search. Keep your eyes open."

Jenny jumped on the seat behind him and they sped away.

Michelle, Cash and the resort staff saddled up on the other machines. No one really talked. Everyone knew this was serious.

Breck sped along an access trail, blasting through the fresh powder. It was pretty deep, even in the trees. Coming out of the forest, he slowed down and parked at the base of Peak Three. The debris field was obvious. A slab avalanche. He could see where it broke loose, up high.

"Let's hope it's done sliding. We don't have much time."

The avalanche had poured down the ski run and took out a bunch of trees in the process. Breck didn't like what he was looking at. It was quiet. Aspen and Brittany were in there somewhere. Buried alive.

"Look!" Jenny pointed at something. A bright orange sleeve. Sticking out of the snow.

"Wait right here, I'll go first," Breck told her. "If it breaks loose again, just . . . try to keep an eye on me but don't take any chances."

The rest of the search crew arrived. They grouped around Jenny, watching as Breck cautiously crossed the surface, his boots sinking in. He kept glancing up at the mountain.

Jenny paced. She looked around again, trying to spot anything that might indicate a survivor. Nothing obvious caught her eye. No ski poles, no skis sticking up. Just a sea of snow. How much oxygen did the girls have under there?

"Screw it." Jenny dashed out to help Breck dig. She called over her shoulder. "Spread out and start looking!"

Cash, despite his whimsical name, turned out to have leadership skills. And avalanche survival training. He passed out the beacons so everyone had one.

"Turn these on in receive mode." Holding one up, he showed everyone what to do. "Spread out arm to arm. Poke the probe in the snow but don't stab too hard. If it bumps into something, we dig."

Breck and Jenny knelt by the orange sleeve. The arm was exposed and as soon as Jenny touched it, the fingers started wiggling. They started digging like crazy. Yellow hair. It was Brittany, the mayor's receptionist.

"Am I in trouble?" she gasped, once they had her face exposed.

"You're not in trouble, you're safe." Jenny wiped the snow out of her eyes. "You're just in shock. Relax, we've got you."

"I'm in big trouble." Brittany started crying. "I called in sick today. I'm gonna lose my job."

"Hey! I've got something." Cash held up his avalanche transceiver. It was beeping.

The snow was deep and settling fast, like concrete. Michelle and the rest of the group surrounded Cash and began probing where the beeping sound was loudest.

"Aspen! Can you hear me?" Michelle called. She felt her probe hit something. "Right here. Everyone dig right here."

Using shovels, they dug quick but careful.

"Aspen! We're right here!" Michelle found a boot and started clawing at the snow. "I found her leg. Get her face clear, she needs air."

"Is she okay?" Breck called. He tried running over but got bogged down, post-holing through the surface up to his knees.

Jenny braced for the worst. She kept working on Brittany, who was able to sit up and watch. Either one of these girls could have broken bones or internal injuries. Or worse, in Aspen's case. There better be an ambulance waiting at the resort when they got back. They were going to need it.

"Aspen!" Brittany called, her voice cracking. "Aspen!"

The snow around Aspen's face was red with blood. Michelle swept it away, the girl opened her eyes and coughed. Her lips were split and her nose was bleeding. But she was alive.

"Daddy's going to kill me."

CHAPTER 23

Who's Hungry?

Danny was down the hall, but Breck hadn't had a chance to drop in. Aspen and Brittany were safe. Alive. The nearest Flight for Life chopper was based in Frisco. Aspen got airlifted. She was in bad shape, coughing blood and abdomen bruises. Maybe internal injuries. The Quandary County Search and Rescue team hiked in a basket stretcher for Brittany. She wanted to ride in the helicopter with Aspen but that was out of the question. There wasn't enough room in there for two stretchers, and the S&R team wanted her neck and back stabilized, just in case.

"I'm going to sue." Eyes red, Aspen's mother Valerie was lying on the couch in the waiting area.

Breck listened politely but said nothing. It was her first coherent sentence since she arrived. The stress and shock were wearing off. Now it was anger. Breck had seen many parents at terrible life moments, just like this. Grief, anger, lashing out, numbness, confusion. It was all natural. The question was, who was she talking about suing?

The automatic doors swished open.

"Where is she?" Mayor Matthews stormed toward the front desk. "My daughter, is she okay?"

Michelle stopped tapping on her keyboard and offered a compassionate smile. "The doctor is with her now. Your daughter is stable and alert. We will have more answers in just a few minutes."

Matthews glared at her, then started to head up the hallway. "What room is she in? You better tell me what room she's in."

Michelle stood up, going professional. She could be formidable when she needed to be. "I'm sorry, Mr. Matthews, but you can't go back there. That is a violation of hospital policy. Please be patient. You are welcome to sit in the waiting area. Your wife is here, too. Right over there."

He spun around and saw Valerie. His eyes narrowed. "Ex-wife."

"I am going to sue that ski resort," Valerie said. Loudly.

The mayor cringed and marched toward her, shushing her the whole way.

"Don't you shush me." Valerie jumped up and jabbed her finger in her ex-husband's face. "I want that whole resort shut down. Now. What idiot is running that place? They should have closed the runs in these conditions. And you better believe I am going to sue. This whole town if I need to!"

"No, you will not." Matthews swatted her hand away. "Now, calm down."

But Valerie slapped him in the face. Pop. Like a firecracker.

"My daughter almost died today. Tossed and crushed and suffocated beneath six feet of snow. Flown through the sky in an emergency medical helicopter, clinging to life. I was ten miles away when I got the call and I dropped everything and drove ninety miles an hour to get here when I did." She looked him up and down. "Nice of you to show up, Seneca."

Seething, she marched through the automatic doors and into the bright afternoon sunshine.

Mayor Matthews looked stunned, silent, eyes glued to the Coke machine.

"I hope she doesn't go far, Jenny's bringing us all sandwiches." Breck wasn't sure what to say. Probably not that. "From Subway." Probably not that, either.

Matthews bristled and turned on him.

"If anyone's getting sued, it's you."

"What are you talking about? I'm the good guy here."

"I should have been the first one you called. How is it, my only daughter just about dies in an avalanche and me, the mayor of this whole damn town, has to hear about it from Mrs. Long? I don't get a courtesy call from the sheriff, but I get a nice sticky note from the librarian."

Now it was Breck's turn to look stunned. "What? I did call you. It went right to voicemail. I left a message."

"Don't give me excuses. Especially when I can prove what an incompetent liar you are right here, right now." Whipping out his cell phone, Matthews tapped on the screen a couple of times.

A mechanical lady voice came through the speaker. *You have one new message.*

The bank. He had been at the bank. With the loan officer. He always shut his phone off when he went into meetings, especially money meetings.

Matthews slid the phone in his pocket without pressing play. "Whatever. You are an epic screw up for a sheriff. That pothead pizza guy could do a better job."

Swish. Jenny came in, carrying plastic bags with wrapped sandwiches. She saw them facing off and stopped in her tracks.

"Who's hungry?"

CHAPTER 24

Foxy Cop Discount

"Thought I was being helpful." Jenny looked to Breck for support, but he was too preoccupied. She tried again. "No mayo. On any of 'em. You know how it goes. You ask for a little mayo and you get half the bottle squeezed on there. Less is more, people."

Breck never locked the Jeep. Well, he couldn't. The lock mechanisms were rusted from forty years of rain, snow, dirt, and grit. But he was so preoccupied he took out his key and tried anyway. It went in and got stuck.

"Gotta be kidding me." He wiggled the key a few times. "There's a can of WD-40 in the back. Behind your seat."

"Oh, look. It's not locked." Sarcasm. Opening the passenger door, Jenny slid the seat forward and patted around. An old Nalgene water bottle. Some Clif Bar wrappers. The WD-40 felt kind of light, but not quite empty. She shook it up and walked around the Jeep.

"Move." Jenny pushed him out of the way and spritzed the key area. It didn't help. She tried again. "Come on, you sucka."

"I swear, no matter what I say or do, Matthews twists everything just to make me look bad," Breck muttered.

He threw some mean looks at the hospital, just as an elderly couple was coming out. They saw him and frowned. The wife took a wadded Kleenex from her sleeve and shook it at him in rebuke. Breck turned away and squinted at the shining white mountains.

"Ever since I've been here, he's been a douche." Jenny spritzed the key again.

It had been three years since Breck hired Jenny as the Deputy Sheriff of Quandary County. At the time, the Sheriff's Office had two other deputies, a dispatcher, three Ford Explorer patrol trucks, and a snowmobile that actually worked. That was the same year the town held a mayoral election. Winner by a slim majority—Seneca Matthews. The man had moved to Quandary barely a year earlier. Long enough to meet the residency requirements.

"His term is nearly up. Somebody else needs to get in there." Breck shaded his eyes. He could see Peak Three from the hospital parking lot. Even from a distance, he could tell where the avalanche slid. "Mayor Jennifer O'Hara. How does that strike you?"

"Sign me up for that." Sarcasm. Jenny went back around and rifled behind the passenger seat again. This time, she pulled out a McDonald's cup and yanked the straw. She brushed past him and used the straw to spray WD-40 directly inside the keyhole. It worked.

"Let's get out of here already." She tossed him the key and threw the can back behind her seat. "That's empty, by the way."

Feeling like an idiot, Breck pulled the Jeep out of the hospital parking lot and headed down the road. The weather had done a one-eighty. Sun was out. The snow was melting fast. Instead of black ice, the tires were kicking up melt-water. It felt good to be driving. Every mile he put behind him, he could feel the tension ease.

Jenny rolled her window down. Cool, fresh air swirled in and made her red hair flip around. She closed her eyes and let out a long sigh.

"I'm starving." They had abandoned their sandwiches in the hospital waiting area. "Too much drama."

Flipping on the blinker, Breck slowed down and pulled into High Country Pizza. He parked next to Freddy's old Honda Civic, shut off the engine and gave Jenny a thumbs up.

"Plan B."

"I'm not eating in this pigsty."

"We'll take it back to the office."

Breck led the way. The entry bell tinkled. Freddy was inside and when he saw them he threw up his hands in mock terror. "Hands up, don't shoot."

"Get a new line. And a life while you're at it." Jenny wasn't in the mood. She leaned to see through the sneeze guard. "All the veggies you got. And *no* pepperoni. I still can't get the smell out of my hair. You need to drive that thing through the car wash—windows down."

Freddy spread a ladle of tomato sauce on some rolled-out pizza dough. He winked at her and sprinkled on mushrooms and green peppers. "Foxy cop discount."

"Not the first time I've been called that," Breck said. He pulled out his wallet. "I'll take the compliment. And the discount."

"You're a riot, man. You should be on stage somewhere."

"Listen up. You still dealing?" Breck was being serious. "Don't lie to me, because all I have to do is ask around."

Freddy held up a piece of spinach as if it were the only kind of leaf he trafficked in.

"Outta the budtender biz. Hey, man . . . whatever happened to them cartel cats?"

As the thought sank in, his eyes went wide, and Freddy scoped out the street through the big store windows, suddenly terrified the cartel men were parked outside. Not paying attention to what he was doing, he dribbled banana peppers into the shredded mozzarella container. Seeing what he did, he carefully picked them back out. Of course, the cheese had an extra pickly glisten it didn't have before.

"Now look what you made me do."

Breck pointed at the toppings. "Put some pepperoni on my half. I still like them."

There were several round diner style tables by the window. Jenny went over and collapsed into a squeaky chair. Three of the legs touched the ground evenly. The other leg was a half inch too short. It was like a rocking chair. "Is it the weekend yet?"

Freddy stuck the pizza in the oven to cook and wiped his hands on a greasy towel. He came around the counter and handed Jenny a big plastic cup.

"Free soda. For the foxy cop."

"Fine with me." She grabbed it and went to the fountain drink machine. She tried the Diet Coke but all that fizzed out was soda water. "I guess it's Mountain Dew, then. How do they make this stuff again? Oh, that's right. Sugar, caffeine, and yellow dye number seven. But why does it taste so good, you ask? Well, the secret is in the embalming fluid."

Jenny glared at Freddy, but he wasn't listening. His eyes were out the front window watching a pickup drive by. The deer in the headlights look again.

"Nobody appreciates my humor."

As she filled up her cup with Mountain Dew, Breck eased into the other chair and laid his forehead on the tabletop. The surface was gritty. He could feel crumbs against his brow. A weekend sounded nice. So did a vacation.

The street outside was clear again. Exhaling, Freddy glanced at Breck.

"How's your bro, bro?"

That made Breck sit up straight. Danny . . .

"Oops."

In the hoopla with the Matthews, the avalanche and the accusations, he had forgotten to check in on his own brother.

CHAPTER 25

Drop Everything

"Just get out of here, Seneca. You came, you saw, now leave."

"Try and be civil, Valerie."

Mayor Matthews hated how his ex-wife spoke to him. Always snarky. What did she have to be so angry about now? It had been two whole years since the divorce. She should be over it by now. Especially since she had walked away with a sizable chunk of his hard-earned money. A nineteen-year-old daughter who barely cheated death should have brought them together. Softened the edge. But while Valerie was a bitter woman who liked to hold grudges, Matthews was a pragmatic man who held the title to her house.

He smiled at the thought.

Valerie thought he was being civil.

"I apologize, Seneca." She gave Aspen a hand squeeze. "Mommy and daddy still love you, dear. And this was certainly not your fault. Not the divorce. And not the horrible accident. Someone will be held accountable, let me tell you what."

Covered in a blue knit blanket, Aspen lay quietly in the hospital bed staring at the ceiling. Both eyes purple. Swollen nose crosshatched in first-aid tape. Her wrist hidden beneath ice packs.

"Can I talk to Brittany?" she asked.

"She's asleep next door, we shouldn't disturb her." Matthews shifted. His feet hurt. He had been standing for hours. Valerie had planted herself in the only chair, pulled up near their daughter's bed, and refused to relinquish it. "You should get some rest, too."

"Have Brittany's parents arrived?" Valerie looked at Aspen but was speaking to Matthews. "Maybe you should go check."

"Maybe I will."

Closing the door behind him, Matthews started down the hallway but paused in front of a sorry pastel painting. A golden pond surrounded by butterflies and cattails. How quaint. Did someone dig this out of a garage sale penny bin?

The Quandary County Medical Center was so small, so clunky, it embarrassed him as mayor. It needed a complete upgrade. It should be a high tech surgical center, a medical mecca for the entire Rocky Mountain region. High-end artwork lining the walls, gallery quality. And how about an actual helipad? The Flight for Life had to land in the parking lot, for crying out loud.

Every winter some B-list celebrities and politicians came to ski. Matthews wanted more. He wanted A-list celebrities. The vice-president. Foreign government officials on holiday. What if they wheeled Brad Pitt down this very hallway after a snowboard wipeout? Quandary had a long way to go to be the next Telluride. But who knows? Maybe they could lure Kevin Costner to buy a couple of hundred acres on the edge of town. That would put them on the map.

"Michelle? Is that you?"

That came from an open door. Matthews peeked in and saw Danny Dyer propped up on pillows. He was hooked to an IV and monitors and looked bewildered.

"Hello Daniel, how are you feeling?" Matthews stepped inside.

"Hey, mister mayor. Like I got run over by a dump truck. One of those big ones." Danny put his hand over his chest bandage and winced. "That's gonna leave a mark."

Matthews studied Breck's brother. The guy wasn't the sharpest knife in the drawer. For a moment, he almost wished him well and left. But why waste a perfectly good opportunity?

"I understand you took a bullet. What happened?"

Danny didn't answer right away and Matthews didn't wait for him to make up a lie.

"Heard it was a robbery. What a world we live in, am I right? Well, you just heal up and as soon as you're able to work those taps, I'll be the first in line. That Ten Mile Milk Stout you serve is top notch."

Relaxing, Danny smiled and licked his lips. "I could use a pint right about now."

"Me, too." Matthews went over to the windows and pulled the blinds. A private conversation was always best when it was private. "I know this is a tough situation. Getting shot, laid up in the hospital. The brewery closed. Losing income every day you're in here. I'm a businessman, I get it."

Danny's soft smile faded.

"Yeah, man. Raw deal."

"It is a raw deal," Matthews said and patted him on the leg. "I want you to know, you've got my complete support. Whatever you need."

He let that sink in. Complete support. It was a good spin of the facts. That's what politicians did anyway. Spin facts. The reason Danny was lying in that hospital bed in the first place was that Matthews hired Mexican cartel *sicarios* to push Danny out of the weed business. Things had gone too far, of course. Matthews didn't want Danny shot. That part was unfortunate.

"I'm a little surprised your brother hasn't stepped up."

"What do you mean?"

Danny leaned forward a little, groaned, and sank back down. He must have just come to. His eyes looked watery and bloodshot.

"If it was *my* brother, I'd drop whatever I was doing and help out." Matthews was still mad at Valerie. For saying he didn't drop everything like she did. But it was a good argument. It wasn't logical, but emotional manipulation was better than logic. "Breck could be keeping the brewery doors open. While you're . . . incapacitated."

"But Breck's a cop. I doubt he's got the time."

Matthews shrugged. "Yeah? Well, what's more important than family? He could quit the sheriff gig in a heartbeat—if he really wanted to." He itched his head like he was confused. "I mean, you got shot, man. That wasn't your fault. Now you're losing money every minute the doors are closed. How long are you gonna be in here? Even when they let you go home, you have to heal up. Take it easy. You can't be doing any heavy lifting. A fifty-pound bag of specialty grain is going to feel like a hundred with a gimpy arm. Maybe even blow your stitches."

Danny listened, his brow crinkling the more Matthews talked.

"I'm just saying. That's what brothers do." Matthews got up and went to the door. He glanced back as if he just thought of something. "If I'm being honest? Maybe Breck's in over his head anyway. Not everyone's cut out to be a cop."

"I don't know," Danny mumbled.

Matthews shook his head, sympathetically, but with a hint of disdain. "You got shot on your brother's watch. Not cool, man."

CHAPTER 26

Savant

A decent night's sleep in his own bed. A bowl of instant oatmeal with brown sugar and cinnamon, and a good cup of homebrewed coffee. Fresh ground beans, four minutes steeping in the French press. A splash of half and half. Just like at the office, the cabinet in Breck's kitchen was stacked with ceramic *Ski Quandary!* mugs. The rest went in an old Stanley steel thermos that wedged perfectly between the driver's seat and the Jeep door.

Breck ducked in the laundry room really quick. His nice Marmot mummy bag had gone through a couple of wash cycles. He gave it a sniff. Satisfied it was no longer contaminated with Freddy leak, he stuffed it in the clothes dryer.

Danny had lied. College kid robbery? The truth was so obvious now. Freddy and Danny were the weed ballers of Quandary. The huff daddies. Danny's only connection to college kids was distributing an illegal substance. So how long had Danny been involved? Freddy, now that made perfect sense. But Danny was in on it this whole time. Breck was blindsided.

It may be legal in the state of Colorado's eyes, but it was still against the law inside city limits. And federal law, too.

As a peace officer, Breck saw the dark side to the drug culture that the average citizen didn't. He had a rant if anyone asked. The heavy toll of addiction. The role played in crime, public safety, and mental health. He had friends who worked in the hospitals in Denver, and they said ER visits had tripled ever since marijuana was legalized in Colorado. And all those modern studies denying it was a gateway drug? Maybe not for everyone, but in his opinion, too many people did make the jump to hard drugs. Black tar heroin. Blue crystal meth. White horse cocaine. And what people didn't realize, was that Mexican cartels funneled ninety percent of America's drugs across the border. He didn't want to see Quandary turn into Juarez.

It was mid-May. The mountains were still white and they would be well into the summer. But even at 9,000 feet, the streets were clear. Melted. Gone in a day. That was it. No more blizzards this year. Breck could feel the change in the air as he locked his cabin door. The willows along the creek were budding pretty good, and the mountain grasses around his cabin were greening up too.

The old wooden porch creaked under his weight. He climbed into the Jeep and wedged the thermos in the door. Breck hated to drink coffee out of insulated travel mugs. They may have lids, but plastic cups made coffee taste plastic. It was a trick shifting gears with his right hand, holding a *Ski Quandary!* mug in his left, and keeping the steering wheel steady with his knees. It was more art than science. But practice makes perfect and he was a knee-steering coffee-balancing savant.

"Alrighty, Danny. Time to 'fess up."

Breck fired up the Jeep. His cabin sat on an open hillside at the edge of a small mountain lake. The waters were dark and choppy. Most of the surface ice from the winter was gone. There was one last ice bar floating in the shadows on the south side, topped off with some fresh slush from the blizzard. It was almost warm enough to take a fishing pole down there. Lean up against that old gray log on the shore, prop the pole up. Have a smoke. Except he was done with cigarettes. Kind of. Neighbors keep saying there were trout. He hadn't caught one yet since he bought the place, but that didn't matter. It was therapy just to sit and stare and nod off.

"Yeah, I need to get down there. Maybe next weekend."

Fishing license from the Parks & Wildlife website. Some bait from the hardware store. He didn't have waders or anything like that. Didn't need all that gear. Didn't want it. Maybe it was better he didn't catch anything anyhow. He wouldn't know how to clean a fish if he caught one.

The CB crackled.

"Come in, Breck. This is Jenny. You there?"

He pulled at the mic to get it unwrapped from the stick shift, like usual. He managed to do it without spilling his coffee.

"Yeah. Go ahead."

"Call came in. Robbery at the hardware store last night. Come pick me up."

The hospital would have to wait. Breck felt a twinge of guilt. He should have just gone over there last night. Oh well. Danny wasn't going anywhere.

"Be there in ten. And hey. Remind me to buy some bait."

Breck rolled his window down. He liked the sound of the gravel road beneath the tires. Ping of rocks hitting the wheel wells.

It was just a dream, wasn't it? Breck knew better. He wasn't going to buy any bait. And he wasn't going fishing anytime soon. He took a quick sip of hot coffee.

Where were those cartel men? They could be all the way in Mexico by now. It was possible they made it out of the state, even with the BOLO. They had plenty of time to get away. Breck was glad Aspen and Brittany hadn't been hurt worse in the avalanche, but it was a distraction. Long enough. The bad guys had all the time they needed and there was nothing Breck could do in a situation like that.

If he had more deputies, things could have turned out different. From the beginning, it would have been different. With more officers patrolling the streets, maybe Danny wouldn't have got shot. No gunmen could have cornered Jenny in the Sheriff's Office, that was for sure. A twinge of guilt knotted up in his gut as he thought about it. She could have been killed. Right there. She shouldn't be alone in that office. Not with a prisoner and cartel men on the loose.

There was only one reason they were short staffed.

The city of Quandary was too small to afford its own police force. So they worked out a law enforcement contract with the Quandary County Sheriff's Office. They paid Breck to patrol the city. They even set him up in the old church building on Main Street for an office.

The county itself didn't have much money, either. Funds came in through property taxes and speeding tickets, basically. So when the Quandary city council reached out for help, it was a good deal. Breck could afford what he needed. Staff. Vehicles. Tools for success.

Until Matthews got elected.

CHAPTER 27

You're Missing Out

The hardware store was a few miles past the turnoff to Freddy's place. It was called the General Merchandise and More. How did the place keep its doors open? It was an outpost, in the middle of nowhere, halfway between Quandary and Alma—an even smaller town than Quandary.

Alma. Breck was glad they weren't driving all the way up there. The town was nice, but the police chief was full of it.

"Don't get so close to the edge," Jenny said.

The ravine. She was seated in the passenger seat, which had a clear view of the drop-off right out the window. With the guardrails down, it made the canyon drive extra exciting.

Jenny tugged her seat-belt to make sure it was latched, and Breck smiled.

"I haven't gone over yet. Not once."

Jenny smirked, but without any humor.

"Once is all it takes."

She was obviously trying to forget about the death drop. It was kind of funny. Whenever she got nervous she lost the ability to chit chat. Her words tumbled out in a runaway monologue.

"Hot diggity damn, this weather is unbelievable. Sunshine and clear skies. Look at those mountain tops. Yo, check it! I think I see an eagle. Look up there! Is that an eagle? It's an eagle, Breck. No, wait. It's just a crow. Or a magpie or something. Man, this weather is *so* nice. I can't believe it. Can you?"

"Sure."

"Won't be long and the monsoon rains are gonna hit. It'll be pouring all the time. Every single afternoon. I need to put this marshmallow coat in storage and dig out my rain jacket. I don't know what I hate worse. Freezing cold or getting drenched."

Jenny wriggled to get out of her coat without taking off her seat-belt.

"I know this thing makes me look like the Michelin Man but I don't care. It's warm and that's all that counts. Style is one thing, function is another. Maybe someday, someone will figure out how to make a coat that looks cute *and* keeps you warm. How about that?"

"How about that."

The narrow canyon road began to get steeper, gaining elevation. Breck downshifted. With that big Corvette V8 engine under the hood, it never lacked power. But it did drink gasoline like a keg-pounding frat boy.

"Open the glove box," he said. "Get the notebook and see how many miles I got left on this tank of gas."

"I will, hold on. This might as well be a straight jacket."

Her arm was jammed in the sleeve.

"Hey, Houdini. Why don't you take off your seat-belt, it'll be a lot easier? Just for a second."

"You have one job. Not to roll this Jeep."

It wasn't working. Giving up, Jenny put her coat back on and wiped the sweat from her forehead. Opening the glove box, she dug out the notebook. She closed her eyes for a second to do the math.

"Another twenty miles left. Then we're screwed."

They left the canyon and with it, the threat of imminent death. They drove past Timber Ridge Road, where Freddy lived, and kept going until the General Merchandise and More came into sight. The store did indeed have more. Besides fishing bait and frozen Snickers bars, it was also a gas station.

"Crisis averted." Breck pulled around to the pumps, which were pretty ancient. They didn't even have a credit card port.

"I'm heading in. I'm getting a bottle of coconut water." Jenny tore off her heavy coat and stuffed it behind the seat. "You want anything?"

"Yeah, get me one."

Jenny gawked at him.

"What? You don't drink coconut water."

"You're right. How about one of those hot dogs. The wilty ones on the rollers."

"Now I know you're messing with me."

She spun around and walked into the building.

Breck got the pump going and cleaned off the windshield with a squeegee. A couple of cars drove by, but the road between Quandary and Alma wasn't busy. It rarely was. It only saw traffic in the fall when sightseers drove through to see the changing leaves. Or Saturdays when weekend warriors were checking out the trailheads.

Jenny stepped back outside carrying a small carton of coconut water and a hot dog in a cardboard tray.

Breck raised an eyebrow. "I was just kidding."

"It's not for you." She sat on the bumper and started working on the hot dog. "You're missing out. This thing is filled with jalapeño cheese sauce."

"You know those are a couple of weeks old, right?"

Jenny took another bite and forced a smile, spitting bun chunks in the process. "Heat lamps, hoses, fertilizer, shovels, rakes."

The nozzle clicked and shut off. Breck hung it back on the pump and twisted the gas cap back on the Jeep. "Somebody wants to do some serious gardening."

Jenny finished her lunch and took a gulp of water. "Sump pump and a generator, too."

"That's quite a list. What else was stolen?"

"Some beer from the cooler. But they didn't even touch the cash register."

Breck turned and studied the General Merchandise and More. The front door was propped open and he could easily see a pane of glass had been shattered. "All that, and they didn't steal the hot dogs? Man, they can't even give those things away."

"I don't feel good about this."

"The break-in, or what you just ate?"

Jenny got to her feet and circled the Jeep a couple of times, looking uncomfortable.

"Yeah, I'm gonna hurl."

CHAPTER 28

Connecting the Dots

"Heat lamps and fertilizer." Breck drummed his fingers on the steering wheel. "You think Freddy is starting up again?"

"Or those cartel freaks. Maybe they're setting up shop in Alma."

Jenny was curled up in the passenger seat with her eyes closed.

"Just puke. You'll feel better."

"And waste five bucks? I don't think so."

It was noon by the time they made it back to Quandary. Breck wanted to check out several forest roads near the General Merchandise and More before heading back. Make a quick patrol of the area, see if they could spot anything unusual. Like a black Range Rover. Or a Honda Civic. They even swung past Freddy's place on their way back down the canyon and knocked on the door. He didn't answer and his car wasn't there either.

Breck guided the Jeep through the canyon. He rolled down his window and hooked his elbow outside. The tires hummed on the blacktop. The ravine was outside his window this time. He didn't have a problem with heights. Not like Jenny. But Breck had spent years rock climbing, ice climbing, and all kinds of technical mountain ascents. Ropes, harnesses, carabiners. Alaska, the Canadian Rockies, the Alps and even a couple expeditions to the Himalaya. But those days were over.

"Hurry up," Jenny gripped the door handle like she was going to open it. "I've got a bottle of Pepto in my desk."

"Two minutes. You can make it."

The summer tourist season hadn't begun yet, so Main Street was still an easy drive. Give it a couple of weeks and it wouldn't be, given the population surge. Quandary always quadrupled, or more. Traffic would halt while some hipster tried to parallel park outside the Starbucks. Herds of pedestrians constantly crossing the street. A never-ending parade of bicycles and motorbikes and RVs. The two-minute drive from the mouth of the canyon to the Sheriff's Office could stretch into thirty.

They passed Danny's brewery. The parking lot was empty. Right about now, his brother should be working overtime to get extra brews fermenting for the business boom. Breck felt bad for him. Bad timing.

"I need to get over to the hospital and see how Danny is doing."

"Wait. It's your turn to write up the burglary report." Jenny cracked open an eye. "You trying to pawn that off on me?"

"Sorry." Breck shrugged. "Brother got shot."

"Lame excuse. How come I always get stuck with the desk work?"

"I'll tell Danny you send your best."

Pulling into the Sheriff's Office parking lot, Breck kept the engine running while Jenny crawled out.

"Hey, Jen Jen. You forgot your coat."

"Yeah, Breck, I'll get it later buddy. Adios."

Jenny was obviously annoyed. It was fun to mess with her.

She went to the office door and as she fumbled with the keys, a big Ford F350 dually with a flatbed trailer stacked high with square bale hay parked out front and honked. Johnny Tibbs jumped out of the driver's seat and waved.

"Good day there, Jennifer." Tibbs always wore nicely pressed collared shirts, jeans and buckaroo style boots. He was wearing a straw cowboy hat, instead of his dark brown one, which was a sure sign winter was over. That, and he had shaved off his beard.

"Talk to Breck." Jenny pushed the door open and went inside.

Johnny Tibbs smiled and tipped his hat, but she was gone. He angled for the Jeep and Breck shut off the engine. His talk with Danny might have to wait a little longer.

"Like a jackrabbit," Tibbs said, nodding towards the Sheriff's Office.

"That's what happens when you ask for volunteers to unload your trailer, one too many times." Breck got out and leaned against the fender. He offered Tibbs a Clif Bar. He always kept a stash of Clif Bars in the Jeep. "You're going to need this if you're throwing hay."

"You kidding? That's what I got ranch hands for." But he took one anyway. He glanced at the office again. "Give that girl a night off. And tell me when it is, so I can take her to supper."

Breck unwrapped his granola bar and ate a bite. He chewed thoughtfully.

"You're not her type."

"Clean cut? Successful?" Tibbs stepped back and gave Breck's Jeep a low whistle, sarcastic. Then he hooked a thumb at the F350. "All the bells and whistles. The good kind. Not the kind that go off when your engine catches fire."

Breck reached over and reclaimed the Clif Bar from Tibbs' hand. "You stop by for a reason?"

"Hell yes. I want to see if that redhead wants to go on a horseback ride with me."

"She's busy."

Tibbs smiled. A little Cheshire, a little Jagger. Then he placed a cowboy boot up on the Jeep bumper. Crossed his arms over his knee.

"City council is meeting in about a week. Our good mayor came over to see me this morning for a pep talk. Asked me how I like that cell tower. Did I get good reception, good WIFI? Reminded me how *he* was the swing vote to get it installed. Mike Jameson wanted it on the ridge above his neighborhood." Tibbs took his hat off and wiped his forehead. He glanced up at the sun. "Is it just me or is it baking hot already?"

"What's Matthews want?"

"Said he wants to get a building permit. For one of those big Clear Span indoor arenas. Metal frame. Covered in canvas. He needs the city council's approval."

"I'm not connecting the dots yet."

Breck finished up his Clif Bar and flicked the wrapper behind the seat.

Tibbs glanced at the Sheriff's Office door again. It was still closed.

"Says he wants to start a horseback riding program for handicapped kids. Wants to work with me to get it going."

Breck wiggled a finger in his ear. "Say what now?"

CHAPTER 29

Locked and Loaded

It turned out propping a ladder against the slanted ceiling of an A-frame cabin was precarious. El Sangrador found that out the hard way trying to string up all the heat lamps. The vibrations from the power drill caused the ladder to shimmy. He was on the upper rungs as it skittered sideways. He hit the floor like a brick.

Zorrero watched the whole thing from the couch, eating a bag of the blood-letter's microwave popcorn.

Having lost his wind, El Sangrador managed a raspy *"¡Ay!"* and lay gasping. His silver aviator sunglasses had flown off and landed all the way by the fridge.

"Maybe a cold drink will help." Zorrero got up from the couch and went to the kitchen area, and pushed the sunglasses away from the door with his toe. Leaning to get inside the mini refrigerator, he extracted a bottle of Coors Light. They had stolen several six-packs from the General Merchandise and More, along with the heat lamps and gardening supplies. He twisted the top off and went back to the couch. "Yes, this does help. That popcorn is so dry."

The blood-letter slowly rose to his feet. When he fell, his leg got caught between the rungs. His shin was throbbing with pain. It was excruciating. The skin felt tingly and hot but he didn't think his leg was broken.

"You should get one of these, amigo." Zorrero held up his Coors Light.

Gritting his teeth, El Sangrador moved toward the fridge, limping as he walked.

They should have stolen an aluminum construction ladder with nice rubber footers from the hardware store. That would have been smart. This one was designed as a loft ladder, heavy and clunky. Made of smooth wood poles, it was more for looks than function.

Putting his sunglasses back on, El Sangrador returned to the task of hanging heat lamps. Someone at the bottom stabilizing the ladder would be much safer, but Zorrero was his lieutenant. He didn't dare make a request like that, despite the chummy comments.

"Here comes another trailer. Those *caballeros* getting ready for all the rich gringos who wanna play cowboy." Zorrero pointed at the front window.

A pickup with a long stock trailer full of horses rumbled past the cabin. There was a lot of activity at the Tibbs Ranch. Cars kept driving in. A big reefer truck had parked by the lodge earlier that morning. Like ants, a line of people unloaded frozen food packages and took them inside. Most of them were clearly kitchen staff, wearing white aprons. They all looked young. College kids, summer jobs.

Zorrero got up and went to the front window to see better. Sipped his beer.

"Careful no ones sees you, commander." El Sangrador slowly climbed up the ladder again. One rung at a time. "This place is supposed to be empty."

"*Cállate, hombre,*" Zorrero said it without much force. It was more of a friendly *shut up*. Regardless, the blood-letter did not pursue the conversation any further.

Twisting an eye-bolt into the hole he had drilled in the ceiling, the blood-letter tied one end of a clothesline to it and climbed back down. He hefted the ladder to the other side of the room and set another eye-bolt, threaded the clothesline through and pulled it taught.

It would be perfect for a row of heat lamps. The A-frame living room looked like a jungle. But all the marijuana plants from Freddy's place were looking a little limp. The sooner they had light and water, the better.

"Here comes another one. A big trailer full of hay." Zorrero pressed his face to the glass like a kid at a candy store. "Hey Sangre, get over here, quick. Look at this nice shiny new pickup truck. F350 diesel Platinum package. Got the moon roof, crew cab, gooseneck. Whole thing's made of chrome. That thing's sixty thousand dollars, easy . . ."

Then he pulled out his cell phone and looked at the caller ID. It was vibrating.

"*Hola?*" He listened for a moment, then hung up. "The coyote is at the trailhead. Let's go. We can get these lamps up later."

The blood-letter came right down, put the power drill on the coffee table, and picked up his Colt .45 with the white pearl grips and rolled the chamber.

"Locked and loaded."

Zorrero snickered. "You watch too many American movies."

CHAPTER 30

Graveyard

Before going to the trailhead to meet the coyote, Zorrero and El Sangrador drove up to Alma first.

The Almart was Alma's answer to Walmart. If the answer was "kind of, but not really." It was tiny, just like the town. But it had groceries. The only other place to buy groceries within a hundred miles was the Safeway in Quandary, but El Sangrador knew that was too big of a risk. The pesky sheriff was down there, waiting. Watching.

So they went inside the Almart and walked the aisles. A radio station with hits from the '80s was playing in the background. Def Leppard was singing about the misuse of confectionaries. *Pour some sugar on maaaaay.*

Still wearing his mirror sunglasses, the Colt .45 sticking out of his belt, El Sangrador pushed a shopping cart. It had a squeaky wheel.

Squeak, squeak, squeak.

He leaned on it for support, because the limp had not yet gone away. His shin still burned from the ladder accident. El Sangrador, despite the broken condition of his moral compass, felt self-conscious about his broken stride. Frankenstein limped in those old black and white B-movies, didn't he? It certainly diminished the image of a hitman impervious to pain. He kept waiting for Zorrero to question his readiness, or mock him, but it had not happened yet.

"May I help you, gentlemen?"

An acne-ravaged teenager was stocking boxes of Lucky Charms onto a shelf. He stared as they went by, ignoring him like he didn't exist. His skin tone was pale, to begin with, but somehow grew even paler. Translucent. It was like he was trying to turn himself invisible.

Squeak, squeak, squeak.

Just past the cereal were canned goods and bags of dried vegetables. Zorrero pointed at a shelf full of pinto beans, yellow peas, and rice.

"Those."

The blood-letter slid his arm behind the beans and swept them all into the cart. Then he did the same with the rice and yellow peas.

Strolling further down the aisle, Zorrero paused to examine the label on a can of Dinty Moore. "If they get it done by the weekend, they can have something special to look forward to."

Bringing the cart close, El Sangrador loaded it up with beef stew, filling the basket area to the top. Zorrero didn't appear interested in anything else. He led the way to the checkout lane.

No one else was in the building. No customers, no manager, no one at the register. The place was a graveyard. The stock boy was frozen, a trembling box of cereal in his clutches. His eyes on the .45 in the blood-letter's belt. It was clear by the look on his face, he believed Almart was going to be *his* graveyard.

Zorrero caught his eye and waved. "We are leaving now. Ring us up."

Trance broken, the kid hustled over to the register and began swiping bar codes. He kept his eyes down, especially avoiding the blood-letter's terrifying silver mirror sunglasses. Even a peripheral glance was clearly too much to bear. He swept can after can of Dinty Moore. Beep. Beep. Can after can. Then beans and rice, bag after bag. Beep. Beep. Beep. His hands left sweaty palm prints on each item as they went by.

Pour some sugar on maaaaay.

CHAPTER 31

Little Buddy

Breck rapped his knuckles on the doorframe and Danny turned to see who it was.

"You look better than the last time I saw you," Breck said. He shut the door behind him. He was carrying a brown paper sack. "Brought you something."

Itching his bushy beard, Danny showed no sign that he cared what was in the bag, but Breck held it up like it was a winning lottery ticket.

"I dropped by the 7-Eleven. Looky here."

He opened it up and pulled out a pack of bottled Guinness.

"What is that crap?" Danny looked pained. "That's the competition, dude. Why would you bring that in here?"

"Well yeah, but . . . it's not exactly swill." Breck set it on the window ledge and patted his pockets. "You got a bottle opener?"

"Get out of here, man."

Breck smiled, but then stopped smiling. Danny was totally serious. Breck put the bottles back in the paper sack and set the whole thing on the floor out of sight.

"Sorry. I would have come sooner, but it's been super crazy. How are you holding up?"

Danny let out a slow, deep sigh. It sounded very similar to a leaky tire.

"Do you know how far behind I am? Summer is about to start and I can't get ready, stuck in here. The brewery is all I got, man. You hear me?"

The blinds were closed, even though it was late in the afternoon. Breck pulled the cords and daylight streamed in. Danny covered his eyes with his hand and turned away.

"Let's let some light in here," Breck said. He meant it more than one way. Nice time was over. "You lied to me. I'm the sheriff of this whole county, and I find out my own brother is selling drugs right under my nose. That same brother just got gunned down by a Mexican cartel. Yeah, that's you. They were trying to put you out of business, Danny. How does that feel? Being in the middle of a turf war?"

Danny kept his hand over his eyes. His jaw was clenched.

Breck waited for his brother to argue. He knew it was coming. But Danny sighed again. Another slow, deep sigh.

"This is what we call a pickle."

"What do you want me to say?" Danny dropped his hand in his lap but looked out the window.

His face had more lines than Breck remembered. The skin tighter across his face. His eyes were sunken in a bit. And here Breck was, yelling at him. A shooting victim. His own brother.

"Remember those family picnics?" Danny asked. He looked like he was going to cry. "Mom made potato salad and ham sandwiches. Sour cream and onion potato chips. I always wanted Lays, so that's the brand she bought. Just for me, cuz that's what I liked. I hated Ruffles. Do they even still make Ruffles? I hope not."

"Yeah, I don't know."

Breck sunk into the corner chair. What was he doing? He didn't need to have this talk yet. Not now. Not like this. A light touch, that would have been the right move.

"Where was that? Do you know?" Danny looked at Breck, pleading. Almost desperate for the answer. "Somewhere near Denver, it's gotta be. I've driven all over trying to find it, but I can't. The creek. That old picnic table. I can't find it . . . I can't . . ."

His brother's face was flushed and the heart monitor was racing. This wasn't fake. Breck looked at the floor.

"Near Mt. Evans. Guanella Pass, I think."

"Remember dad? Panning for gold. I think all I ever found was Fool's Gold, but he said it was real and he was proud of me. Me, Breck. Proud of . . . *me*." Some tears dripped down Danny's cheek. He was barely keeping it together. "I'm such a screw-up."

"Naw, man. You're not."

Danny cleared his throat and blotted his face with the bed sheet.

"Can you help me out?"

Breck glanced up, with a firm nod. "Whatever you need."

"The brewery. I need you to take over. I can't run it like this. If we don't get the doors open, I'm sunk."

It took Breck off guard. "I've got a full time . . . there's a lot going on right now. A lot of responsibilities. As sheriff. You know?"

Danny's face went flat. He smirked a little and shook his head. "That's what I thought."

The heart monitor slowed, going back to normal. Breck got out of the chair, coming closer, and sat on the edge of the bed. "Hey, I'll think of something. Okay? It's not over."

Danny looked him in the eye.

"Quit."

"Quit what?"

One of the nurses pushed open the door. "Mr. Dyer?"

Both Breck and Danny replied simultaneously, "Yes?" The nurse's name tag said 'Melinda.' That was it. She was one of the paramedics that day at the brewery. Breck kept thinking her name was Brenda for some reason.

"Your heartbeat was rapid. I just wanted to check in but I see you are fine." She looked at her wristwatch. "It's four o'clock now. I'll bring you a dinner tray in an hour, okay?"

Danny shrugged, so she stepped back into the hallway.

Breck waved. "Thanks, Brenda."

She frowned. "It's Melinda."

"I knew that."

She left the door open. They could barely hear her soft footsteps as she walked away. All the nurses wore the same white lace-up shoes. Breck shifted his weight and started to get to his feet. It was time for him to walk away, too.

"Take that crap with you." Danny was talking about the Guinness.

Breck picked up the paper sack. The bottles clinked.

"Everything's gonna work out fine, little buddy."

"That's what dad always said." Danny frowned. "You're not dad so don't act like it."

They always watched *Gilligan's Island* reruns as a family. Pizza slices on paper plates and plastic TV trays. Whenever there was a serious problem, a bad grade, or a bully at school, their father always said that. To both of them. Whoever needed to hear it the most. *Everything's gonna work out fine, little buddy.*

"Sorry." Breck wasn't sure why he said it. It just came out. "I'll check in again tomorrow, okay?"

CHAPTER 32

Tangy Bouquet

Danny was mad at him. For what exactly? Breck couldn't just quit being sheriff. There was too much happening, too much on his shoulders. Danny of all people ought to be cheering him on. Catch the bad guys who tried to kill him. They were still on the loose. Who knew, they could even circle back into Quandary and cause more trouble. Anything was possible.

That reminded him of something. He looked up and down the hallway. Where was the hospital security guard? He mentioned it to Michelle when they first brought Danny in. Dangerous times. They needed to be extra vigilant.

The hospital relied on a private company. Maybe the word "company" was generous. It was called Security Expert Services, but the only expert Breck had ever seen was a middle-aged guy with a beer belly and a goatee, a can of pepper spray on his belt. An ex-TSA employee from Denver International Airport. Breck never asked why he quit the airport. Presuming he quit.

Whatever was going on, the hospital was an easy target. What if those cartel men wanted to finish the job? What was stopping them from walking right in the building? Danny wasn't the only one in danger if that were to happen.

Whatever the reason for the lax security detail it was a good enough reason to have a conversation with Michelle again. Maybe he could even ask her out on a second date in the process. To a real restaurant. Right that wrong.

Breck went down the hallway to the front desk, but Michelle wasn't there. It was Belinda. Brenda. Melinda.

Midstride, he spotted Valerie Matthews trying to feed a dollar bill into the Coke machine and veered in her direction.

"This piece of junk." Valerie tried again, but the dollar bill was too wrinkled.

Passing a trash can, Breck threw away the paper sack full of Guinness.

"Here, I think I have a dollar."

He took out his wallet and gave her one of his. It worked. She hit the Diet Coke button and a can clunked into sight.

"Thank you, sheriff. This is for Aspen."

"How is she doing today?"

"They want to keep her for observation. One more night. The doctor is going to release her in the morning." Valerie actually smiled.

It was an expression Breck had never seen her make before. Without the mayor in the room, she seemed like a different person. The combativeness was absent. The barely-suppressed loathing. In that smile, Breck saw a healthy, genuine mother's concern.

"Good to hear it."

"I can't believe I almost lost her." Valerie shook her head in disbelief. "It doesn't feel real, does it?"

It did feel real to Breck—because he had been there. The search. The fear and desperation. Racing against the clock. Digging Aspen out of the snow with his bare hands. Bloody snow covering her face. Was she breathing? Would she need CPR? Or would she need a body bag?

It was better Valerie didn't know those details.

"If she hadn't been wearing that avalanche beacon . . ." Valerie shuddered. Then that motherly look faded. "I can't believe they haven't shut that ski resort down. These conditions are deadly. You're the sheriff of this county. Can you make them shut it down?"

"That decision is up to the resort owner, unfortunately." Breck tried to choose the right words to sound professional. And avoid an argument. "I wish I had some jurisdiction there but the ski runs are on National Forest land. They lease it from the federal government. I can certainly make a recommendation but ultimately it's their call."

Valerie listened but did not lash out at him.

"I thought that National Forest is public land? This is a public safety issue. Maybe they need to hear from the public." She turned and headed to Aspen's room, Diet Coke in hand.

Breck checked the time on his phone. It was 4:20. The classic weed code.

"How about a chat with Freddy."

Breck went out to the parking lot, got in the Jeep, and drove straight to High Country Pizza. The little bell above the doorway tinkled and Freddy looked up from behind the counter.

"Ah, man. What now?"

"Where were you last night?"

Freddy looked fidgety. "Denver, man. Drove down yesterday morning, got back today. Why? What did I do?"

Denver? That could be verified. Breck had some contacts at the Department of Transportation. They could check the traffic cams at the Eisenhower Tunnel.

"So you didn't break into the General Merchandise?" Breck watched him closely.

Freddy was hard to read. He always acted like he was up to something sneaky. He had that perpetual deer in the headlights look. Even when he wasn't doing anything wrong. It was amazing the man's conscience hadn't flamed out years ago.

"No. Definitely not."

"You fibbing to me? You know I don't like fibs."

Freddy chuckled. "I got doughnuts at the Krispy Kreme on C-470, man. The receipt is in my jacket."

"You went all the way to Denver and back for doughnuts?"

"Krispy Kreme, man. Krispy Kreme."

The jacket was hanging on a coat rack. Breck almost stuck his hand in the pocket, but he had a mental flashback of his nice Marmot sleeping bag after Freddy had slept in it. Damp. Gritty. Tangy bouquet of pepperoni and pee.

"I believe you."

CHAPTER 33

Cat Clock

There was a U-Haul parked halfway up Boreal Pass Road.

The afternoon sun was high in the southern sky. Fluffy white clouds were starting to build along the mountain ridgeline. Like a scene from *The Sound of Music*. But instead of Julie Andrews in a black dress and white apron, a sweaty man in blue jeans and a t-shirt got out of the U-Haul. A tire iron in his hand and a handgun in the other.

El Sangrador slowed down and stopped, the gravel crunching beneath the Range Rover's tires. Zorrero rolled down the passenger window.

"Commander Zorrero?" The driver was short and stocky, with a pitch-black mustache.

"Sí."

The driver's eyes darted like a hummingbird, suspicious of a trap, but his head didn't move. It was like talking to a cat clock. Zorrero nodded at the U-Haul. There was a padlock on the back. "Open it up."

Both El Sangrador and Zorrero got out of the Range Rover. Unlocking the padlock, the driver rolled up the heavy door. A dozen men and women were inside. Cowering. Moaning. Blinking in the bright light.

"Get out, *mi* little *poblanos*." Zorrero snapped his fingers.

They looked like a group of captives. Which they were, more or less.

"Where are my babies?? My *niños?*" It was a young woman, and her husband put his hand over her mouth and whispered in her ear to please be quiet, for the sake of the Blessed Virgin.

"I already paid your coyote the full price. What was agreed upon." Another man spoke, with gray streaks in his hair. To make his point, he turned his pants pockets inside out. "I have nothing more to give."

The driver ran his fingers over the tire iron, stroking it like a kitten.

"Welcome to the *Estados Unidos*. All is well, my friends. Your children are safe, *señora*, and you will see them soon." Zorrero put his hand on the driver's shoulder. A warning not to damage his laborers. "But first, there is one more thing you must do. To earn your freedom."

He crossed the road and pointed at a faint footpath winding into an aspen grove. The tall white trees were starting to bud. There was still snow in the forest, snowbanks here and there. Hard crusty piles, refusing to melt.

"Up this trail, there is a hill on the mountainside where the sun shines most of the day and fresh water trickles down from the heights. There are shovels and saws and tools. As soon as we clear a field, and plant *las hierbas*, your obligation to Los Equis shall be considered fulfilled."

The man with the empty pockets bowed before Zorrero, his hands clasped. "Señor. *Por favor, por favor.* My knees are full of arthritis. I walk with a cane. There is no way I can hike up that long ol' trail. Have mercy on a decrepit old man, señor."

"Shall I have mercy, El Sangrador?" Zorrero gave the blood-letter a blank look.

There was a time when El Sangrador would have simply shot such a man and herded the rest up the trail like goats. But with his own shin still throbbing from that accursed ladder, he felt a strange reluctance to strike. Was this what the priests referred to as compassion?

The driver felt no such reluctance. Swinging his tire iron, he knocked the man across the skull. He dropped like a stone. His scalp split open and blood poured out.

Zorrero gave the blood-letter another look. Quizzical this time. But El Sangrador said nothing. It was better to never show weakness. In his moment of contemplation, he had nearly forgotten that lesson. Pulling out the pearl-grip Colt .45, the blood-letter shot the fallen man several times in the body until he was absolutely still.

The other captives huddled together, eyes filled with terror. The señora screamed, her voice echoing off the ridge.

"It is okay to scream," Zorrero said, magnanimously. "There is no one for many miles."

The señora finished her scream, then pressed her face into her husband's shoulder. Allowing her to blubber was good, in Zorrero's mind. It infected the others with just the right amount of fear and helplessness. The dead man would reinforce obedience, as well. They would be eager to prove they were dedicated laborers now, after seeing such a thing.

It would not take long to clear the hillside of rocks and brush, with such dedication. Then they could hoe the earth and plant the marijuana from Freddy's cabin in the fertile soil where it would get plenty of natural sunlight. It would be a good start for his new business. Not only would there be plenty for the stoners of Quandary county. That was just a fraction of the business to come. From this hillside, they would ship out bushels of weed across the state, and beyond. In the back of the Range Rover was a box of seeds. Enough to plant a crop a hundred times bigger. Perhaps a thousand times bigger.

All under the protection and beneficence of the Los Equis cartel. Zorrero was Commander 23. His territory was central Colorado. But Zorrero wanted more. To stretch for the sky. The sun. The moon. One day he would be *El Jefe* of Los Equis itself.

"Follow me." Zorrero entered the aspen grove.

CHAPTER 34

Illusion

The Subway in Frisco. For breakfast. *What is wrong with this guy?* Mayor Matthews wondered.

"If they're serving meatball sandwiches at this hour, I swear . . ."

It was seven in the morning. He should be in bed, not traveling down the highway to meet Mike Jameson for breakfast. Not there. Matthews could have chosen the Starbucks back in Quandary, or the Blue Moose. That was a lot closer for both of them. But this was a strategic move.

Parking the BMW against the curb, he thumbed a quarter into the meter. No surprise—Mike Jameson was already there, sitting at a booth by the window, tapping on the glass.

"I see you, chunky," Matthews muttered. He waved pleasantly and headed inside.

"I bet you didn't know they served breakfast, did you?" Jameson grabbed Matthews hand and shook it like he was strangling a cat. "I can't believe you wanted to meet here. I thought you hated Subway."

"Nonsense. They make delicious food."

Then Jameson got pensive.

"I hear Breck's brother took a bullet. Tragic. Simply tragic."

"It certainly is. Very sad. Now, what do you recommend?" Matthews eyed the menu. He was about to take a bullet, himself.

"Bacon, egg and cheese flatbread. Make sure you get extra mayo. You won't regret it."

They ordered their sandwiches and then settled in the window booth. The sun was barely up. There wasn't much traffic on the road outside. A utility truck parked next to Matthews' BMW, within striking distance of a door ding. A small crew, dressed in orange safety vests and hard hats, came inside and formed a line at the counter. Matthews was wearing a suit coat and tie. He felt overdressed. Out of place. Behind enemy lines.

"How are sales, Mike?" Matthews could ask that and be genuine.

"Things always pick up this time of year. Everyone wants to ride a mountain bike right about now."

Everyone but you, Matthews thought, sipping his coffee. It was an irony of the highest order. Mike Jameson owned the mountain bike shop in Quandary—Mikey's Bikeys. The guy was rotund. To put it mildly.

There was a clock on the wall above the potato chip rack. As soon as it hit ten after seven, Matthews' cell phone rang. Brittany, right on cue.

"Sorry Mike, let me turn this thing off." He thumbed the volume all the way down and put it back in his pocket. "It's just the governor. It can wait."

That impressed Jameson. Which was the goal.

"Oh my, well if it's the governor . . ."

"No, Mike. I won't take his call. Not while we're talking. Besides, we're in the middle of breakfast and I want to eat it while it's hot." Matthews knew how to make a show. To help sell the illusion, he took a big bite of his breakfast sandwich. Mayonnaise oozed out and he grabbed a napkin. "That's . . . tasty."

"You really ought to reconsider putting a Subway into City Hall. Half the building is empty. Think of the lease money, if nothing else." Jameson held up his sandwich like an Olympic trophy. "We wouldn't have to drive all the way to Frisco, either. Chew on that."

Oh, I'm chewing on something right now. But Matthews feigned earnest reflection. This was too easy. "By the way, how is the cell reception at Mikey's Bikeys?"

"Patchy." Jameson leaned into his straw and took a pump of Sprite.

"What if I told you we could fix that?" The cell tower above Johnny Tibbs' dude ranch was a spicy subject. And like the queen on a chess board, it could be moved where it was most useful.

"Really? How?"

"There's really only one way, given how tight our city funds are. We take another vote on that cell tower. This time, I'll vote with you. We tried it where it is. It's not a good location. Quandary would get better reception if it was sitting on the north end of town."

"This day just keeps getting better." Jameson looked amazed. "But what about Johnny? Won't he pitch a fit?"

"Well, that's the only way forward that I can imagine—unless we can generate some major tax revenue. Then we can afford a second cell phone tower in Quandary."

"Tax revenue? I hear ya." Jameson held up his Subway napkin like it was the American flag. "We build it, people will come."

Matthews smiled like it was a good idea. Then he snapped his fingers.

"Or . . ." Bait and switch. "Cannabis is legal in Colorado, why isn't it legal in Quandary? And it is *big* business. Denver and Pueblo are making so much money they can't see straight. Hand over fist, doobie over joint. Think of all that tax money. We're talking a million bucks year one. Guaranteed. With that kind of dough, we can afford two cell towers and everybody's happy."

Jameson thumbed the rest of his sandwich into his mouth, chewing. Thinking.

It was time to drive this home.

"You know why Breck's brother was shot? He was selling marijuana and somebody tried to rob him. If marijuana was legalized, crime would actually go down. Check the statistics in Denver. If people can't have something, they'll break the law to get it. But if the law allows it, then there's no reason to shoot anybody. You just go down to the legal dispensary and buy some. Times are changing, Mike. Let's get ahead of the curve."

Matthews held his breath.

"What does Breck think?" Jameson asked.

Spinning the truth was one thing. An outright fabrication was another. But if a little lie was what it would take, Matthews would go there.

"Oh, he agrees. We had a good chat about it at the hospital."

Jameson sucked on his straw again but the Sprite was gone. He pulled off the lid and stared at the ice.

"You know what? Let's just move Johnny's cell tower," Matthews said, matter-of-factly. "Tear it down, put it up by your bike shop. Come what may, Quandary needs better cell service. Tibbs is a complainer and complainers complain. Am I right?"

"No, hold on. I don't want to make Johnny mad. I'd rather find a way to finance a second tower. And if Breck's on board so am I. Get me that Subway and I'll get you legalized weed. That's *two* sources of tax revenue. Problem solved." Jameson glanced over at the sales counter. "You want another one? I'm buying."

Matthews' flatbread breakfast sandwich only had one bite taken out of it.

"You gotta try the steak and cheese next! You won't regret it." Jameson squiggled out of the booth. "Finish that up. I'll be right back."

CHAPTER 35

Father Knows Best

Matthews had more than one reason to go to Frisco. After choking down his breakfast, he bought a handheld GPS from the local mountaineering shop. It was lemon yellow. About the size of a cell phone. Garmin brand—only the best.

Then he drove to Valerie's house. That very morning, Aspen had finally been released from the hospital. Sent home. But she chose to go home with her mother. It stung a little. Matthews' big house on Eyrie Road felt empty. He missed seeing his daughter on the couch, texting. Or texting over a slice of pizza at the dining room table.

The big elk head above the fireplace mantle would be his only company now. And time was ticking away. College was going to start in the fall. The university in Boulder. Far enough away that he wouldn't see her except for Christmas and spring break. Maybe. Presuming she would ever want to ski again. The avalanche had shaken her up quite a bit.

Parking in Valerie's driveway, Matthews got out and looked around the neighborhood. He had never actually been there before. Paid for it, yes. Seen it, no.

Right through the pine trees, blue waters were lapping against the rocky shore in the morning sunshine. Seagulls in the sky. Whereas Quandary was tucked up in a mountain valley, Frisco was spread out along the edge of a reservoir. Quiet, peaceful, with a view of the water. It was worth every penny—of the second mortgage he just took out. Even though he despised her, Matthews had to admit Valerie had good tastes.

Aspen's Volkswagen Beetle was parked out front. He had bought that for her the day she got her driver's license. He'd never forget the look on her face. She thought he was the Best Dad Ever, back then.

"She's asleep." His ex-wife opened the door before he could ring the doorbell.

By the look on her face, she was not pleased to see him on her porch. But Valerie always had that look on her face.

"I just want to see her. Make sure she is okay."

"Keep your voice down, Seneca." It was a harsh whisper. Valerie stepped outside, and quietly closed the door behind her. "Of course she's not okay. Every time she closes her eyes, she has nightmares about that horrible avalanche. Maybe now that she's home, in her own bed, she can finally get some rest."

"Her *home* is with me. She hasn't lived here since she graduated from high school. She moved out, Valerie. To get away from you."

"She moved out so she could be closer to the ski runs." Valerie looked him up and down. "You're a credit card, Seneca. A walking talking credit card."

It never ended. Matthews rubbed the bridge of his nose. He might as well leave. She wasn't going to let him in the house and Aspen did need to rest. That much was true.

"Daddy?"

Aspen stood in the doorway, dressed in pajamas and fuzzy slippers.

"Go back to bed, honey." Valerie turned around, surprised to see her standing there. She obviously didn't hear the door open. "This is just a bad dream."

"Stop being mean to each other, I can hear every word."

The swelling was worse. Her nose looked like it might explode. Matthews held out his arms and she came out for a hug.

"I'm sorry, ptarmigan." It was a nickname he hadn't used since she was little. She looked so young and helpless and broken. But she was a Matthews. Tough. Strong. Resilient. She needed to bounce back. What could he say to get her to bounce back like a Matthews? "Why don't we go shopping later today?"

"She doesn't want to go shopping," Valerie said. "She needs rest."

Ignoring her, Matthews smiled hopefully. "Would a new car make you feel better? A hatchback with a ski rack on top. We'll buy new skis, too. How does that sound?"

Valerie couldn't believe what she was hearing. Her face went dark.

"Oh, daddy, stop." Aspen looked bleak. "I just wanna sleep. But . . ."

She trailed off.

Taking her by the shoulders, gently, Matthews gave her a father-knows-best eyebrow arch. "I know you went through something awful. But don't let it win. You hear me? We need to get you back in the saddle. This weekend, you and I are going skiing together. I won't take no for an answer."

"Well, I've heard enough." Valerie took Aspen by the arm and led her inside. "Daddy has to go the hell to work."

Click—the door latched shut. *Click*—that one was the deadbolt.

It was the right thing to say, even if it was hard to hear. Matthews knew it. The best way to cure a nightmare was to confront fear. The world was a cold hard place, and it could chew Aspen up and spit her out if she didn't take the initiative. He would make sure she did. Despite her mother's attempt at enabling the fear. Because that was what Valerie was doing, and she didn't even realize it.

Matthews stepped off the porch and got in the BMW. The yellow Garmin GPS lying in the passenger seat caught his eye. He opened the seat console. The sticky note with the coordinates was still there. Zorrero was a pro. It was like he disappeared off the map. Breck was so clueless.

Taking out his phone, Matthews sent out a text.

Is the garden open yet? I'd like to come see.

Backing out of the drive, Matthews rolled his window down and explored the neighborhood. He found a parking area at the reservoir. There were already sailboats in the water. That was something he always wanted. A boat. But not a sailboat, a speedboat.

His phone beeped.

Not yet. Set up a temporary greenhouse. Wait for an invite.

CHAPTER 36

Dude Was a Putz

"**Y**ou got new wheels?" Breck was sitting at his desk in the Sheriff's Office when Jenny came through the front door. Pushing a mountain bike. "Now, this I was not expecting."

She was sweaty and a little out of breath. Propping it against the wall, Jenny unclipped the chin strap on her bike helmet and set it on the kitchenette counter. Next to the coffee maker was a dusty case of plastic water bottles. She grabbed one and took a few gulps.

"What?" Jenny was defiant. And surprisingly alert.

"I thought you might have been taking a sick day. After that General Merchandise GI shanghai. Guess I was wrong."

"That, my friend, was a wakeup call." She held her arm up and flexed her bicep. "Time to get back into shape."

"I see."

Breck picked up the landline and started dialing.

Jenny ignored him ignoring her.

"Zero sleep. It's like, 7 A.M., and I'm propped up on my couch gargling acid reflux. Pounding through my second bottle of Tums, I come to realize I can't eat that crappy junk. I'm not in my twenties anymore. Not if I intend to lay down and sleep at night like a normal human being."

Breck held up his hand like he was stopping traffic. "Hi there . . . you. Is Michelle working today? Okay, thanks." He put his hand over the receiver and whispered. "It's *Belinda*, right?"

"What are you talking about?" Jenny squinted at him, waiting for more. But there wasn't anymore. "So I start walking down

Main Street and just keep on going. All the way past Safeway, not even sure where I'm going. Forty-five minutes later I'm at Mikey's Bikeys and I'm buying me a dang mountain bike."

Breck held up his hand again. "Hi, Michelle. It's Breck, down at the Sheriff's . . . yeah, it's me . . . yeah, not too many Breck's are there?"

While he was stumbling over his small talk, Jenny took the water bottle over to her desk. It was irritating. Breck and Michelle. They had barely gone out on one date, maybe a year ago. Couldn't he just get to the point? Act like a sheriff perhaps? She chugged the water bottle, crinkling it in her fist.

"I just wanted to say, it couldn't hurt to amp up security at the hospital. Are you still using that TSA guy?" Breck cleared his throat quietly and shifted in his seat, listening. Nodding. "Griffin? That's his name? First or last? . . . First name. Okaaay. Here's the thing. There are some suspects involved in Danny's shooting that have not been apprehended yet. I imagine the chances are remote, but Danny could still be a target. Well, a remote chance, like I said . . ."

Deciding she had had enough of the Breck & Michelle Show, Jenny spun around and rifled through the papers on her desk. The forms for the General Merchandise and More robbery were done. The accident report on the avalanche was done. As she sorted everything, she came across the BOLO for the cartel men's Range Rover. They were probably in Mexico by now, but it was still their best lead. Maybe it was time to follow up again. Why not?

There were only two ways out of Quandary. Besides a network of forest roads, half of which led to old mines or nowhere at all. North through Frisco, or south through Alma.

She started with Frisco. Picking up her desk phone, she hit Line Two and called the State Patrol. They didn't have anything new to report, so she dialed up the police chief in Alma. Jenny wasn't looking forward to the conversation. Chief Maxwell Waters. Dude was a putz.

Alma was a small mountain town, higher in elevation than Quandary. Just across the county line. Only two cops in the entire police department, just like Breck and Jenny were the only ones holding down the fort at the Sheriff's Office. But the boys in Alma only had to patrol one tiny town. Breck and Jenny had an entire county to look after.

"Chief Waters, this is Deputy O'Hara. If you have a minute, I'd like to follow up on that BOLO we put out earlier this week. Black Range Rover. Two Hispanic males, mid-30s. Possible cartel connection. Armed and dangerous. You got anything?"

Sitting up straight, Jenny waved the BOLO form to catch Breck's eye. "Okay, hold on. Let me put you on speaker. Breck is right here."

Breck hung up with Michelle, just as Jenny put the Alma police chief on speakerphone.

"So are you saying you *did* see a black Range Rover?" Jenny asked.

Breck came over to see what was happening.

"Chief, do you have something for us?"

The line was silent for a long moment. They heard him sigh and rustle around on the other end. Hemming and hawing.

"Alright, here's the deal. Yesterday afternoon, there was a black Range Rover. It parked at the Almart. Two individuals went in there, bought some groceries and came out."

"Yesterday?" Breck was stunned. "Were they Hispanic males?"

"Well, these two folks were indeed people of color. Quite possibly Hispanic in nature. I could not say with certainty, and I would hesitate to conjecture."

"Conjecture? What are you talking about?" Now Jenny was stunned. "We sent out a BOLO. Why didn't you call us the moment you spotted them?"

Chief Waters made some kind of unintelligible noise. Jenny frowned at it. What was that supposed to be? A whale giving birth?

"Are you at the dentist?" she asked. "Because it feels like we're pulling teeth here."

"Here's the deal, deputy. Yes, two Mexican men in a black Range Rover bought groceries at Almart. The stock boy said they purchased pinto beans, yellow peas, and cans of Dinty Moore beef stew. One had a pearl-handled pistol in his belt but we are an open-carry state. Maybe he's worried about bears. This is bear country, deputy. And who am I to approach two men of color without due cause?"

Breck and Jenny stared at each other. Jenny mouthed, *Is he serious?*

Apparently, he was because the chief kept on rationalizing.

"Now, this may be a small town, but we are full-fledged officers of the law up here. We take our duty seriously, and we are sensitive to the many needs of our community and nation. Just because a couple of non-white males came through here doesn't make them criminals. I had no cause to detain or question them. That would be racial profiling. That would be wrong."

"It's not racial profiling. It's criminal profiling." Breck was in disbelief. "You had an All-Points Bulletin. With vehicle and suspect descriptions. Your job is to follow the evidence. Did you at least run the plates? Tell me you ran the plates."

The chief didn't like that.

"Don't tell me how to do my job. We are not racists in my department, sheriff. And no one is going to accuse me or my team of racial profiling."

He hung up. Breck leaned over and poked the phone till it stopped humming.

"What the hell was that?" Jenny started pacing. "Holy crap. Those cartel freaks didn't drive off to Mexico. They went to Almart and bought lunch."

The front door opened and two people came inside, a man and a woman. "My name is Bill Chisolm and this is my wife Libbie. We're Brittany's parents. We'd like to speak with someone about that avalanche."

Breck grabbed his keys and his coffee thermos and headed past them. "Jenny, I'm heading up there. Can you chat with the Chisolms?"

Holding her tongue, Jenny mustered up as pleasant a smile as she could.

"Happy to help."

But she wasn't. She wanted to catch bad guys, not catch grief from angry parents.

CHAPTER 37

Iceberg

"We got cameras. Let me show you the security footage."
The Almart manager led Breck into the store office and typed on his keyboard until a video appeared on the computer screen.

"I appreciate your help." On the drive up to Alma, Breck considered stopping by the police department first as a courtesy. Maybe smooth things over. But time was of the essence, and Chief Waters had hung up on him. That wasn't very courteous.

"It'll take a second. Got to get to the good part." The manager clicked the mouse, skipping the video forward to the right time code.

While he waited, Breck glanced at the stock boy. Standing quietly in the doorway. The kid was short and thin as a rail, gaunt even, wrapped in an Almart apron that was way too big for him. Could have been a burial shroud.

"You okay?" Breck asked. "You look a little pale."

"It's just my skin tone." He fiddled with his apron.

"These guys threaten you?"

"Not really." The stock boy untied the apron strings and then re-tied them. "It was just . . . it was something about 'em. Made my skin crawl."

Let's not talk about your skin, Breck thought. He could count the kid's veins. Both the blue and the red ones. "You want to wait outside? Get some sun?"

Strings untied again. Strings re-tied again. "Naw."

"Here we go," the manager said.

The camera was above the registers. The footage was full color and clear as day. Two Hispanic males were buying a cart full of dried goods.

"I recognize that one." Breck pointed at Zorrero.

Gray dress pants, white open-collared shirt. Trimmed black mustache and a slick haircut. Seated at Freddy's kitchen table smoking a cigarette. A gun on the table. A Glock. And then someone hit him in the back of the head. Now Breck had a face to go with the pistol-whip. Silver aviator sunglasses. Tall. Muscular. Probably ex-military, like so many cartel men were. The Colt .45 with white grips was obvious on the security footage. Sticking out of his waist belt.

"They paid with cash?" Breck asked.

He could have waited to see it for himself. But it was taking a long time to get there. Can after can of beef stew. Can. After. Can.

The stock boy swallowed. "Yes, sir. That guy had a really thick accent. The tall one never said a word. Just stared at me. With those sunglasses."

"You didn't get any names, then? Did they speak to each other?"

"Not really."

Breck studied the screen again. At least the security footage was decent.

"Can you do a screenshot and email it to me?"

The manager clicked the mouse a few times. Breck took a business card out of his wallet and set it on the desk. It had the Quandary County Sheriff's Office email address on it. Jenny should have it by the time he got back.

"Did you see which way they drove when they left the parking lot?"

"Out of my way."

Breck turned to see Chief Maxwell Waters shove past the stock boy, his sidekick Officer Rhodes in tow. The room was barely bigger than a broom closet, and it was a tight squeeze with all of them inside.

"What are you doing here, Dyer?" Then Waters pointed an accusing finger at the store manager. "Don't tell him nothing."

The manager was unimpressed, obviously. He hit the send button. "Check your inbox."

"I saw that, *Greg.*" Waters swiveled the accusing finger over to Breck. "You are out of your jurisdiction, Dyer. You crossed the county line a mile back. When you're in Alma, you're in my little corner of the world. You got a warrant to show me?"

Rhodes smirked. "You just pissed in the wrong pond."

Breck looked at him for a second. Carnival clown. He didn't see the coin slot. Probably around back.

"I only need a warrant if someone isn't cooperating."

Waters turned on the manager again. "Tell him he needs a warrant, *Greg*."

One of the other security cameras on the computer screen showed the back of the building. A white box truck was backing up to the dock. Greg shrugged apathetically. "The iceberg is here."

"I gotta go." The stock boy squeezed past Officer Rhodes and disappeared.

Waters glared at Breck. "*You* gotta go."

In a dramatic sidestep, they both moved to one side so Breck didn't have to squeeze past them as the stock boy had.

Since he already had what he needed, Breck left. A dozen snarky comebacks came to mind but he kept them all to himself. Despite their flawed logic and hypersensitivities, and their territorialism, Breck hated to see tension between law enforcement agencies. That kind of conflict didn't serve anyone's interest—except the lawbreakers.

Waters and Rhodes followed him out to the parking lot and watched him get in his Jeep. Breck leaned out the window. One last try.

"You do realize these men are armed and dangerous?"

"Innocent until proven guilty. Now stay out of Alma."

CHAPTER 38

Eleven Live Ones

The last time Zorrero and El Sangrador were at the cultivation site, it was blanketed in snow. How quickly things change. Now, green grass covered the hillside. Scrub bushes were leafing out. There was a freshness in the air.

But winter's memory was right there for all to see, clinging to the peaks above them. And the memory of death was fresh, too, for the laborers had been forced to carry the dead man up the trail.

Zorrero was pleased. Everything was going so well. Ahead of schedule, even. As the people filed out of the forest, one by one, he set them each to a task. Some to clear rocks and chop away the foliage. Some to erect a shelter with pine branches and a big blue tarp. Others to bury the dead.

Besides the señora, who pined for her children, there were several other women. Their task was to bring water from a nearby stream with 5-gallon buckets. For watering the crop, quenching thirst and cooking the meals.

The last laborer emerged from the forest trail. A head count—eleven workers in total. Even if he had to execute another one or two, the grow field would be ready in a matter of weeks.

Of course, none of them would be allowed to leave at that time, simply because the marijuana was in the ground. The product must be faithfully maintained. A drip system of hoses would need to be laid out and overseen, for the rains may be inconsistent. Fertilizing. Pruning. Bud removal and packaging. It would all require much care.

The entire summer would be very busy. And even when autumn arrived and the high country changed color and the growing season ended, the workload would not ease. Every hand would be required, perhaps more. Perhaps they would need to employ the coyote's service again. For the mayor would install a Clear Span building inside the Quandary city limits. A massive greenhouse. To which they would relocate the entire operation. A major endeavor!

The laborers did not know any of this, nor would he tell them too much too soon, lest they lose heart. Alas, the señora would not be seeing her young *niños* anytime soon.

It was a strange thought. Transitioning from an illegal operation to a legal operation. A drug cartel operating *within* the confines of the law. Who could have foreseen this day? America. Land of opportunity, indeed.

Zorrero paused his thinking, peering down the trail.

Where was the blood-letter?

He hiked up last to make sure there were no stragglers or escape attempts. But everyone was accounted for. Eleven live ones. One corpse. The coyote had taken the U-Haul and returned to Monterrey. So where was El Sangrador?

Rolling pine and fir and willows covered the mountainsides. The footpath zigzagged down the slope, quickly swallowed in the enormity, the vastness of it all. Could he have gotten lost? That would be shameful. Perhaps Zorrero might need a new *sicario*. One with a stronger inner compass. One who could be relied upon not to lose his bearings.

A black crow cawed somewhere.

CHAPTER 39

Miraculous Malverde

Alone in the forest, where no one could see or hear, El Sangrador eased onto a soft patch of pine needles and groaned. Sweat beaded his face. His leg felt like it was on fire.

In the course of his twenty-eight years on Earth, the bloodletter had been shot thirteen times. All thirteen occurred on the same occasion.

When he was young, he got pinned in a firefight with a rival cartel in the leafy streets of Ciudad Juárez. He hid behind a Ford Pinto, terrified, while bullets flew everywhere.

That day, he had been wearing a fourteen-karat necklace imprinted with the image of Jesús Malverde, the patron saint of *narcos*. El Sangrador was a *halcone* at the time, a falcon of the street. But he was flushed out like a quail.

With fervency and great fear, the young *halcone* sought Malverde's intercession.

"O, Miraculous Malverde, pray for me. Jesús Malverde, listen to me."

Disoriented, he ran headlong into the fiery spray of a machine gun. A hundred rounds rained through the sky. He felt his body rattled and tossed by the bullets. Yet somehow he raced to safety, intending to lay down and die in the presence of his lieutenants. The cobblestones his deathbed.

Pulling his shirt off, it was discovered that not one bullet pierced his body! Many had grazed his arms, his legs, his neck. The burns were everywhere. He had been hit with enough bullets to pulverize his innards, yet they did no damage worse than cigarette burns.

It was a miracle.

When the truth of the intercession was clear to the lieutenants, he was embraced. Rewarded with rank and authority. El Sangrador wore the necklace night and day, ever after.

Sitting up, the blood-letter slowly rolled up his pants leg. The skin was swollen and purple.

Falling from the ladder in the A-frame had been painful. At first, he was certain no bones got broken. As the days passed, his limp persisted but was slowly getting better. Until he began hiking up this steep mountain trail. Now he wasn't so sure. Maybe it was broken after all. He probed the skin gently with his fingertips, half-expecting to see a bone shard tear through. But there was only pain and discoloration.

It had been a struggle to keep up with the laborers. Slower and slower he walked. His breathing became difficult. They zipped right up the zigzags like it was nothing, and the blood-letter lost sight of them entirely. He shaded his eyes and looked up the steep slope. Could he make it all the way to the top?

El Sangrador was terribly thirsty.

Reaching into his shirt, he touched his fourteen-karat necklace. He traced the image with his fingertips.

There was no glory in a swollen leg. Not like the machine gun baptism in the leafy streets of Ciudad Juárez. But the situation was grim, regardless of its absurdity. What if he expired right there? Died of thirst, alone in the woods?

"O, Miraculous Malverde, pray for me. Jesús Malverde, listen to me."

He clenched the necklace, ashamed of his foolishness. A ladder in a cabin. Was that to be his demise? Not gang violence? Not a rival cartel? Zip-tied and hung from a beam by his neck, or chopped up and pieced out for the vultures to pick at in the sun? But a ladder in a cabin?

Thunder rumbled. He opened his eyes. Dark, flat-bottomed clouds were gathering overhead. Suddenly, rain fell. Cold drops of rain. Holding out his tongue, El Sangrador felt refreshed. Revived.

Soaked to the core, he rolled his pants leg down again and stood. The pain was not so bad now. The pine needles would not be his deathbed. He was destined for greater things than this. With quiet assurance in his heart, his AR-15 a crutch, the blood-letter boldly returned to the trail.

CHAPTER 40

Vulture Boos

Suddenly soaked, Valerie Matthews led the protesters inside the ski resort's big lobby. One moment it was sunny. The next, rain cascaded from the sky.

"Avalanche! Close it down! Avalanche! Close it down!"

The chant was catchy. Simple. It conveyed the message even though their big poster-board signs had turned into streaky mush.

The protest group was not so much a group as a cluster. It consisted of exactly five people. Valerie and Aspen, Brittany and her parents. The girls chose not to chant, as this was not their idea. Even so, the concerned parents' outcry echoed across the big vaulted corridor. That was because no one else was inside. Except for the employees working the food court and gift shop, everyone was outside skiing.

Given the general emptiness, the protest chant faded into a heartless mumble in a matter of minutes. Until a maintenance door swung open. The young resort manager, Cash, wheeled out a laundry cart full of white cloth towels embroidered with the ski resort logo.

"Avalanche! Close it down!"

"We *are* closing it down." Cash passed out towels so they could dry off. "The slopes are melting. Even with the fresh snow we got from that blizzard, I doubt we can stretch it another weekend. This rain is gonna do us in."

As if he sent out a psychic announcement, a bunch of skiers marched in from the slopes. Elbows and clatter, it was a race for the food court to claim tables and seats. The last ones in the door realized their misfortune. With no place to sit, they murmured and trolled around like vultures. Wet vultures.

"Avalanche! Close it down!" Valerie waved her sign at them but received a chorus of vulture *boos*.

Cash offered her a towel.

"Mrs. Matthews, I don't think there's any avalanche danger now."

"Well, I guess we can all go home then, huh?" She bristled. "Who is in charge of this place? Is it you?"

Brittany gripped her father's arm, a plea. "Can I go now?"

But he just patted her hair like she was a little girl.

Cash looked at Brittany and Aspen sympathetically. The girls were obviously uncomfortable with the protest and the attention they were getting. Everyone knew who they were. Some reporter had put their Facebook profile photos in the local paper. The avalanche had even made the news in Denver.

"Glad you two are okay. That was a close call. It doesn't get closer than that."

Brittany kept staring at the entry door like she was going to bolt.

"I need to get back to work."

Her mother, Libbie, tried to give her a hug but Brittany slipped out of it.

"We drove all the way up from Littleton just for this. Don't you think this is important?"

"I'm going to get fired."

"Brittie, we don't want anyone else to get hurt on this mountain. Do you?" her father asked.

She rolled her eyes.

"We had avalanche beacons, dad. Skiing is risky. Besides, it was our own fault. Maybe we shouldn't have gone out so soon after a blizzard. I gotta get back to City Hall. The mayor is going to bust a vein. I told him I was meeting you for lunch. *That was two hours ago!*"

Bill Chisolm smiled softly but was unmoved. "You were lucky. Very very lucky. And don't you think the ski resort should have closed the slopes until the danger had passed? It wasn't your fault. It was theirs."

The implication was not lost on Cash. He closed his eyes and his face relaxed into a dreamy smile.

"What are you doing?" Aspen whispered.

"Beach barbeque in Maui. A coconut Mojito."

Brittany started to cry. Her parents circled around her even tighter, all arms and hugs. Which made her cry even harder. She squirmed but they didn't let her escape.

"It's going to be okay, Brittie."

Valerie shook her sign at the food court again. More boos.

Brittany sobbed. "I don't want to be the bad guy. I like skiing. People are going to hate me."

"Is anyone hungry?" Cash opened his eyes. "I've got High Country Pizza on speed dial. What do you like? Pineapple? No charge. The resort is going to pay."

Between the avalanche, the boos, and Cash's penchant for faux pas, Valerie was incensed. "You are absolutely right about that. The resort *is* going to pay. You'll be hearing from my lawyer."

"Mom, no." Aspen paled.

"Hush, honey. This is how grown-ups settle arguments."

Cash took out his cell phone. "Everyone likes pineapple."

Wheeling her new mountain bike through the big glass entry doors, Jenny came in, soaking wet. Her long red hair was caked to her head and shoulders.

"Give me one of those." She took a towel from the laundry cart and wiped her face. Eyeliner was everywhere. "So I got a complaint. Somebody called about the protest."

Giving Cash a steely stink eye, it was clear who Valerie suspected.

"It wasn't me." He put a finger in his ear so he could hear better. "Hello? Freddy?"

He walked around to find better reception. The rain was interfering with the signal.

"It wasn't him." Jenny wrung her hair out. She turned and pointed outside. They could see a silver BMW parked in the rain with its running lights on. "An anonymous caller."

"Seneca!" Valerie ran over and pounded on the glass. "I see you!"

The headlights flicked on and the BMW peeled out, disappearing in the haze.

CHAPTER 41

Bread and Butter

Hustling up the concrete stairs, Seneca Matthews slipped inside City Hall and hid his wet jacket on a hook behind the office door. Checked a mirror to fix his hair. Hearing footsteps, he dropped into his desk chair, grabbed a pen and pretended to be writing.

"Is that you, mayor?" The librarian, Mrs. Long, peered in the doorway. "I thought you left."

"What's that?" Matthews glanced up, feigning innocence. "No. I've been here since 8 A.M., Mrs. Long."

Her brow furrowing, Mrs. Long tried to align the given facts. "Strange."

Giving her a semi-charming yet impatient smile, Matthews held up the pen to show her. As if it settled any and all mysteries regarding his whereabouts. "I've got a ton of work to do before the city council meets. What do you need?"

"Strange."

Mrs. Long, her brow still furrowed, turned and padded back to the library.

She didn't *need* anything. The woman was a busybody. An 83-year old busybody. *When is she going to retire?* Matthews wondered. The library was the worst place for her since no one ever checked out books anymore. She could find all the chitty chat she needed at the old folks' home in Frisco. If she would only give up the library gig. Or give up the ghost, for that matter.

When secrecy was required, it was bad enough working around Brittany. Her desk was right there at the front door. The girl was actually easy to sneak past, given the constant lure of Instagram and Facebook, but Mrs. Long had eyes like a hawk. And an identity-theft phobia which kept her from even touching the smartphone her grandkids bought her. If it didn't come through a landline, she wouldn't answer it.

Matthews heard the front door creak open.

"Brittany? Can you come in here please?"

Slowly, Brittany peered into his office. "I'm sorry, Mayor Matthews. My parents made me do it."

His face contorted into cartoon confusion. "Do what?"

Her face contorted into genuine confusion. "The protest at the ski resort. You know."

He shrugged. "I'm not sure I do. What are you referring to? I wasn't aware of any protest at the ski resort."

"Weren't you . . . there?"

Holding up the pen again, Matthews tried the same stunt. "No. I've been here since 8 A.M., Miss Chisolm. I've got a ton of work to do before the city council meets. Can you tell me why you didn't show up for work today? And why I shouldn't fire you?"

Her lip quivering, Brittany's emotions got the best of her again. Tears leaked down her face.

It was exactly what he hoped would happen. Setting the pen down, Matthews folded his hands on the desk in front of him.

"Perhaps I'm being too harsh. I'm sorry, Brittany. You've been through a rough week and I had no call to speak like that." There were times he wished he were a better actor. Like Brittany. Were these tears real? Perhaps. And perhaps not. Either way, it reminded him once again that emotions always trumped truth. Whether it was tears or outrage. That was how arguments were won.

Standing up, he went around and ushered her to a nice leather chair in the corner. There was another way arguments were won—deception.

"Sit down for a moment. It's okay to cry." He went back to the desk and sat on the edge. It was a tactic he often used. To loom. It made the person sitting in the chair feel small and insecure. "So your folks are at the ski resort, protesting."

He handed her a Kleenex.

"I asked them not to, but they did it anyway. They're going to sue the resort. For not shutting down the ski slopes after the blizzard."

Matthews scratched his jaw, reflecting on the avalanche. Or pretending to.

"Hhmm. Well, they do have the *legal* right to file a lawsuit. And I certainly understand their concern as parents. Aspen nearly died in the avalanche, too." He picked up a framed photo of Aspen that was sitting on the desk. From his peripheral vision, he could tell Brittany was watching. This was his bread and butter. "But if they sue the resort, there's a good chance it will have to close down for good. If that happens, this town will lose its biggest source of tax revenue. A lot of people will lose their jobs."

He almost added, *starting with you.* But that was the wrong approach. For now, at least.

Brittany blew her nose. "I don't want that to happen."

"Neither do I." Matthews put Aspen's photo back. "Not to mention, what about the skiing? Everyone loves skiing. I'd hate to see the place shut down. What would people do? Drive all the way to Vail?"

The girl's eyes were red but the tears had stopped. A calmness was settling over her. It was sinking in. He could tell.

She wadded up the Kleenex and threw it in the trashcan.

"Maybe I can talk to them. My parents."

Bread and butter.

CHAPTER 42

Freebie

"Three pineapple and ham." The cardboard pizza boxes had gotten wet and warped in the rain. Freddy's Civic wasn't exactly waterproof, either. "You must be starving, dude."

"This is a peace offering." Cash counted out some money. "High Country hiring? Cuz I may need a new career at this rate."

Curious, Freddy looked down the corridor. Valerie Matthews and the Chisolms were marching around the food court, chanting again now that they had an audience.

"Those cats look full-on ticked."

Cash shrugged. "That's Aspen's mom. And Brittany's parents. Trying to blame me for that avalanche."

Avalanche! Close it down! Avalanche! Close it down!

"That's a drag, man." Then Freddy winked. "You need any-thing *else?*"

Surprised, Cash glanced around but no one was close enough to hear.

"I thought you got busted, bro."

Setting the pizza boxes on the floor, Freddy patted his coat pockets. They were bulging with product.

"My grow house got raided. But I just found a new supplier down in Denver. Everything, man. White Rhino. Sour Diesel. Blue Dream. Nothing less than absolute bomb weed. I can huff that cheeba all day."

"Ganja?" Cash turned around to see where the redhead depu-ty was, but she was gone and the protest was a good distraction if nothing else. He pulled out his wallet again with a smile. "I'll take a forty-bag right now, if you got it, man."

Freddy traded a thick bag of marijuana for two twenty-dollar bills.

"Let's go hotbox my Civic."

"Wish I could. But I'm on the clock."

His smile faded as he looked back at Aspen, sitting on the floor next to a fake palm tree. Alone. Arm in a sling. Bruises everywhere. She looked so sad.

"That your girl?" Freddy asked. "Chick looks pretty messed up."

"Aspen about died in that avalanche. Stuck in the hospital for days. Tell you what, she could use a hit of this reefer. If I could talk her into it."

Cash bent down to pick up the pizzas, and Freddy knelt next to him. He pulled out a Ziploc baggie full of yellow and blue pills.

"What's this?" Cash asked.

"Something better than reefer, man. A couple of these makes the pain go bye-bye." Freddy scooped out a handful. "Freebie. Gotta take care of your girl, man."

Cash tucked them out of sight, picked up the saggy boxes, and headed down to the food court. He threw Freddy a nod.

"Peace, out."

CHAPTER 43

That Old Chestnut

"That freak show mayor."

Breck looked up to see Jenny, completely soaked, standing in the doorway.

"What did he do now?" Breck asked.

Squishing with every step, Jenny started to bring in her mountain bike but hesitated. "I ought to chuck this thing in the dumpster."

Breck went into the jail cell full of split wood and chose a few pieces for the potbelly stove. "Let's fire this thing up. You'll dry out pretty quick."

"We need a decent budget so we can get a decent patrol car so I can get where I'm going with a little dignity." *Squish, squish.* "Thanks to Scrooge McDouche. And get this. The reason Brittany's parents stopped in this morning was to tell us they were staging a protest at the ski resort. Wondered if they needed a permit."

While she talked, Breck wadded up a piece of newspaper and stuffed it in the stove, beneath the wood. He looked around. "Where did the matches go?"

"So, maybe half an hour later I get an anonymous caller. Complains about an anti-avalanche protest. People with signs chanting in the parking lot. Says it's making people mad and there could be violence. Maybe the Sheriff's Office needs to shut it down. Hint, hint."

Leaving a trail of wet footprints, Jenny went to her desk and pulled open a drawer. It was empty, so she slammed it.

"Aw, come on. I had a change of clothes in here. What did I do with 'em?"

"Check the other desks, maybe."

There were three other desks. Back when they had two other deputies and a dispatcher to run the phones, they were used for more than just storage. Jenny started opening and slamming drawers. Matthews sure had done a number on their budget. She sometimes felt like a ghost, wandering around the old church. Stone walls echoed. Those empty desks. The morning sun in the stained glass lit up the jail cells with a field of colors.

Breck spotted the matches by the coffee maker. "Hey, you want some hot coffee? It'll do the trick. Warm you up."

The coffee pot was half-full from the day before.

"Love me some sludge," Jenny said.

He poured it out in the sink. "Give me a *little* credit."

"What I need is to go home and take a hot shower. Binge-watch Netflix for the next forty-eight hours." She sank into her chair with a low miserable groan. "My legs are killing me. I haven't ridden a bike for years. What was I thinking?"

She watched Breck poured fresh coffee grounds into the coffee maker, hit the go button, and take the matches over to the potbelly.

"The quote-unquote anonymous caller didn't realize we have caller ID." Jenny squeezed her hair. Water splattered on the floorboards. "City Hall. It was Matthews. He claimed to be a concerned citizen and tried to disguise his voice. It was like a bad episode of Sesame Street. Just like Freddy did, remember? Anonymous calls are not all that anonymous, boys. What a couple of idiots."

Getting his laptop, Breck brought it over to her desk.

"The Almart manager emailed a screen grab from the security footage."

He opened his browser and brought up the photo. Zorrero and El Sangrador at the register. "That guy up front. Mustache. He's the one I saw in Freddy's cabin. Silver Shades—he's got to be the one who snuck up behind me."

A twinge of fear shot through Jenny's gut.

"That's them."

She knew those faces. So much of that night was a blur. But some of it was crystal clear. Like the big ape with the sunglasses leveling a semi-auto AR-15 at her brainpan.

Jenny leaned forward, frowning. "Either they're really hungry, or they're stocking up for the long haul."

The coffee maker clicked off. Hearing it, Breck went over and filled up two *Ski Quandary!* mugs. Predictably, he poured a little half & half into his. She always drank hers black as night. No matter how bad the coffee tasted. And the office coffee always tasted pretty bad. It was another victim of their tight departmental budget.

"They paid in cash. No names. Hardly talked." Breck brought the drinks back to Jenny's desk and gave one to her. "And of course, Chief Waters lives and breathes by that old chestnut, *If you see something, don't say anything.* We're lucky we got this photo at all."

Jenny cradled the mug. It was warm but she hardly felt it, staring at the cartel men.

The man with the mustache. He had been wearing black gloves that night. Treated her with kid gloves. Like a toddler. Like the gun in her hand was just a toy. *Shhh, shh, shh. You won't get hurt. Not today.* And poor Freddy. Poor ding dong Freddy. Crawled right under that jail cell cot, his sky-blue Converse shoes sticking out. She thought for sure they were both dead.

Jenny felt her stomach flutter again. The stock boy was in the frame, scanning a can of beef stew. Eyes down. Back rigid.

"Did they do anything to that poor kid?"

CHAPTER 44

Hard to Believe

Brittany's voice came over the telephone intercom. "Alma Police Chief Waters on line one."

Mayor Matthews instantly picked up the phone. "Maxwell."

Getting up from his desk, Matthews stretched the phone cord as far as it would go. It was close enough. He tapped the door closed with his toe. Wouldn't it be nice to have a button on his desk that shut the door electronically? The governor had one of those, down in Denver.

"That sheriff of yours is ticking me off."

There was a colonial-style gridded window behind his desk. Matthews sat down and swiveled around so he could look outside. There wasn't much to see, besides the red brick of Blue River Bank. Wouldn't it be nice to have an office in a building that wasn't a glorified strip mall? A second-story suite with a panoramic view of the mountains? And a button on his desk that automatically closed his door. Well, that was all going to change. Plans were already in motion.

All kinds of plans.

"You just hang in there, Maxwell. Be patient."

"He waltzes into my town any time he wants. Don't give a rip about jurisdiction. Telling me how to do my job. Do you know he accused me of racial profiling?"

"It won't be long. As soon as you announce you're running, you will have my full endorsement."

"The election is next year. I don't know if I can put up with him that long."

Matthews shifted the receiver to his other ear and spun around to make sure the door was still closed. To be safe, he lowered his voice.

"You may not have to."

"What can you do? You can't fire a duly elected official."

Matthews was starting to get annoyed. This was the exact same conversation they had every time they talked privately. As a general rule, Waters was both repetitive and annoying. But he was malleable. That was a big selling point. Because Breckenridge Dyer was not.

"What was Breck doing up in Alma?"

"Whoever robbed his brother, he thinks they came through here. I get it, it's personal. And for that reason, I'm being very nice about the whole thing. But now he's harassing the fellows at Almart."

"Almart?" Matthews asked.

"Couple Mexican guys. And Breck didn't even bother calling me to ask if it was okay to question Greg. Let alone see the security footage without a warrant. Just because they're Mexican, doesn't make them drug lords. Or whatever it is he thinks."

Drug lords? Waters didn't even know what he was talking about. But Breck did. And if he was in Alma looking at security footage in a grocery store, then Zorrero had gotten sloppy. That wasn't good. Matthews' mind raced. If Breck somehow tracked Zorrero down and arrested him, the entire business plan would go belly up. Maybe worse. Accusations would fly. The mayor, working with a Mexican cartel? Legalizing cannabis to set up a massive marijuana greenhouse and dispensary in Quandary? No matter how he spun it, it wouldn't look good come re-election time.

"Here's what's going to happen," Matthews said, slow and steady. "I'm going to hang up and call the governor. I might not be able to fire our little sheriff but he can. Or at the very least get the DA involved. Open an investigation. If Breck's own brother has been dealing drugs illegally inside the city limits, how could Breck not know? I find that hard to believe. And so will the governor."

"Let's assume Breck gets fired. They still got one deputy left in the Sheriff's Office. That red-haired gal. O'Hara will get the job, not me."

"Only to fill Breck's shoes during the remainder of his term, then the position of sheriff is up for a vote. Besides she's probably involved, too. Even if she isn't, it won't matter. A department-wide corruption investigation? The governor will want a fresh face in there. That's gonna be you."

Waters went silent. Matthews could hear him breathing, so he knew he was listening.

"I'm hanging up now, Maxwell. And you . . . go delete that Almart video."

CHAPTER 45

Big Fat Caramel Frap

After a hot shower, Jenny went into her kitchen and stared inside the refrigerator. There were a lot of lost causes staring back at her. She dragged the trash can over. Half a jar of spaghetti sauce, feathered with mold—gone. A plastic tray of green gooey organic salad—gone. Very expired milk, with a cottage cheese floater—gone.

She tossed a wilted cucumber, and then examined a foil-wrapped breakfast burrito from the Blue Moose. Sniff test fail.

"That would have been good. A week ago."

Suddenly free to be seen, Jenny realized there were glass shelves in the refrigerator. How about that? A carton of coconut water was in the door. She took it to the couch and dug the TV remote control out of the cushions.

"Let the marathon begin."

The place was a rental. One bed one bath. It was maybe 500 square feet but it was all she needed. And all she could afford.

The clothes dryer was in the kitchen next to the clothes washer. Which was next to the stove. It hummed and clinked and pinged. Her uniform was in there.

"Saturday night. Party hard."

She tried to watch Netflix for a while but she had too much on her mind. Throwing on some jeans and a flannel shirt, Jenny rooted through a pile of shoes in her closet looking for a matching set. Hiking boots. That would work.

What time was it? It was only 7 P.M. She locked the door and started walking. Her mountain bike was chained to a lamppost, like a pit bull in a junkyard. Abandoned and despised.

Low gray clouds with wispy tentacles crept along the ridges. Jenny couldn't see the mountain tops, but at least the rain had quit falling in town.

Where was she going? Danny's brewery? Still closed. Who knew when it would open again. Danny was still in the hospital, recovering from a gunshot and all the complications that came with it. The guy played with fire and got burnt. Jenny shook her head thinking about it. What was the allure, exactly? Getting stoned. She hated feeling out of control. Even a light beer buzz. One beer was plenty for her, never two. There was too much danger out there to let her guard down. Even for a second.

Jenny turned around and headed the other direction, avoiding water puddles. Starbucks was open. An old 1800s era Victorian home converted to a café. Bright yellow, hard to miss.

There were a lot of refurbished Victorian homes in Quandary. Just like most of the mountain towns in Colorado. She liked the Old West vibe. Maybe she'd get a Frappuccino and give Netflix a second chance. See if *Tombstone* was on there. Or *Open Range*.

Jenny kept an eye on every car that drove by. There were a ton of SUVs on the road and half of them were black. Each time she saw one, her gut tightened. Her 9-mil was in her purse but she wished it was even closer. Like in her hand. But that might not go over so well in public, dressed like a civilian.

"Even when I'm off duty, I'm on duty," she muttered.

Starbucks. Aspen was sitting at one of the patio tables alone. Jenny almost went over to say hi, when Cash came out carrying two drinks and joined her.

Heading inside, Jenny went to the register and was relieved to see that there was no line. Once tourist season hit, she wouldn't set foot in here again. A barista in a green apron came up to the register.

"What can I make for you?"

"A big fat caramel frap."

"Venti?"

"If that word means obscenely overpriced, then yes."

Wandering around the store, Jenny pretended to check out the various coffee beans and mugs for sale while she waited. But she was really looking out the window. Aspen and Cash were still out there. Talking quietly. Jenny could tell Cash was trying to get Aspen to smile, but it wasn't working. It had been a rough week for the girl. Jenny was so glad to see her out and about. Alive. With someone who cared.

Jenny hadn't been on a date for a long time. Most of the single men in Quandary were just passing through—climbers, hikers, skiers. There was Freddy. Gross. Danny? No thank you. Breck? That would be weird. Never date cops or co-workers and Breck was both. It would only lead to trouble when things fell apart. And things always fell apart. How about Mayor Matthews? His marriage was over. Jenny laughed out loud, and the barista looked up.

"Sorry, I'm not laughing at you. I was thinking of a joke."

The guy had an ego the size of Texas, alternately charismatic and annoying, but Johnny Tibbs wasn't too hard on the eyes. He was always hitting on her. *Jennifer.* He called her by her full name. It was a half-step between deputy and Jenny. Maybe deputy was too formal and Jenny was too friendly. At least he wasn't spooked by the badge. A lot of guys were. Whatever. But maybe sitting at a patio table with Johnny Tibbs' Texas-sized ego would be better than sitting on her couch alone, sipping a caramel frap and watching *Tombstone* again. Well, no. That was a ridiculous thing to say. *Tombstone* was amazing.

She headed home.

CHAPTER 46

American Proverb

Dawn had taken its sweet time. But it had finally arrived.

Through squinted eyes, the big blue tarp stretched out over El Sangrador's head could be mistaken for the big blue sky. Given the random perforations and general leakiness of the material, it might as well have been. For all the good it did.

After that heavy thunderstorm, a soft drizzle settled in for the night. How many times did he wake up and move his cot? His pillow was a plastic Almart bag filled with spare socks. His blanket, a coat. It was all soaking wet.

Sitting upright, the blood-letter placed his feet on the ground and weighted his bad leg. It was tingly and numb but he could walk. He reached in his shirt and felt the golden necklace with the image of Jesús Malverde. Then he reached for a glass bottle with the image of Jose Cuervo.

"Buenos días." El Sangrador whipped around to see Zorrero sitting in a folding camp chair, wide awake. He looked damp and unrested and displeased. "Give me that."

He held out his hand, wiggling his fingertips.

El Sangrador had yet to take a swig of the tequila. The cork was out. That was as far as he got. But the blood-letter did not complain. He never complained. That would be seen as a flaw in character. Not just any flaw, but weakness. The worst sin of all. At least the blood-letter had managed to reach the camp without limping too bad. That final slope, the zig-zags leading to the grow field, was steep and tricky. But Malverde had interceded on his behalf and sent the cooling rain to ease his pain and strengthen his spirit.

Except the rain had persisted—long after El Sangrador had arrived safely at camp.

The leaky tarp was a nuisance. For both men. No matter where they dragged their cots, big wet drops fell in their eyes and woke them. It was a relentless nocturnal game, full of cursing and fits. It must have looked silly, had anyone seen, but no one had. The laborers had huddled in the forest on the far side of the grow field. They had no tarp but were given a roll of plastic garbage bags to use as ponchos.

In lieu of a cooked breakfast, for the fire pit was soaked, El Sangrador yearned for a swig of tequila. It was a suitable substitute. Warm him up. Reduce the tingling in his shin. But it was not meant to be, for the bottle was nearly empty.

"For you, señor."

El Sangrador dutifully handed over the tequila.

Zorrero drank it down and threw the bottle into the trees.

"This is unacceptable." Beneath his camp chair was a duffel bag. He pulled it out and looked inside. All his spare clothes were wet. "I am the commander of this entire territory. Shall a commander sleep like a dog? In this leaky doghouse? Like all those little doggies out there?"

"No, señor."

"How will you fix this injustice?"

El Sangrador snapped his fingers. "There is the cabin. Where the plants are. We can sleep in real beds, in great comfort, and return here every morning."

It was the first thing out of his mouth and he instantly regretted saying it. The cabin was miles away. That meant a great deal of hiking. Back and forth. Up and down. He should have suggested getting a nylon tent. There was much to be said for a good tent. One of those big family sized kinds with aluminum poles and zipper flaps that keep the rain and mosquitoes out. Vestibules for muddy shoes. Netted windows—they could watch the workers from inside, where it was shady. And drink tequila all day. The blood-letter silently chastised himself for speaking without thinking.

Zorrero's phone beeped. He read a text and frowned.

"It is the mayor. He says the sheriff tracked us to that grocery store." He put his shoes on and laced them up. "That pesky sheriff. Now he knows we did not leave this area. We must be extra careful."

The blue tarp was sagging. It was so low it almost touched Zorrero's head. He slid out of the camp chair, stooping, and crept outside without grazing his head on the wet plastic.

"We cannot stay at the comfortable cabin. Too risky with *la policía* prowling around."

El Sangrador could agree with that. He suspected the sheriff would redouble his efforts to hunt them down now. They had shot his brother, after all. The beer man. It would be wise to stay off the roads as much as possible. Even the back roads. The A-frame was located on the Tibbs Ranch, which was a few miles out of town. Off the beaten path, but still, all it would take was one cowboy catching a glimpse of the Range Rover.

Following Zorrero out from beneath the droopy tarp, the blood-letter straightened up and looked around. Everything was glistening with fresh moisture. The pine, the mountain grass and willow branches, the jagged granite stones. The sky was pink and clear and he spotted some robins dancing around in the freshly tilled earth.

"Just to be safe, maybe we should bring all the cannabis up here," El Sangrador said. "The workers have cleared enough ground already, we can plant them pretty quick."

He checked the time. The laborers had not yet risen. The early bird gets the worm, wasn't that an American proverb?

"Plus, we can go buy a tent," he added. "A real nice one. Some new sleeping bags that are dry. There is a place in Frisco that sells camping gear. And we can stop by the sandwich shop, it's right next door."

He was already tired of pinto beans and yellow peas.

The blood-letter hoped Zorrero would agree. It would be a risk driving on the highway in the daylight. But it was a Sunday morning. The sheriff would not be working. No one would expect them to drive boldly through town, up the highway to Frisco, buy a tent and a sandwich, and drive boldly all the way back. And even if they were spotted, El Sangrador would have both the AR-15 and his Colt .45 with the pearl grips.

Zorrero combed his fingers through his wet hair and tucked in his shirt.

"Let's get off this cold rainy mountain."

CHAPTER 47

Pluck the Day Like
a Chicken

Weaving the SUV between the pine trees, El Sangrador pulled in next to the A-frame and parked. It was a good hiding place. If anyone at the Tibbs Ranch might happen to look across the pasture, they would not see the vehicle.

Zorrero used a heavy bootjack made of welded horseshoes he found on the porch to prop open the back door of the cabin. While El Sangrador began transferring cannabis plants from the living room to the SUV, Zorrero went straight to the mini fridge. There were still a few bottles of Coors Light in there, from when they robbed the General Merchandise and More.

"It's the little things." Zorrero wrung off the bottle cap and drank half of it at once. He handed one to the blood-letter. "Carpe diem."

He sat down on the dusty couch and smiled. That sheriff. He was probably driving around Alma looking for them. What a fool. If Zorrero wanted to, he could walk right into that police station and kill that sheriff at his desk. The redheaded deputy, too. The bodies they could dump in the streets as a warning. The government would fear them and leave them alone to do business.

That was the way of the world.

How many times had he done just that? The last time was in Reynosa. Body pieces in garbage bags. Dumped at a gas station. It was a clear message for his rivals as they battled to see who would control the city, a major trafficking route. The Gulf Cartel had splintered and various factions fought fiercely over the turf. Zorrero caught one of the rival commanders and personally chopped him up. It had the desired effect. Other commanders went into hiding and Los Equis prevailed in Reynosa. From Piedras Negras to Nuevo Laredo, their reach grew long. Drugs and human cargo flowed across the border.

And now, here he was in this sleepy little mountain town in America. His only rivals, the pizza man and the beer man. They had been easy to deal with.

"Señor." El Sangrador came in the door, with a look of concern. "Some *muchachas* are cleaning the other cabins."

Zorrero finished his Coors Light and set the bottle on the coffee table.

"We are lucky then, coming here when we did."

Working together, the two men loaded the rest of the potted plants into the SUV. Just like at Freddy's cabin. There was barely enough room for them this time, as they had grown a little taller already. The A-frame had served its purpose. A temporary greenhouse while the field was cleared of underbrush and stones.

Zorrero climbed into the passenger seat, but El Sangrador hesitated.

"What about the lamps and hoses?"

"We don't need them no more."

But El Sangrador went back inside the cabin again. He returned with the couch blanket with the black bear eating honey stitched on it. He stuffed it beneath the driver's seat and got inside.

"In case we ever sleep in this car again. Last time I was freezing."

It was a kitschy blanket. But Zorrero did not chastise him. He understood his concern. Especially after the cold wet night beneath the leaky tarp. What rotten conditions for a commander of his stature to endure. Zorrero was irked. His clothes were wrinkly and damp and his skin was starting to chafe.

The blood-letter put the SUV into gear and slowly inched through the pine trees and out onto the road. He braked, unsure which way to turn. Right would lead back up Boreal Pass Road to the trailhead. Left would take them to town.

"We can take these plants up to the grow field now." He licked his lips. "Or we can go buy a tent in Frisco like we talked. Get some tequila and a tasty sandwich."

It was true. Their conversation earlier did revolve around those things. While the tequila was appealing, the thought of sleeping in a tent was not. Zorrero wanted better accommodations. A mattress and four walls. This A-frame cabin was perfect, but it was no longer an option. It belonged to the Tibbs Ranch, and with the summer so close it was no surprise a cleaning crew had been sent. They were getting the rental cabins ready. For bankers and lawyers and politicians who wanted to come to play cowboy.

"Head into town."

Driving past the ranch, Zorrero spotted a lot of activity. Indeed, there were several young women walking among the rental cabins. Carrying buckets and mops and brooms.

"We are lucky they did not clean yesterday."

El Sangrador touched his necklace. "Malverde."

Leaning forward, Zorrero caught sight of Johnny Tibbs' big silver Ford pickup truck. Parked by a big wood barn. Spotless. Shining in the sun. The flatbed trailer was still hooked up, and a couple of young men in Stetsons and chaps were unloading the hay bales.

He wondered if it had a fifth wheel? A nice truck like that could haul any trailer. Like a big RV camper rig. Every time the cartel men drove through Quandary, or up to Alma or Frisco, they saw old retired couples with white hair driving pickups with camper trailers. Up and down the highway. Not a care in the world.

That's what they needed. A camper. Parked at the trailhead. That would be much more comfortable than a musty nylon tent. It could rain all day and Zorrero wouldn't care.

He handed the blood-letter another Coors Light.

"Carpe diem."

El Sangrador glanced at him curiously. "What does that mean again?"

"It means to pluck the day. Like a chicken."

CHAPTER 48

Happy Campers

The Tibbs Ranch was only five miles outside of Quandary, but the road was narrow and windy and it took a good half hour. Eventually, Boreal Pass Road popped out on Main Street—right next to the Quandary Brewery. Still closed for business.

"All that good beer inside, no one to drink it." Zorrero rolled the window down and flung his Coors Light bottle into the parking lot. "That is the real tragedy here."

On a Sunday morning, almost every place was closed except the Blue Moose café. There were a lot of cars there. El Sangrador wished they could stop and enjoy a warm meal, perhaps some eggs and coffee, but the Sheriff's Office was a stone's throw away. With its ever-present snowmobile and big green dumpster. Perhaps the sheriff himself was in the Blue Moose at that very moment, eating eggs and coffee. Or the redhead deputy.

Besides, the cleaning crew at the Tibbs Ranch nearly stumbled upon their operation that very day. Their good luck was holding. Why tempt fate?

The road widened north of town, just past the Safeway, and turned into highway. There wasn't much in between Quandary and Frisco—except the Continental Divide Motel and Campground.

Zorrero perked up the moment he saw the sign.

"Pull in here."

"Are you certain? We still have a long way to go to Frisco."

"Forget about that."

Zorrero clapped his hands like a kid in a candy store. Behind the motel, there was a large campground filled with RV campers.

Rows and rows of them. It looked like many people were there to stay, with their belongings strewn about. Many were so determined to stay that they hung signs with their names on them.

Welcome to Our Campsite — The Larsons.

Happy Campers — Tom and Phyllis.

Chillin' and Grillin' — The Mitchells' Home Away from Home.

As they drove around the campsites, El Sangrador shook his head, marveling. Such fancy pickup trucks, everywhere they looked. And luxury trailers. Some even towed along an extra Jeep Wrangler or an ATV. Glaring symbols of American pride, prosperity, and selfishness.

"*¡Fíjate!*" Zorrero slapped the center console like a snare drum. A big F350 Ford dually, just like Johnny Tibbs' truck. It even had an oversized camper attached with a fifth wheel trailer mount. Bird wings were airbrushed on the side, the word *Raptor* above the hitch. "We are birds of prey, are we not? This is the one, Sangre."

El Sangrador was confused. What about Frisco? Buying a tent? And a sandwich?

"Hop on out." Zorrero unbuckled his seat belt. "I'll meet you back at the trailhead. We can park that whole rig right there and live like kings."

Obediently, the blood-letter did as he was told. Zorrero got in the driver's seat and drove the Range Rover right back into Quandary, abandoning him at the Continental Divide Motel and Campground. He walked around for a few minutes to get his bearings.

The motel itself was small. Just a row of doors, facing a small concrete swimming pool that smelled like sulfur. Several kids rode around on bikes, chattering and shouting at each other.

The blood-letter chose a picnic table where he could study the Raptor. Beneath an awning, there was camp furniture, a propane gas grill, plastic ice chest. All surrounded by a thicket of tiki torches. They even had a satellite dish on the roof.

All day he watched the Raptor. As suspected, an elderly couple came out and sat in the camp chairs. They grilled hot dogs for lunch and ate potato chips. Then they put on wide-brimmed sun hats, rubbed on a thick paste of sunscreen, and read books all afternoon.

What a life they were living. Nothing to do. Nowhere to go. Relaxing in camp chairs and grilling hot dogs sounded very nice.

El Sangrador walked into the motel office and paid for a room. The elderly couple would surely go for a walk or a swim in the stinky pool. Eventually. And when they did, he would make his move. But what was the rush?

Perhaps he would go for a walk, himself. The Safeway wasn't too far away. They sold hot dogs and potato chips. Perhaps they sold books there, too. El Sangrador was a Louis L'Amour fan. Perhaps they had Louis L'Amour, and he could relax and read and eat hot dogs all day.

CHAPTER 49

Yellow

Sunset turned the clouds orange. The lake was calm, and in the still waters, Breck watched the sky's reflection. The first stars, pinpoints in the blue expanse, shimmered in the depths.

He reeled in his fishing line. There weren't any trout in this lake.

The lapping sounds were faint against the gritty shore. How long had he been sitting there, his back against the old gray log? He must have nodded off because his neck was sore and the last thing he remembered the sun was still above the ridge.

Taking his pole, Breck walked back home. It was just up the dirt road from the lake, not a far walk at all. He looked up at the surrounding ridges. Most of the snow was gone below timberline. The peaks, however, were coated in the white stuff. Maybe he would find time to go snow climbing this year. Bust out the crampons and ice ax. They were gathering dust in his basement, which was a downright travesty. The couloirs would be in perfect shape in just a few weeks. Late June, early July. Compact and stable for a safe ascent.

It was so easy to forget that the danger was real. Poor Aspen, Brittany. Those girls almost didn't make it out of the backcountry alive.

Going inside, he put the pole in the closet and went over to the kitchen cabinets. He got out the coffee beans, the grinder, and the French press. What time was it? He started to look at the clock but something else caught his eye.

The answering machine. The little red light was flashing. Cell service was patchy at his place even on a good day, and it was a good day, but people usually rang the landline if they wanted to reach him. Someone had tried.

"Breck . . . Johnny Tibbs. Thought I'd let you know, one of my rental cabins was busted into. Nothing was stolen. Just the opposite. I got a dozen new heat lamps now. The barn cats will appreciate them next winter."

Heat lamps? In one of Tibbs' rental cabins? Breck set the coffee beans down and grabbed the phone, jabbing in Tibbs' number. Just like Freddy's cabin—he used heat lamps to keep his crop of cannabis warm and happy. Until it got stolen.

Breck touched the back of his head, where the cartel man had struck him. Just as easy, it could have been a bullet to the brain.

"Yellow?"

Whenever he answered the phone, Tibbs always said *yellow* instead of *hello*. It was pretty lame, but Breck had no time for lame. Tibbs had a Mexican cartel problem now. He just didn't know it.

"Hey Johnny, I'd like to take a look at that rental. Can you keep your people out of there until I swing by?"

"Too late. Housekeeping already scrubbed it down. Those cabins have been sitting all winter collecting dust, and I got paid guests arriving first thing in the A.M. Summer season is right around the corner, amigo."

Rubbing his brow, Breck tried not to sigh audibly. Tibbs just obliterated a crime scene to make a buck. Of course, the guy didn't know what was going on. But even so, a break-in should set off red flags at the very least.

"Tell you what. You're a busy man," Tibbs said. "Why don't you send Jennifer out here and I'll show her what's what. Give her the down-low."

Breck gritted his teeth—not cool, Johnny Tibbs.

"Listen up. Have you seen anything suspicious?" Breck asked. "Cars? People? If they had heat lamps in there, that means they were using the cabin as a greenhouse."

"Who's they? And what the hell were they growing in my rental unit?"

"You know I can't discuss the details. Let's just say some very dangerous men. And it ain't cilantro. Keep your staff away from that cabin, alright? And don't let anyone move in there. Can you tape it off until I get there?"

Tibbs chuckled, but it was humorless.

"Sheriff, you know what I'm looking at right now? Golden frame. Hung on the wall above my desk—the Second Amendment. All my boys pack a six-gun at all times, and half of 'em carry rifles when they ride. If anyone's dangerous, it's Johnny Tibbs."

Breck looked at the clock. It was getting late. By the time he got out there, it would be too dark to see. The way Tibbs was talking, it would be a wasted trip anyhow. Any evidence was bleached, swept and gone. And if the cartel men weren't using the cabin as a greenhouse anymore, if they cleaned out the plants, they weren't coming back. Not to that particular cabin, anyhow. Where else would they go? And why?

"Just be careful, Johnny. Tell your staff to be very careful and report anything suspicious to me immediately, alright?"

"We have a motto out here. Shoot first and ask questions later." There was impatience creeping into his voice. "Now if you'll excuse me, I've got a ranch to run."

Click. He was done talking.

Breck hung up the phone and picked up the bag of coffee beans. But he was too distracted and just stood there, mind reeling.

He should drive out there. Maybe the housekeepers missed something. Or there might be evidence around the A-frame somewhere, on the ground or the deck. At the very least, it would be smart to drive around the area and see if the neighbors saw anything. There weren't many homes beyond the Tibbs Ranch, but there were a few tucked back in the forest.

He almost called Jenny. But it could wait until morning. She deserved a full weekend off-duty, why spoil that now?

The cartel men. First, they came through Quandary. Then groceries in Alma. Now the Tibbs Ranch. One thing was for sure. They were sticking around.

CHAPTER 50

Doctor Grade

There was a knock on the door. Standing on her tiptoes to see through the peephole, Aspen flipped on the porchlight. It was Cash.

She opened the door and let him in.

"Hey." Cash leaned in for an awkward hug. Aspen allowed it.

Looking past her shoulder, he studied the house. The kitchen was down the hall, dimly lit. There were no lights on in the living room, either. The television was on mute, flickering images and shadows.

"Your dad's place is ten times as big."

Aspen shut the door, made a beeline for the couch and curled up with a big pillow.

"Where's your mom?"

"She went to yell at daddy."

Crossing the living room, Cash sat down on the couch, too. There was some kind of real-crime murder mystery on TV. A bloody garage in nowhere suburbia. A man in pinstripes, eyes both pleading and skeevy. Interviews with family members, their faces filled the screen—serious, tearful, suspicious.

"The husband did it. It's always the husband."

"That's not funny."

Aspen took out her phone and started scrolling. The glow from the little screen lit up her own face—serious, tearful, suspicious.

Cash squeezed her sock. "Just kiddin'."

The swelling was starting to go down in her nose, but the bruising around her eyes looked even darker. The sling was wadded up on the end table. Her wrist was still bandaged but her fingers were working well enough to text.

"Are you feeling any better?"

She shrugged.

"I brought you something." He tried to catch her attention by bobbing his head a little. It worked, and she looked over at him. "It's medical, so don't freak out."

He pulled out a plastic Ziploc baggie. Inside were several hand-rolled joints.

Aspen sat up, alarmed. "I don't smoke and I never will."

"You sure? I do it all the time."

But she pulled the pillow tight and stared at the television again.

A jailhouse interview. Narrator seated in a chair, legs casually crossed, a look of disbelief on his weathered face. He knew. After a thousand jailhouse interviews with a thousand skeevy eyes, the truth was as plain as day. Crime scene photos. Bloody knife on the kitchen tile. The man in the pinstripes mouthing the words. *I didn't do it. It wasn't me.* There was nothing new under the sun.

"You got jacked up pretty bad, Aspen. I know, I was there. I was the one who found you, remember?" Cash quietly put the marijuana back in his jacket. "Something like that can mess with your mind, too. Dark places and stuff."

Getting up, Aspen went into the kitchen and got a glass out of the cabinet. She turned on the faucet and filled it with water. She set it on the kitchen island and started opening drawers, rooting around.

"You got a headache?" Cash asked.

He came over and leaned on the island, watching.

"If we turn on a light, you can see better."

"No. That'll make it worse."

A soft blue light emanated from the digital display on the refrigerator. It made Aspen look blue.

"I can't find the aspirin. I don't know where mom keeps it." She slammed the drawers. Frustrated, exasperated. A tear shot down her cheek but she wiped it away just as quick. "I'm fine."

"No, you're not." Cash glanced down the dark hallway, at the front door. "Listen. I know you don't want to get baked, and that's okay. Don't do anything you don't wanna do. But let me help, Aspen. I'm here for you—no one else is."

From his other pocket, Cash produced a different Ziploc baggie. Full of little pills. The ones Freddy gave him.

"What are those?" Aspen asked.

"Aspirin ain't gonna cut it. This is doctor grade." Cash pushed the baggie across the kitchen island. "Some of these will make it all go away. Trust me."

Aspen closed her eyes and rubbed her temples.

CHAPTER 51

Burning Daylight

Since she lived so close by, Jenny was always the first one at the office. So when she wheeled her mountain bike into the parking lot, she was surprised to see Breck's Jeep was already there.

"What time did you get here?" She slung her bike helmet on the coat rack. Now that Jenny didn't need her puffy marshmallow winter coat, the coat rack looked pretty sad. Like a Charlie Brown Christmas tree. "It's barely 8 o'clock . . . on a *Monday*."

Breck was rummaging through the evidence locker. It was literally a locker. A gym locker with a padlock. He held up a box of latex gloves.

"We need to order more of these. And have you seen the crime scene tape? I can't find it anywhere."

"Behind the coffee filters." Jenny pointed at the cabinets in the kitchenette. "We have a crime scene?"

"Tibbs Ranch. One of the rental cabins. A bunch of heat lamps hanging from the ceiling. Johnny called it in last night."

Jenny's eyes went wide.

"The cartel duo. Are they holed up in there? Holy crap." She drew her Luger and dropped the magazine to check the loads.

Breck opened the cabinet and pushed aside the coffee filters. Sure enough. A roll of crime scene tape. "What's this doing in here?"

"It's a little message—stop buying Folgers. It's a crime." Jenny holstered her gun. It was clear Breck wasn't gearing up for a shootout. "So what's the deal? Are the wonder twins up at Johnny's place or not?"

He put the roll of tape and the gloves into a backpack with a *Quandary County Sheriff's Office* logo sewn onto it. Along with some evidence bags. He zipped it up. "A little half n' half and it tastes just fine."

She went to the tac closet and got out a box of 9mm rounds. She hefted it in her palm. "Dude. It's called taste buds. Get some."

Breck smiled. Sometimes, Jenny could be funny. Since the department budget was so thin, decent coffee went out the window. Really, it all came back to Mayor Matthews. No patrol car. Broken snowmobile. Staff cuts. Bad coffee.

"I have a french press at home. Whole beans. I grind my own coffee."

"Well, Brecky's got game." She wiggled her cell phone. It was 8 A.M. on the nose. "And we're burning daylight. Let's go already."

Slinging the backpack over his shoulder, Breck grabbed the Jeep keys off his desk and headed for the door. But before they could leave, the office phone rang. Jenny ran back and answered.

"Sheriff's Office, Deputy O'Hara."

Even from the doorway, Breck could hear a frantic voice coming through the receiver. Someone was having a bad morning.

"Val, slow down." Jenny waved Breck over and pointed furiously at the CB like it was a bomb. She covered the mouthpiece for a second. "Call Michelle and get an ambulance out to Valerie Matthews in Frisco. Her daughter is unresponsive."

Dropping the backpack, Breck ran over to the radio.

"Valerie, stay on the line," Jenny said. "Tell me if Aspen is breathing. Check her breathing right now. Can you do that?"

"Michelle, come in. This is Sheriff Dyer and I have an emergency situation." Breck paused to see if she would respond. The hospital always kept their CB on. The State Patrol, Search & Rescue, and the ambulance all relied on it. And so did they half the time. Breck knew Michelle would be listening. And she was.

"Breck, go ahead."

"We need an ambulance to Valerie Matthews' house in Frisco. Aspen Matthews is unresponsive and . . . hold on."

He glanced at Jenny for more information. Valerie was sobbing and shrieking and in complete shock. Her voice rose and fell and Breck couldn't quite hear what she was saying.

"Talk to me, Val . . ." A look of relief washed over Jenny's face. She gave him a thumbs up. "So Aspen *is* breathing. Good. Keep her on her side and wipe away that foamy discharge. Keep her airway clear. She could choke if you don't."

Breck went back to the CB to finish his thought. "Michelle. Aspen is breathing, but unconscious. Her mother is on scene. I am heading over there right now. I'll meet the ambulance when it gets there. Breck out."

He patted Jenny on the shoulder to get her attention. Showed her his Jeep keys. "I'm going over there."

She nodded but kept talking on the phone. Her voice calm and even. "Don't hang up, Valerie. Stay on the line. An ambulance is on its way, and so is the sheriff. Help is coming. You're not alone, I'm right here with you."

CHAPTER 52

Awful

It only took ten minutes to get to Frisco from Quandary, but it felt like forever. Could Aspen hang in there that long? What happened? She was *just* in the hospital—now she was going back again.

A long time ago, Breck and Danny fixed up the Jeep. Back when they were on better terms. Dropped a big block engine under the hood. Swapped out from a 1970s Chevy Corvette. It was Danny's idea to install racing gears instead of a timing belt. Of course, Breck didn't do much of the work. He barely knew the difference between a crescent wrench and a pair of pliers. But Danny knew what to do.

Most Jeeps had a four-cylinder under the hood with a top speed of fifty-five. Not this thing. In a heartbeat, Breck was doing ninety.

All he had for a police siren was a red and blue LED light bar, affixed to the windshield frame above the visors. He reached up and pressed the on-button. The strobe pattern danced across the hood and the pavement. Breck hammered down the accelerator and shifted gears. Maybe he could cut that ten minutes down to five.

Digging out his cell phone, Breck held it above the steering wheel so he could find the Mayor's number without veering into oncoming traffic.

"Come on. Pick up."

But it went straight to voicemail.

"Matthews, this is Sheriff Dyer. There is a serious health emergency concerning your daughter and an ambulance has been called. I am heading over there, too. I need to speak with you right now. Call me."

He tossed the phone on the passenger seat. Maybe someone else had gotten through already. Jenny was probably still keeping Valerie calm. She was good at that. She was good at a lot of things. Which was why Breck had kept her on the payroll long after the city council slashed his budget. And kept slashing. Further and further, month after month. He didn't tell her this, but Breck even docked his own paycheck to keep Jenny around. He couldn't do the job alone, that was for sure.

Finally, Frisco. Speed limit signs went from 55 to 35, and the forest gave way to tourist shops and restaurants. Easing off the juice, Breck was relieved to hit the traffic lights green. The clock was ticking. He weaved through the neighborhood until he spotted Valerie's house and mashed the brakes. Skid marks in the driveway.

The front door was locked. He banged on it and rang the bell at the same time.

"Sheriff's Office! Valerie, it's me. Breck."

The ambulance wasn't there yet. But he knew he would beat them, no surprise. The door swung open and Valerie grabbed his wrist, dragging Breck inside.

"Thank God, thank God!" Her face was soaked with tears and runny makeup. She could barely talk. "Hurry! Please, she's . . . she's . . ."

Aspen was in her bedroom. Lying on the bed. Valerie had rolled her sideways and jammed pillows around her to keep her that way.

Checking her neck for a pulse, Breck was relieved to find one. But it was weak and her breathing was shallow. Her lips and fingers were a light blue color. Saliva and vomit were on the bed sheets.

"Aspen. Can you hear me?" He checked her eyes. Pupils dilated. "Does she have a medical condition? Blackouts? Alcohol abuse? Drugs? Is she on any meds? . . . Valerie?"

Exhausted and disoriented, Valerie sunk onto the bed next to her daughter and dropped the phone from her hand. Jenny was still on the other end.

"I don't know. I don't know."

A gurgling sound. From Aspen's mouth. Then it stopped just as suddenly. Breck leaned down and listened for a couple of quick seconds. Then he rolled her on her back, pinched her nose and began giving her CPR breaths.

"What's going on?" Valerie shook Aspen's legs. "Aspen! Aspen! Wake up!"

Breck paused and listened. Nothing. More CPR breaths. Where was that ambulance?

Just as the thought crossed his mind, two paramedics appeared in the bedroom doorway. Nurses from the hospital. Same ones that showed up at the brewery when Danny got shot. They wheeled in a stretcher.

"We'll take over now." It was Melinda. She was wearing a name tag this time. Opening a medical kit, she put a plastic CPR mask over Aspen's face and began squeezing air into the girl's lungs. "Help us get her on the gurney."

As they were strapping her onto the stretcher, Breck looked around the room. What had happened here? The curtains were closed. Laptop closed. A cell phone with a pink polka dot cover on the nightstand. A glass of water and a Ziploc baggie full of blue and yellow pills. Breck grabbed the baggie. This was it. Obviously. He handed it to Melinda.

"Take these with you. Can you analyze them?"

"We will pump her stomach at the hospital and see what's in her system. But I guarantee you this is oxycodone. Well, the yellow ones for sure."

They were quick and loaded Aspen in the ambulance in a matter of sixty seconds. Valerie climbed inside too, clutching her daughter's leg. The look on her face was awful. Breck closed the door and the ambulance drove off in a blast of sirens and flashing lights.

And then it was silent. A light breeze off the lake. Sunshine. A seagull flew over, watching him.

Breck wiped his mouth with the back of his sleeve.

"Good times."

CHAPTER 53

Wheelhouse

"I thought real cowboys only drank black coffee." Mayor Matthews raised an eyebrow at Johnny Tibbs' latte.

Tibbs took a frothy sip and *ahhhhed*. "When did *you* take an interest in handicap kids? I thought the only thing in your wheelhouse was you."

"Touché." Matthews gave him a crisp nod of concession. "And it is that very perception that I aim to change because it is a far cry from the real Seneca Matthews."

He loosened his tie, took off his suit jacket and slid it over the back of his chair. Casual. Relatable. That was the new visual. The optics. And it all started here with Johnny Tibbs in a busy Starbucks on a Monday morning.

"The Tibbs Ranch. Biggest outfitter in the county and there ain't one person in town that doesn't know who you are. You're a brand people trust." Matthews tried to avoid a patronizing tone. He made it ooze genuine admiration. *Ain't* was a good touch. "Listen. You've made your money, and so have I. We're kings in our own castles and that's a good thing. But maybe it's time to be more than that. Give something back. Help the community we live in and love."

He could sense Tibbs was watching him carefully. For a tell. A crack in the façade. An eye tick or a quake in the voice. But Matthews had rehearsed his talking points. The arc of his spiel. For that's what it was.

"Therapeutic horseback riding. It's where they put handicap kids on horses and it does a world of good. For everyone involved."

He pulled a packet out of his briefcase and set it on the table. Photos of Aspen riding horses. The building plans. A picture of some poor kid in a wheelchair for good measure. "Now look. If we work together we can make this happen right here in Quandary. You know horses, so you can help with all the practical decisions. The how-tos and the what-nots. And I will personally cover the expenses of the indoor arena. The whole thing. It won't cost you a dime."

Legalizing marijuana. It was a tricky sell. Chunky had been easy, but the cowboy would be much harder to convince. But if Tibbs truly believed Matthews' had a heart for helping the community, if they were buddy-buddy, he might budge. What better way to get to a cowboy's heart, than with a horse? And a little tug on the ol' heartstrings.

Matthews tapped his finger on an arena diagram.

"Look how big that is. Big enough for a lot of horses and therapists to do their thing. Mom and dad can watch from the observation area. Couches. A fridge full of ice cold Pepsi Cola. Maybe a latte machine? Big heaters in the arena so they can ride all winter long. We're taking care of people, Johnny. That's what this is all about."

Big heaters in the arena—so he can grow cannabis all winter long. *That's* what it was all about. Convert it to a greenhouse, shut the riding program down. Or shove it onto Johnny Tibbs' plate, one hundred percent. He had a big enough ranch to run the whole show, didn't he? *Show some heart, Johnny. Help those poor crippled kids . . .*

"We can do a lot of good for this community if we work together." Matthews rolled up his sleeves while he said it. The metaphor was a little too obvious, but he did it anyway.

Tibbs finished his latte. He took off his straw hat long enough to comb his short hair with his fingers. Then he put it back on.

"I ain't gonna lie to you. I was not expecting this from you. Sounds like a good cause. I can get on board with that. Count me in."

"We're not done talking, partner." Matthews pointed at his empty cup. "Stay put. Round two is on me."

He went over to the counter and loudly ordered two lattes. Better than choking down two Subway sandwiches back to back. Why couldn't Jameson have a latte addiction?

CHAPTER 54

Sour Day

Carrying beach towels over their shoulders, Tom and Phyllis Nickles passed through the gate at the Continental Divide Motel and Campground's hot springs swimming pool.

"Rotten eggs," Phyllis said, scrunching up her nose.

"Every time we come here, it's the same comment." Tom set his towel on a lounge chair and settled in.

"Well, it stinks to high heaven."

"You're welcome to wait in the camper. I'm going to take a dip."

Shuffling around the kidney-shaped pool to the shallow end, Tom eased his foot into the water and flinched. The temperature was hot, indeed. But once he got in there, it would be worth it and he knew it.

Phyllis opted for the lounge chairs. She sat down, stretched out and began flipping through a house-flipping magazine.

Tom hated those magazines. They were so expensive these days. And cleverly displayed right next to the registers at the Safeway store. Every time they went down there to resupply on groceries, Phyllis just had to buy one. He could never talk her out of it, no matter what he said. Tom felt guilty buying a package of Tic Tacs—they used to cost a quarter not too many years ago. Now they were over a buck!

The smell of sulfur dioxide was strong. But it was no different than the geysers at Yellowstone. Sinking in up to his neck, Tom took a seat on the underwater concrete stairs. It was his favorite spot in the swimming pool. He could relax and let his legs float.

He had bad knees and the temperature helped with circulation. Kept the blood flowing.

"Look what they did to this old farmhouse, Tom." Phyllis held up the magazine, but he was too far away to see. "There is a chimney from an old wood stove in the kitchen, and they exposed the brick. What a hoot. I want to do that at our house."

"We don't have a chimney."

Phyllis turned the page and her face lit up. "You should see these before and after photographs. Then you'll change your mind about the whole thing."

"There's nothing to change my mind about. We don't have a chimney."

Tom dipped his whole head underwater for a moment. When he came back up, he noticed a Ford pickup truck rolling by with a Raptor camper trailer. A man with silver sunglasses and short dark hair was behind the wheel.

"Would you look at that, Phyllis. An F350 and a Raptor fifth wheel camper trailer. That young man has got the exact same setup we do."

He glanced at Phyllis. She was ignoring him. She was pouting, he could tell. She always pouted if he didn't sound enthused about a magazine article or a passage in a book she was reading. It would be a sour day if he didn't change the subject quick. He pointed a dripping finger at the passing vehicle.

"Follow your bliss, young man! Go confidently in the direction of your dreams. Live the life you've always imagined." He glanced at Phyllis again. "That's Henry David Thoreau."

The magazine was in her lap—she was paying attention now.

"That's our pickup truck and camper."

He stood up to get a better look. It certainly did look like their pickup and camper. Same colors. Satellite dish. Florida plates. It even had a sign above the trailer door. *Happy Campers — Tom & Phyllis.*

"Son of a gun!" Climbing the pool stairs, Tom hustled as fast as he could. But the air at 9,000 feet was much thinner than it was in Orlando. He sunk down onto a lounge chair to catch his breath. "Where's your cellular phone? We need to call 9-1-1."

"It's in my purse." Opening her purse, Phyllis rooted around inside but couldn't find it. "I know I put it in here. Right after I finished my Cracklin' Oat Bran. You saw me put it in here, didn't you Tom? I *knew* we should have gone to Gunnison."

Tom wheezed but held his tongue. She was always losing things in her purse. If it wasn't the phone, it was her sunglasses or their keys or the antacid tablets. Every summer they alternated locations, between Quandary and Gunnison. Phyllis preferred going there, for she enjoyed the view of the reservoir. But Tom liked it better here. There wasn't a hot springs pool at the RV campground in Gunnison, and the water did wonders for his knees.

"Hurry up, he's turning onto the highway." But it was too late. Their truck and camper trailer sped away, and quickly faded into the distance. "Tell the police I got a good look at him. That hooligan must have swum up the Rio Grande. I know an illegal alien when I see one."

CHAPTER 55

Blaze of Glory

"**B**reck, you there?" It was Jenny.

Unwinding the cord from the gear shift, the usual CB circus, Breck got the mic free and pushed the talk button.

"Just left Frisco. It was dicey, but Aspen is alive. They're taking her to the hospital now."

"Good. That was not fun."

There was relief in her voice, but Breck could tell there was something else on her mind.

"What's up?"

"I got another 9-1-1 call. This one came from the Continental Divide RV campground. Keep your eyes out for a stolen camper trailer with Florida plates. Raptor, with an F350 dually up front."

Breck looked in his rearview mirror.

"You know what, I just passed the motel a minute ago. I can turn around and go take a statement."

"Better yet, keep driving. They called it in just a second ago, so the vehicle has gotta be on the highway. Probably a mile or two ahead of you. And get this. They described the perp as a Hispanic male with silver sunglasses. Well, not in those words exactly."

The cartel men kept turning up in surprising places, but then always disappeared into thin air. If that stolen camper rig was on the highway . . .

"I see it!" Breck gunned the Jeep. The Corvette engine purred like a Tiger. "Heading south into town. Just went by Safeway."

Breck flipped on the light bar and pulled up behind the trailer. He honked his horn a few times, since he didn't have a proper siren, and crossed the double yellow line so the driver could see him in the side mirror.

"Come on, pull over. You know you want to," Breck mumbled.

But the Raptor did not. Mile after mile, it kept ambling towards Quandary. There was just enough oncoming traffic that Breck couldn't pull alongside or get ahead of it. Then the highway funneled into Main Street and they entered the city limits, passing by the tourist shops.

Breck checked the speedometer. Now they were down to 10 miles an hour and the guy was still trucking. If they had a second patrol car, Jenny could set up a roadblock. Wouldn't that be nice?

"I can't get him to pull over. He's heading right down Main. We're passing Starbucks now. Look out the window, you'll see us go by here in a couple of seconds."

As he drove past the Starbucks, Breck noticed another Ford F350 dually. It was Johnny Tibbs' truck. And it was parked right next to Mayor Matthews' BMW.

A couple blocks down, the Raptor passed the Sheriff's Office, the Blue Moose, the Quandary Brewery, and kept right on going out of town.

Jenny's voice crackled over the radio. "I saw him. It's definitely our guy."

"Alrighty. I can barely make my mouth say these words, but . . . can you call Chief Waters up in Alma? Ask him to set up a roadblock at the other end of the canyon. I don't want to play road rage with that big truck."

Breck hung up the mic and downshifted. The road angled above the ravine, getting steeper with every twist and curve. Time to play the long game. Now that he was certain it was the cartel gunman, Breck knew what he was dealing with. This wasn't an average car thief. There would be no gentle pull over, no peaceful surrender. No hands up, aw shucks, you got me. This was a desperado in a desperate situation. And he was driving a powerful truck with a lot of weight. If Breck tried to shoot the gap and get ahead, the guy could easily swerve into him. Plow the Jeep into the cliffside. Or knock him into the ravine. It was better to stay on his tail and flush him into a trap.

"No dice, Breck." Jenny sounded ticked. "Waters told me to get a dictionary and look up the word *jurisdiction*."

"You gotta be kidding."

"I told him to get a dictionary and look up the word *ass-hat*."

As the incline increased, the Raptor slowed down even more. Not exactly a *Smokey and the Bandit* style car chase. Even so, Breck backed off a little for safety. With the guardrail gone, the canyon road was an extremely dangerous place to be doing this.

"Let's see how this pans out. I'll try and force him to stop once we get past this drop-off. I may have to shoot out his tires."

"Please be careful, Breck," Jenny said. "You know he's a killer. Hundred percent chance he's armed."

They exited the canyon and Breck tried to pass the RV but each time he tried the vehicle swerved. It was a narrow two-lane road and the cartel man was anticipating Breck's moves.

"Alright, pal. We'll do this at the top of the pass."

The road would get steep again in a few miles after they passed the General Merchandise and More. It zigzagged up switchbacks until it topped out at the high point. Red Mountain Pass. There was a dirt overlook up there. It was basically a wide spot in the road. What about cutting around the RV at that point, zip ahead, and shoot those tires before he could pick up speed?

Suddenly the brake lights lit up. The Raptor slowed and turned onto a narrow dirt road. Change of plans.

Breck grabbed the CB.

"He's not going up the pass, Jen. He just turned onto Tarryall Creek Road."

The Raptor was kicking up enough dust that Breck could barely see it.

Jenny's voice came back over the radio.

"What's he doing? Taking a scenic mountain drive?"

It was a good question. Breck knew these forest roads. They led all over the place and back again, like a spider web. Some of them got pretty bumpy and rutted. One wrong turn and that big trailer would get stuck. But he could guess what was going on. Chances were, this guy was leading Breck deep into the back-country, far from help—and then it was on.

Guns out. Last stand. Blaze of glory.

Breck had his .44 Special. It could punch out a hole the size of a baseball. It just wasn't all that accurate at a distance. It was designed for close quarters. In the Almart video, the guy was armed with a pearl-handled Colt .45. If that was all he had, they could shoot it out Old West style. But the night he waltzed into the Sheriff's Office, Jenny said he was carrying an AR-15. That changed everything. A powerful long-distance rifle with a scope versus his Rossi .44? Breck didn't like those odds.

CHAPTER 56

Radio Hiss

The Jeep started chugging and sputtering. Breck looked at the gas gauge. The needle was on full, but of course, it was. It was broken.

The Raptor kept on going up the dirt road. After a minute, it disappeared around the next bend in a cloud of dust. The sound of its rumbling wheels and diesel engine dwindled into silence.

It was over.

Breck pounded the steering wheel with the palm of his hand. "This crap wagon."

He had a love-hate relationship with the Jeep. A vintage 1977 CJ7. He was so stoked the day he bought it. Classic. Authentic. There wasn't a cooler vehicle on the road. But it was old and had its problems. Not being very mechanically minded, Breck tried to learn as things went wrong. And things did go wrong. Leaky fuel lines. Mystery electrical fluctuations. Clutch went out. Starter burned up. Power steering died. How many times had he been on the side of the road? Danny always seemed to know what to do, and when he didn't, they towed it to the four-wheel shop in Frisco.

With each successful repair, Breck was deliriously confident it was back up to par. Seaworthy! Roadworthy! Ready to roll! Until the next breakdown.

But running out of gas was just embarrassing.

Normally he kept a studious eye on the mileage, but between Aspen's OD and the Raptor robbery on the way back, he didn't even think about his fuel tank. Now, here he was. Stranded in the middle of the National Forest. Once again, the bad guys had vanished.

The CB. He didn't want to, but he had to. Breck reached for it, his hand moving in slow motion. Halfhearted tug on the tangled cord. What other choice did he have?

"Uh . . . Jen . . . you still there?"

The response was quick, her voice tense. "Yeah, of course, I am. Did you catch him? Are you okay? What happened? What's going on? Talk to me."

Breck closed his eyes.

"I ran out of gas."

"Say what? Can you repeat? Repeat that last part, please."

Breck leaned forward and rested his forehead on the steering wheel. This was so bad.

"I ran out of gasoline. Can you . . . drive out here with a fuel can?"

Radio hiss.

Breck knew she was trying to figure out if he was serious.

Radio hiss.

"Jen?"

"Well, I can't exactly bring you a fuel can on my mountain bike. I'll have to call somebody with an actual motorized vehicle."

If the Sheriff's Office had a patrol car, Jenny could drive out there herself. If she had a livable wage, Jenny could afford to buy her own car. The only other vehicle they even had was that broken-down piece of junk snowmobile. Even if it was working, the snow was gone. And a snowmobile without snow was like a Jeep without gasoline.

Breck thumped his head against the steering wheel a few times. Ridiculous. There had to be some kind of federal grant they could apply for. Having to rely on the Quandary city council for funding was nuts. Something had to change.

"Can you put out a BOLO on that RV?" Breck asked. "These forest roads go everywhere. Who knows where they're heading, but I bet they'll wind up in South Park. Maybe the staties will come through for us."

Breck hung up the mic. Automatically, the cord knotted up around the gear shift.

What was it, noon maybe? How many miles had he driven— and where was he exactly? Somewhere on Tarryall Creek Road. In the middle of the National Forest. Feeling like a complete idiot.

Kudos, cartel monsters. Kudos on a smart play. Run out the clock on the dumb cop with the fifteen-gallon tank and the broken gas gauge. Maybe Danny was right. Quit the sheriff gig, run the brewery. A lot less stress and the pay was probably better.

CHAPTER 57

Dance, Puppet

"I'll need a building permit to get this arena started," Matthews said. "It needs an upvote from the city council."

"Won't be a problem at all." Tibbs picked up his phone and checked the time. "Well, I guess I better head on back to the ranch. First week of a busy season."

People who checked their cell phones during business meetings. That irritated Matthews. It was rude and showed disrespect. Matthews always gave people his full undivided attention and turned his own phone *off.*

But today he held his tongue. He needed Tibbs on his side. Getting the building permit was a major piece in an intricate puzzle. A criticism about basic cell phone etiquette might derail the conversation and jeopardize the whole production.

But Matthews was the puppet master. Tibbs was the puppet. He gave the cowboy a charismatic buddy smile. Dance, puppet.

"A busy season is good. It's what we both want. People buy what we're selling, that means tax money flows right into the city coffers. Helps this community." Matthews held up his finger like another thought just struck him. "Speaking of tax money. Medical cannabis. It's been on my mind for a long time now, and it's something the city council should take seriously. Even recreational cannabis. Hell, the times are a changing, Johnny. What the people want, the people should have."

Tibbs frowned. "Well, I don't know about that."

An easy smile of self-assurance. A poo-poo wave of dismissal. "Is it even a drug, really? More like beer than cocaine, don't you think? But either way, the big winner here is Quandary. You hear what kind of tax money Denver pulls in these days? Pueblo? They are rolling in cash, my man."

Before Matthews could massage the pitch any farther, Tibbs' phone started ringing. And etiquette be damned, he answered.

"Yellow?" A smile. "Why, Jennifer. Glad you called, this is a nice surprise. What can I help you with?"

Matthews drowned a grimace in his latte, with a few lukewarm gulps. Johnny Tibbs—cowboy, businessman, Lothario. The momentum of this conversation just got hamstrung by a redhead.

"Breck ran out of gas?" Tibbs slapped his thigh, his face brightening. "Where is he? Tarryall Creek Road? Tell you what, Jennifer. I'll drive out there right now and take him a couple of gallons if I can take *you* out on a horseback ride. How 'bout it?"

Breck ran out of gas? Matthews couldn't believe what he was hearing. It was another example of gross incompetence. Or at least he could spin it that way to the governor. It was just a matter of time before Breck was out of office. And the sooner the better.

"Naw, I got time. Just sitting here at Starbucks. Our good mayor loosened up the purse strings and treated me to a vanilla latte . . . Yeah, he's sitting right here, hold on." Tibbs handed the phone to Matthews. "It's for you."

Matthews almost hung up without even saying anything. Whenever the deputy called him, it was always something pathetic. Like during the blizzard, when Breck got out of radio range and the girl lost her nerve. And now Breck ran out of gas and needed a rescue. What could she possibly have to say at this point? It was bound to be a complaint about finances. No money, no patrol car. Predictable.

"What is it?"

"Mayor Matthews, this is Deputy O'Hara."

"I know who it is. What do you want?"

"Your daughter was just taken to the hospital. Are you aware of the situation?"

"What? What the hell are you talking about?" Matthews stood up and looked around as if expecting to spot Aspen sitting at a nearby table.

"Your daughter was found unconscious this morning and they took her to the hospital. Valerie called 9-1-1, and Breck was first on the scene. It appears to be an overdose."

"Overdose? On what? Aspen doesn't do . . . why didn't you call me immediately?"

"Breck did call you. Didn't you get his message?"

Matthews pulled out his phone and turned it on. The voice-mail icon popped up. *One new message.*

CHAPTER 58

Big Wigs and Fat Cats

When he saw Johnny Tibbs' big Ford truck purring up Tarryall Creek Road, Breck wanted to shoot himself.

He should have put in a request. Send Freddy. Bring a pizza in the process. Breck was starving and he was all out of Clif Bars. The box behind the passenger seat was full of wadded wrappers. He must have eaten the last one already.

Breck stood up and brushed pine needles off his pants. How long had he been sitting under that tree? Hours. The cartel man in the stolen Raptor was long gone now. What a joke.

Tibbs climbed down out of the cab and pulled a red plastic jug from the bed of his pickup. He was all grins.

"Howdy, sheriff."

Breck took out a twenty from his wallet but Tibbs ignored it. He unscrewed the gas cap on the Jeep and started pouring fuel in the tank.

"This is called gasoline. You see this little pipe? It's called the gas tank. Now the trick is . . . you gotta fill it all the way to the top."

Maybe Breck should have just walked. It would have taken all day to hike out to the highway, but he could have hitched a ride back to town. What was worse? A ride in a murder van, or getting roasted by Johnny Tibbs?

"So Jennifer called me. I was in the middle of a high powered executive meeting. A board room full of big wigs and fat cats. But the world won't stop spinning if ol' Johnny Tibbs has to step away for a sec and help out a friend in need. Stranded on a lonely road.

No food, no water. Oh hey, you thirsty? Check the console of my truck. Brought you some apple juice—it's in the sippy cup."

Breck tried to stuff the twenty-dollar bill in his shirt pocket, but Tibbs wiggled away.

"I won't take your money. You need that more than me. I'm on the city council, remember? I've seen your annual budget and it ain't much to look at."

That was it. Breck had had enough.

"Whose fault is *that?*" He put the cash back in his wallet. "Did you know there's a Mexican drug cartel setting up shop in Quandary? They shot Danny, pointed a rifle at Jenny's head, broke into Freddy's house and stole all the marijuana plants he was growing. What do you think I'm doing out here? I had them. They stole an RV at the Continental Divide Motel and were trying to outrun me. And now they did because I ran out of fuel. All because I have no operating budget to speak of. How am I supposed to chase the bad guys without a patrol car, Johnny? That's on the city council. That's on you."

Tibbs screwed the cap back on the gas tank. The grin was gone.

"What the hell are you talking about? A Mexican drug cartel? Is that who broke into my rental cabin?"

Breck stared at him.

Tibbs took the empty gas can back to his truck, and set it in the bed.

"Listen. What if we legalized all that junk? That weed. Matthews says the city will get a windfall of tax money. Then you'll get your budget. Hire a dozen deputies. Get a whole fleet of cop cars."

"Matthews tell you that?" Breck shook his head, disgusted. "His own daughter just OD'd on opioids. And he wants to legalize drugs."

That made absolutely no sense. Matthews had been a thorn in his side for nearly four years. It had started out slow, subtle. A critical eye on his expenditures. A concern with overspending. Then it kept getting worse, and somehow the city council members fell in line with him. Followed his lead. Most of them were business owners. They took a seat on the council out of a sense of civic duty. Community pride. But they weren't cutthroat politicians. Not like the mayor was.

Was it a personal thing? Did Matthews dislike Breck so much that he wanted him to step down out of spite? Breck couldn't recall any major arguments or friction. Not at the beginning. But whenever the topic of marijuana came up, it was clear they were in different camps. Why couldn't he see how destructive drug addiction was? Maybe he could if he had seen Aspen lying there, barely breathing, soaked in her own vomit.

"You sure you don't want that apple juice?"

Smiling again, Tibbs leaned inside his truck, opened the console, and brought out a tin of chewing tobacco. Copenhagen. "You dip?"

"No."

But giving up cigarettes was not easy, and Breck was almost tempted to try. If it was anyone else than Johnny Tibbs making the offer, he would have taken a pinch.

"Oh, guess what? I talked Jennifer into going horseback riding with me."

CHAPTER 59

The Corner Chair

It was midafternoon when Valerie finally, unwillingly, vacated the corner chair.

"I have to use the restroom but don't you *dare* sit in this chair. It's mine, Seneca." Valerie flicked Matthews in the chest as she walked out of the hospital room. "When my baby girl wakes up, I want to be the first person she sees. I'm her mother, for Pete's sake."

As soon as she was gone, he took over the corner chair.

The hospital. Again? Aspen still had purple bruising around her eyes from the avalanche, although it wasn't as bad. The swelling in her nose was down, too. Her wrist was still bandaged, but that was the least of her problems now.

How could Valerie have left her alone like that? Even for a moment. The girl had nearly been crushed to death. That was bound to take a psychic toll. She should never have been left alone.

If this was anyone's fault, it was Valerie's. And Breck's. Even if his call went right to voicemail, he should have dialed Brittany at City Hall. She would have been able to tell him the mayor's schedule, explain that he was meeting with Tibbs at Starbucks. Then Breck could have called the coffee shop and talked to the manager, and that manager could have come to his table and whispered in his ear that he had an urgent phone call.

Matthews checked his phone. He listened to Breck's voicemail. Yeah, okay, so the man tried once. One single phone call. But he was the mayor. Of *Quandary.* In a family emergency, any competent sheriff wouldn't have given up until he got through. Matthews hit the delete button.

"Daddy?"

Aspen's eyes were open.

"Oh, ptarmigan, you're okay! Daddy's here." He leaped up and gripped her good hand tight. Petted her hair. It was all knotted and bunchy. Didn't Valerie care enough to brush her unconscious daughter's hair?

"I'm sorry daddy . . ."

"Sorry? For what, honey?" He held his breath. Was his daughter suicidal? How did he miss the signs? She had been shaken up after the avalanche. Maybe her thoughts took a dark turn.

"I only took a few. I promise."

She looked so young like she was twelve again. Twelve years old—that was the year he caught her eating a bowl of Lucky Charms right before dinner on Christmas Eve. Spoiled her appetite. And her mother had spent the whole day cooking. A crown roast with apricot sauce. Eggnog sweet potato casserole. He was so mad, he didn't let her have a chocolate reindeer muffin, even though they had candy cane antlers and a cinnamon red candy nose and Aspen had been staring at them all day. Not until they were opening presents the next morning.

Aspen had the same look on her face.

"What did you take?"

Aspen lowered her eyes. "I thought they were pain pills. And I had such a bad headache and my nose hurt really bad. I'm scared, daddy."

Matthews relented. She was too fragile. He wished he had a chocolate reindeer muffin to give her.

"Mr. Matthews?"

He turned and looked. It was the nurse, Melinda.

"Can we speak in the hallway?"

He gave Aspen a kiss on the forehead, went into the hall and closed the door behind him.

"What happened?" he asked. It was a harsh whisper.

"Your daughter was brought in unconscious this morning. There were prescription pills next to her bed, so an overdose was suspected. We pumped her stomach."

"She's not on any prescription."

"There were two substances, both synthetic opioids—oxycodone and fentanyl."

Matthews was stunned. How did Aspen get a hold of opioids?

Melinda let it sink in for a moment. "Those drugs are 100 times stronger than morphine, Mr. Matthews. And they are illegal without a prescription. She is lucky to be alive."

Directly across the hallway was Danny Dyer's room. Breck's brother. He was sitting in a wheelchair in the doorway, clutching an IV pole on wheels, watching.

"Is the girl gonna be okay?" Danny asked. His eyes were watery. Teary even.

"Mr. Dyer, I'll be right over to check on you." Melinda smiled softly at Matthews. "I have to check on another patient. Excuse me."

Where was Valerie? Matthews looked up and down the hallway. Did she fall in the toilet? Now he would have to repeat this information to her, all over again, and he wasn't sure he heard everything right. His brain felt a little fuzzy. How could this happen? To his little ptarmigan? Well, he was going to find out. Right now.

Going back inside, Mayor Matthews sat on the edge of the bed and held her good hand again. But this time, he had a serious look on his face.

"Aspen. Where did you get those pills?"

She cringed. She didn't want to say.

"Aspen? Tell me right now. This is very important. Those were illegal prescription pills that were very very dangerous."

She began to cry, but suddenly sniffed away the tears and looked up at him. A look of realization. "I almost died, didn't I?"

"Yes you did, honey."

"It was . . . my boyfriend." She paused, trying to recall what happened. "I was watching TV. My head was hurting so bad but I couldn't find the aspirin. Cash came over. He wanted to help. He . . . he had some joints. Said it was medical marijuana and everybody smoked it. But I told him no. Then he showed me a bag of . . ."

She yanked her hand out of her father's hand and reached for a tissue.

Matthews felt a cold anger wash through his body. Cash. The floppy-haired surfer boy that ran the ski resort? That little piece of garbage.

"And where did Cash get them?"

She squirmed up into a sitting position. Her face was flushed. The Matthews rage was boiling up inside her, as well. He knew that look.

"Cash gets everything from his dealer. It's the guy who delivers pizza. Freddy."

Footsteps. Valerie was coming.

Immediately, Matthews went over and sat in the corner chair.

CHAPTER 60

Omaha Stakes

Carrying a chainsaw on a horse was a little awkward. But clearing trails was his job, and Laramie didn't want anyone to think he couldn't figure it out.

Laramie wasn't his real name. It was a nickname he gave himself. His real name was Duane and he was from Omaha. But Laramie sounded much more cowboy, and that was the vibe he was going for.

His freshman year of college was over. Colorado State University in Fort Collins had the best veterinary program in the country. Laramie was going to be a vet. A large animal vet. Horses, specifically. His family owned a feedlot in Omaha, and he had grown up around cows. But Laramie was sick of cows. He could have gone home for the summer and worked the feedlot, but he happened to notice an advertisement in the back of *Western Horseman* magazine for wranglers at the Tibbs Ranch in Quandary, Colorado.

The minute he arrived, he was put to work unloading hay from the boss's flatbed trailer. Every moment was busy. There was so much to do. Oiling tack, cleaning corrals, filling grain bins. Learning all the horses' names was a full-time job all by itself.

Laramie would be leading trail rides all summer long, so he needed to learn the herd quick. Each horse had its own personality, its own skill set. Mr. Tibbs expected his wranglers to pair each ranch guest with the right horse. If someone got pitched off it could cost the wrangler his job. The stakes were high, there was a lot to learn, but it was all solid horse experience. The Tibbs Ranch was as different from the family farm as night was to day, and Laramie already knew he was never going home again! Well, maybe for Christmas.

The first guests had already arrived, just that very morning, and were unpacking their bags in the A-frame cabins. But before there could be trail rides, the trails had to be cleared of debris.

His boss, Johnny Tibbs, pulled the crew together for a staff meeting. Who wanted to clear trails? Every winter, snow, and wind brought down trees and broke off branches and someone needed to ride out there with a chainsaw and open the trails again. It was a good way to learn the trail system, too.

Getting paid to ride a horse through the National Forest? This was the high country of Colorado! A far cry from the feedlots of Omaha.

Laramie jumped at it.

Which was how he found himself alone on a mountain ridge, late in the day, and all turned around.

The afternoon had been a blur of hard work. He chopped and sawed his way through dozens of tree trunks, mounds of branches, and he even shoveled through some crusty snow banks. But somewhere along the line, the trail split a few times and curved and the one he was on now seemed to simply dead-end at a rocky granite bluff.

From a gap in the trees, Laramie tried to spot the cell tower. Mr. Tibbs had warned him not to lose sight of it.

Even though the sky was clear, Laramie heard a loud boom of thunder. Then his horse collapsed, right beneath him! Jumping out of the saddle, Laramie tried to get out of the way. A thousand-pound horse going down—it could crush him like a tomato.

Then he noticed a giant hole in the animal's flank. Blood began squirting and a twist of intestine bulged out like a giant spaghetti noodle. The horse gasped and groaned, and then promptly died.

That wasn't a lightning strike. Someone just shot his horse out from beneath him. Some dummy just thought he shot a deer. Crouching down, Laramie made a dash for the rocky bluff. There were boulders to hide behind. And it was a good thing he did because the shooter took a second shot. Bark splintered and flew everywhere.

"Hey! Stop shooting!" he called.

But a third shot swept the hat right off his head. Dropping to the ground, Laramie crawled as fast as he could. Around boulders and tree trunks and scratchy underbrush. Wait a minute. This was not hunting season. Nowhere near it. Whoever was shooting at him was trying to kill him.

Maybe he got off the trail, and wound up on some old coot's private property. But if so, there were no signs to indicate it. Maybe it was a gold mine, and somebody thought he was a claim jumper. Whatever the reason, Laramie didn't waste time trying to figure it out.

Wiggling between some rocks, the young wrangler tried to get his bearings. The shooter was downhill, judging from the way his hat flew off. The top of the ridge wasn't too far away. If he could just get on the far side he could make a run for it.

Laramie grabbed a stone and lobbed it. It arced through the air and clocked an old hollow log. On elbows and knees, he crawled uphill, staying among the boulders.

Risking a look, Laramie inched forward to see. He spotted movement. A man with a rifle. Slithering between the trees. Gun trained on the hollow log.

Laramie ducked back down. This might be his one and only chance. He had to run for it. Should he try? Or just stay put? His hands were trembling.

Omaha wasn't sounding so bad now.

CHAPTER 61

Cygnus

In the Rocky Mountains, so high in elevation and so far from the Front Range city lights, the constellations wheeled across the night sky, staggering and innumerable. Just like in the deserts and canyons of northern Mexico. El Sangrador loved driving the highway from Chihuahua to Ojinaga at night. How many times had he driven that road? A cigar in hand. A trailer full of immigrants or heroin or meth, destined for the fruited plains of America. It was a breathtaking journey.

Those same stars, just as staggering and innumerable, lit up the mountain ridge. He could count all the pine cones in the dirt like it was daytime. But the light was ghostly, serene. That was how it made the blood-letter feel. Ghostly. Serene. All the cumbersome cares of the world melted away. He was alone in a time between times.

El Sangrador paused near a tall brown pine tree. It was dead but still upright, ruined by pine beetles. He examined the spot where his bullet had hit. The bark was gone, the size of a paper plate.

That cowboy kid. Jumped from the stones like a jackrabbit, hopped over the ridge and vanished. He must have been an Olympic distance runner because even with his rifle scope the blood-letter quickly lost sight of him.

His bootprints were easy to track. Deep impressions in the soft spongy forest floor. The kid was wearing buckaroo boots with high underslung heels. El Sangrador knew that style of boot was only meant for saddle work. They were not running shoes. That boy's knees must hurt terribly by now.

El Sangrador's own shin was starting to hurt again, and if he hoped to make it back to the grow field camp he must yield the chase.

All this hiking around. How he wished he was back on the asphalt road between Chihuahua and Ojinaga. The window down, the smell of diesel fumes and cigar smoke, and more stars than he could count.

Climbing back over the familiar ridge, El Sangrador looked forward to lying in his cot and sipping Jack Daniels until the sun came up. He preferred tequila, but it was the only kind of liquor in the old folks' RV.

He had found a perfect hiding place for the RV, near the trailhead. There was an old mule path heading up a gully and they parked it there, just off the main road. The Range Rover, too.

Zorrero was captivated by the F350 and sat in the driver's seat for hours, chattering about the features. The switches on the dashboard. The fabric on the seats. The special transmission. TorqShift six-speed, whatever that was. It was all jibber jabber to the blood-letter. He did like fancy vehicles, but he was not as concerned with the specifications like Zorrero was.

The camper itself was just as nice, although strangely, it was loaded with frugal sundries. Except for a box of Kellogg's Cracklin' Oat Bran, generic off-brand foods dominated the pantry. There were heaps of fast food napkins and ketchup packets. Little motel soap bars in the bathroom. El Sangrador got excited when he found a bunch of cigars in the glovebox, but then he realized they were Swisher Sweets—a cheap and unsatisfying brand. However, the most odious discovery was the liquor cabinet. It was stocked with the cheapest of American whiskey. Jack Daniels. But cheap American whiskey was better than no whiskey at all, so he hiked several bottles up to the grow field. It would help pass the time.

Claiming it as his command post, Zorrero stayed with the RV. He was surely sleeping comfortably on the supple mattress in the bedroom compartment. Propped up on pillows, watching the big screen satellite television. A bowl of delicious Cracklin' Oat Bran. All there was to eat on the mountain was yellow peas and pinto beans.

But El Sangrador was used to deprivation.

In the bright starlight, he had no problem finding the grow field again. The laborers had done well clearing away the brush and stones, and cultivating the fertile soil. They even had all the cannabis from the pizza man's cabin planted in the ground already. Hoses had been laid out carefully along the crop rows and pierced so water could seep out at a controlled flow rate.

Hauling the sump pump and generator from the General Merchandise up the trail had been hard work, so the cartel men rewarded them with a feast of Dinty Moore beef stew. El Sangrador took a can for himself but saved it for later. He could only savor a good meal when he was by himself and could let his guard down. It was sounding pretty tasty at the moment, after the long chase.

Almost there. The blue tarp was nearly invisible in the dim light. He was feeling tired now. Maybe he would wait till morning to cook his beef stew. As he approached the tarp, the blood-letter nearly tripped over something.

A rough wooden cross. It was made from pine branches and someone had hung a rosary on it. To mark the grave of the dead man. When did they do that?

That first day, El Sangrador instructed them to bury the body near the trail, a grim deterrent against any foolish attempts at escape. But the cross and rosary were new. They must have constructed it while he was tracking the cowboy kid on the far side of the ridge. Probably the distraught señora. Her wailing had rarely ceased and she pestered the blood-letter incessantly. Her *niños*, she needed to find her *niños*. But he would not let her go search for her children. She would likely never see them again. They all wanted things they could not have. El Sangrador wanted a decent cigar and a bottle of high-end tequila. But such was life.

Pausing at the grave site, he looked up at the night sky once again. There was one constellation that looked exactly like a cross. Cygnus, right overhead. Right above the grave. Right above the leaky blue tarp.

God was a mystery to El Sangrador. Why would he take such an effort to craft a world of such beauty, only to curse it with suffering for one and all? Even Jesús himself was crucified by the Roman soldiers. It was a conundrum. But questions like that were for the priests to debate. No matter the answer, the world would keep turning. Until it turned no more.

Pulling back the crinkly tarp, the blood-letter could now lie in his cot and see the night sky without obstruction. The giant cross.

The Big Dipper. The Seven Sisters. All of them rotated around the North Pole like the world of suffering rotated around the God of sorrow.

It was fascinating to watch.

CHAPTER 62

Business Is Blooming

Valerie took Aspen home. Again. Matthews was hurt that his daughter preferred her mother's home to recuperate in after a crisis, but he knew better than to argue too much. Besides. He had enough to juggle already.

After he helped Aspen into her mother's car and watched them drive away, Matthews went into the 7-Eleven and bought some AAA batteries. Then he sat in his car and stared across the mountain valley. Snowcapped summits were twinkling in the morning sunlight. The ski runs were still white with hard-packed snow, too. Narrow white fingers splayed out across the green forested slopes. But he knew ski season was over. The greatest single source of revenue the town had was shutting down. Now, it was up to the tourist shops and the mountain guides to pick up the slack. The Tibbs Ranch was a big part of that, luring white collar hacks to dip into their financial portfolios and spend, spend, spend.

Matthews texted Zorrero. *How is business? We need to talk.*

The cartel men were supposed to be growing cannabis. Were they? If they couldn't get it done, he might have to find someone else who knew what to do. There were plenty of rookies and hobbyists out there. Like Freddy and Danny. But Matthews had his sights set on a much bigger operation. Something much more involved than two local stoners could handle. Who knew the professional cannabis trade better than Mexican *narcos*? The United States might run on corn and oil, but drugs were the backbone of the national economy down there, for crying out loud. But he hadn't heard any updates recently. Did they run off with Freddy's plants? Or were they holding up their end of the deal?

Right on cue, a text came back: *Business is blooming. Come see.*

He set the phone down and pulled out the yellow Garmin GPS. He put in fresh batteries and turned it on. Plugged in the coordinates. He started the BMW and started driving.

It was like a treasure hunt. He passed the Blue River Bank and High Country Pizza, turned onto Main Street, then onto Boreal Pass Road. Winding into the woods, he passed the Tibbs Ranch. Then the blacktop turned into dirt and the road started gaining elevation. It was a slow drive, but scenic.

Matthews couldn't remember the last time he took a mountain drive simply to enjoy the view. He wasn't even sure he'd been to Boreal Pass before. This all looked unfamiliar. Maybe he would bring Aspen and Valerie up for a family picnic one of these days. There were plenty of grassy places to pull off.

Checking the GPS, Matthews slowed down and looked around. He was close. Suddenly a man stepped out of the trees and waved. It was Zorrero.

"Is this the right place?" Matthews asked.

"Drive up the gully. Park next to the RV."

He pulled aside some uprooted bushes, exposing a rough path leading through an aspen grove. Matthews drove between the trees, careful not to scrape against the trunks. Sure enough, there was a pickup with an RV camper trailer, and Zorrero's black SUV. Matthews shut off the engine, got out and looked around, confused.

"Where is all the marijuana?"

Zorrero opened the RV door. "Oh, it's not down here. It's up on the hill where it gets plenty of sunshine and personal care. Got a whole crew workin' on it. Come on into my *cantina*, let's shoot some whiskey."

Matthews followed him inside, slid into a booth seat while the cartel commander poured glasses of Jack Daniels.

"Don't be shy, I got plenty." Zorrero clinked cups. *"¡Salud!"*

They gulped their drinks.

"You look like a man with a problem." Zorrero poured a second round. "I can see it in your eyes."

Matthews sighed and nodded. He did have a problem. They both did.

"My daughter was taken to the hospital yesterday."

"A father's worst nightmare."

"Yes. *Gracias,* my friend." This time, Matthews took a small sip of the alcohol. Why gulp it down if the man was just going to re-fill it? And Zorrero had his hand on the bottle like he was ready to pour again. "She was given some pills. Dangerous pills and she overdosed and almost died because of it."

Zorrero gulped his drink, listening. His face was flat. Whatever he was thinking, he wasn't letting it show.

Matthews continued. "She got those pills from a dealer in Quandary. A dealer we are both familiar with."

This piqued the cartel man's interest. He leaned across the Formica kitchen table, causing the leg poles to wobble. "Better not be the pizza man. He promised me to my face he would not sell no more."

Matthews took a tiny half-sip. "The pizza man."

The muscles in Zorrero's jaw tensed. Something about his face made Matthews' gut knot up. Maybe he shouldn't have said anything. Maybe he should have made a police report with Breck and let him take care of it. This was starting to feel like a bad idea.

"I don't want you to do anything drastic. But can you give him a scare?"

"A scare?"

"That's all it will take. The guy has no spine, and he's in way over his head. I don't want any bloodshed, that's unnecessary. What we're doing here . . . this is *almost* a legal enterprise. Once I get the city council to legislate support for cannabis businesses, and the greenhouse gets built, we'll both be very rich men. The money will flow like a faucet. Some small-time pot dealer won't even matter."

Matthews realized he was talking too fast. The words were tumbling out. He took a breath to steady his nerves. Zorrero had assured him that there would be no violence when they first agreed to work together. But there had been violence.

"You would think seeing his beer friend shot dead would have been enough persuasion."

"Well, yeah, it shook him up." Matthews felt a little confused. "But the good news is that Danny's going to be fine."

Zorrero leaned on the Formica table again. Eyes rock hard. "The beer man did not die?"

Matthews shook his head, an awkward icy feeling creeping over him.

"No. He's still in the hospital, but he didn't die. That would have been tragic. It was an *accidente*, right? . . . Hey, how about that garden tour? Love to see it."

CHAPTER 63

Short-Staffed on Square Dance Night

Filling out forms took up so much time. Jenny was busy typing on the laptop, lost in a haze of paperwork. The 9-1-1 calls each required a form with time stamps and transcriptions. The retired couple from the motel, Tom and Phyllis Nickles, dropped by the office and talked her ear off. Phyllis, who had a piping high-pitched fever voice, rattled off a mental checklist of their travel trailer valuables. And the not-so-valuables. A box of Cracklin' Oat Bran cereal which was worth four dollars, and three home improvement magazines she had purchased for ten bucks each. She was constantly interrupted by Tom snapping his fingers in frustration and mumbling about the high price of Tic Tacs. Jenny maintained a professional demeanor, though it took all she had to keep from slapping them both.

Breck was sulking. He spent half the day out in the parking lot tinkering on the snowmobile. Jenny knew a six-year-old child with a Lego fetish had a better chance of repairing the solenoid than Breck did. But hey, the guy had been humiliated. She cut him some slack and avoided any conversation beyond small talk.

A reflective flash outside the window caught her attention. Looking outside, she saw Johnny Tibbs' pickup pull into the parking lot. Any excuse was a good excuse to shut the laptop, so she did.

Jenny opened the door and leaned against the door jamb as Tibbs jumped out of the truck. Breck shrunk behind the snowmobile. It was obvious he wished he was invisible.

"It's that round silver thing in front of the seat." Tibbs threw a cocky grin at Jenny, complete with a theatrical wink. "Called a gas cap. It's where the gas goes."

Slowly, ever so slowly, Breck stood up straight. He wiped the grease off hands on a red shop rag. It was almost as red as his face.

"You need something?" Jenny crossed her arms. Poor Breck. Would he ever live this down? "Or, you just stopping by to remind us you're a pain in the ass? Cuz we haven't forgot."

Tibbs' smile vanished.

"I'm here to report a missing person. One of my wranglers rode out the day before yesterday to clear trails, and never made it back to the ranch."

Jenny realized he was done kidding around. She felt a little sorry for what she said. But not sorry enough to apologize.

"You go look for him yet?" Breck asked.

Tibbs nodded.

"Yep. Me and some of the boys saddled up and rode the trails. Saw a bunch of fresh sawn logs, which was the kid's job . . . but we didn't find him. Of course, those trails go back quite a ways and tie into a network of hiking trails. And there's a bunch of old mines, too. Who knows? I'm sure he just took a wrong turn somewhere."

Cracking open the dumpster, Breck threw the rag inside.

"I'm a little busy with this solenoid, but why don't you head inside and fill out a missing person report. Jenny, you want to type it up?"

"Not really."

"I ain't got time for a sit-down." Tibbs turned around and started to climb back in his truck. "I'll get one of the office gals to call you with the kid's contact info, his folks' number, home address—all that jazz. I'm up against a full schedule of trail rides, fly fishing and square dances. Every day that kid don't come back, is another day I'm short-handed."

"Short-staffed on square dance night?" Jenny smirked. "Would you call that hell or high water?"

Breck started to sink back down behind the snowmobile when they heard a car horn honking. A Honda Civic came flying down Main Street and pulled in next to Tibbs' truck. Triangular sign on top. *High Country Pizza—We Deliver.*

It was Freddy, but he wasn't delivering pizza.

"Forget about that paperwork, Jennifer."

Tibbs stepped back down and wiped the dust off the Civic passenger window with his palm. Laramie was sitting inside, wide-eyed and white as a sheet. "Here's my missing wrangler."

He yanked open the door, with an impatient look.

"Where's your hat?" Tibbs looked the kid up and down. Shirt and knees smudged with dirt and pine needles. "And where's your horse?"

Seeing how dazed the young wrangler looked, Jenny came over to check on him.

"Are you okay?" she asked. "What's your name?"

"His name is Doug or Duane, I think." Johnny passed his hand in front of Laramie's eyes. "Deer in the headlights."

"You don't even know his name?" Jenny asked.

Tibbs shrugged. "He's from Laramie. I know that much."

Kicking the driver door open, Freddy jumped out and ran straight to Breck. He looked just as terrified as his passenger did.

"Yo, man. Those cartel cats are back! And they're out for blood, man." He grabbed Breck by the sleeve. "What about those relocation programs? Where they give you a new name and a new job at a Dairy Queen in Kansas? I want one of those."

"What are you talking about?" Breck asked.

Freddy pointed at Laramie. "Found this kid wandering around on the side of the road, way up in the canyon. Those cartel cats tried to snuff his pipe, too. Oh, God. This ain't right."

CHAPTER 64

An Old Shoe and a Pepperoni

Inside the Sheriff's Office, Jenny wheeled over one of the spare chairs from the extra desks. Without a word, Laramie sank into it. The boy's lower lip was quivering and he looked like a train wreck. She knelt in front of him, trying to catch his eye.

"Just relax. You're safe."

Tibbs looked at his watch. "How long is this gonna take?"

Jenny scowled. "Go get him a water bottle out of the fridge, *Johnny*."

Freddy wouldn't let go of Breck's sleeve. Every time Breck took a step, Freddy was right there like a smelly shadow. At the mention of water, his tongue shot out like a lizard. "Dude, I am so freaked right now. Got the PTSD, man. Can I get one, too?"

"What you can do is get off me." Breck pried his fingers loose and pointed at the cot in the jail cell. "Go. Sit. Stay."

Poor Laramie. The kid was still in shock over what he went through. Couldn't these clowns shut up for two seconds? Jenny showed him the badge that was clipped on her belt.

"Hi, my name is Jenny. I'm a deputy sheriff. I understand you were hitchhiking and Freddy picked you up in his car. I know it smells like an old shoe and a pepperoni had a baby in there, and I'm sorry you had to endure that."

She smiled. It was a gentle joke, and it seemed to work. The young wrangler's eyes came into focus. The badges. The jail cells. He started to regain his color.

"Why were you on the road in the canyon?" Jenny asked. "Were you lost?"

The boy blanched as the memories came back.

"Trees everywhere." His voice was a hoarse whisper. "It was so dark for so long. But I didn't stop—I couldn't stop. I kept going. Then the sun finally came up, but all I saw were more trees. So I just kept walking and walking but the sun went down again . . . and then, I found the road."

Jenny waited, letting him relive it in his mind. Whatever he had gone through, it had not been pleasant. And even though it was painful to talk about it, they needed to know what happened.

"Why were you walking in the forest?"

Laramie started hyperventilating. His face twisted up and he gasped for air. Jenny touched his shoulder.

"Johnny says you were clearing trails. Did something bad happen?"

He nodded, barely getting his words out.

"Some guy shot my horse. And then he shot at *me*. A bunch of times. I ran for it and he chased me over the ridge but I got away."

Freddy wandered into the jail cell. He laid down flat on the cot and pulled Breck's sleeping bag over his head. Breck saw it happen and frowned.

"What did he look like?" Jenny asked.

"Tall. Mean looking. He had a black military rifle with a scope. He was wearing silver sunglasses. That's all I remember."

Returning with a cold water bottle, Tibbs handed it to the young wrangler. Laramie unscrewed the lid and drank the whole thing.

"Did you shoot back?" Tibbs asked. Jenny glared at him, but he glared back. "What? All my boys carry revolvers. This ain't the fairgrounds and we ain't giving pony rides. We're the real deal."

Crinkling the empty plastic bottle, Laramie squirmed.

"I left my pistol at the bunkhouse." He avoided looking at his boss. "With that big chainsaw, plus the bow saw and hand ax, it was all too much to carry . . . I was afraid I'd shoot my horse on accident."

Breck motioned to Tibbs and Jenny, and they all went across the room to talk. There was a topographical map of the county pinned on the wall. He placed one finger on the Tibbs Ranch and one finger on the canyon highway.

"Here's where he started and here's where Freddy found him. It happened somewhere in between."

Jenny stared at the map. They were looking at a lot of back-country and a lot of it was rough terrain. Peaks and ridges. Creeks and drainages. It was all National Forest, too. A massive amount of land to search on foot.

"Some idiot just shot one of my horses," Tibbs said. "That was a two-thousand-dollar gelding."

"It wasn't just anybody," Breck said. "The gunman he described matches one of our cartel suspects."

"In the middle of the dang woods?" Tibbs looked skeptical. "You sure?"

There was a muffled moan from the jail.

Breck glanced over and frowned. Freddy had completely zipped himself inside the sleeping bag. "I might as well burn that thing."

Jenny studied the map closer. There was nothing back there. No roads or houses. No reason for a cartel gunman to be hiking in the woods, let alone shoot at an innocent horseback rider. It didn't make sense. They stole Freddy's plants. Bought groceries in Alma. Hijacked an RV. What were they up to?

Her eyes went over to Freddy—pothead, stoner, dealer, grower. And suddenly she knew.

"A grow field."

Breck raised an eyebrow. A look in his eyes. Was he impressed? He took a closer look at the big map.

"A grow field . . ." He traced a circle around the whole area with his finger. "If there's a grow field up there, how are we going to find it?"

"That is a crap-load of ground to cover." Jenny whistled softly. How many square miles was that? She didn't want to know.

Tibbs spread his hands, carnival barker style.

"We can always saddle up some horses."

But Breck cringed. "I hate horses."

Tibbs winked at Jenny like he had earlier in the parking lot. Theatrical. "Well then, how do you feel about single-engine aeroplanes?"

CHAPTER 65

Fly the Friendly Skies

The Quandary County Airfield. It was in an open meadow north of town. There was a concrete airstrip, hangar, and an orange and white striped windsock on a flagpole. That was it.

There wasn't an official parking area except for the pavement around the hangar. Johnny Tibbs' truck was already sitting there, so Breck pulled in next to it.

The airfield was another one of the mayor's drumbeats of dissatisfaction. Breck could hear it now. *Has anyone in this town ever flown into Telluride? If we ever hope to see Bono on the tarmac in Quandary, we need a private concourse with an executive lounge, leather couches, CNN and sparkling water.* It was far-fetched. They couldn't even afford their own police department. And barely paid Breck enough to keep the lights on.

"You nervous?" Jenny asked.

Going mime, Breck gave her a fluttering Pierrot expression and clutched at an invisible pearl necklace.

"Hmm . . . that was pretty." Jenny zipped up a light jacket.

Breck pulled out a pair of binoculars. Messed with the focus. Low clouds were bunching up on the mountain tops. It was going to rain. With the rain came thunder and with thunder came lightning. What safer place than a flying tin can with Johnny Tibbs at the stick? Breck was nervous, but he wasn't going to say it out loud.

The big overhead door began folding upwards. Inside the hangar, they saw a small white single-engine aircraft. Two side doors propped open. It had a smooth bullet curve shape to the body design, and Tibbs was standing on the wing.

He called and waved. "Jennifer, how does co-pilot sound? You're up front with me."

Jenny pushed open the Jeep door and rolled her eyes at Breck. "Let's go fly the friendly skies."

She headed into the hangar. Seeing his prey approach, Tibbs jumped down like a panther.

"What about those rain clouds," Jenny asked. "Not a fan of turbulence."

Tibbs laughed like it was the funniest joke he'd ever heard.

"This is a Cirrus SR22. Turbocharged. It'll knife through them clouds like butter. Why don't you do the pre-flight walk-around with me? I'll give you the grand tour and put your mind at ease."

He tried to put his hand on the small of her back, but Jenny swatted him off.

"How did I get myself into this?" Breck mumbled.

The 7-Eleven had been out of Clif Bars, so Breck bought a box of Power Bars instead. He put as many of them in his pockets as he could fit. If that plane cratered in the middle of nowhere, he was going to be prepared. For anything. Johnny Tibbs had those Alferd Packer dead fish eyes.

Heading inside the hangar, Breck wiggled the wing. The whole plane rocked.

"Didn't you just get your pilot's license last year?"

"Two years ago. Same year this plane was built." Tibbs wasn't as amused with Breck's comment as he had been with Jenny's. He climbed back up on the wing and offered Jenny his hand. "This baby just passed its Annual Inspection. Plus, it's got a full tank of gas. Not everyone can say that. Can they?"

Jenny got into the front seat and put on a headset. To get in the rear seat, Breck had to crawl over the pilot's seat. It was a tight squeeze. There wasn't much leg room.

"Do you serve peanuts or pretzels?"

Ignoring him, Johnny Tibbs flipped a few switches and taxied onto the runway. Without warning, he gunned the engine, and Breck felt his stomach sink as the plane lifted off the ground.

The town of Quandary. It looked pretty tiny from the sky. Toy cars on Main Street. Black specks heading in and out Safeway like a busy little anthill. Breck took out the binoculars. He could see the green dumpster in front of the Sheriff's Office. The chair-lift at the ski resort. The mayor's shiny silver BMW at City Hall.

The highway stretched away south of town, through the steep narrow canyon. In the distance, Breck could make out the switchbacks leading up to Red Mountain Pass. And Alma, a glittery patch, miles away. But Tibbs banked east, toward the cloudy peaks and mountain ridges.

Breck spotted an open meadow with horses. They were flying over Johnny's ranch.

"There's my cell tower." Tibbs leaned close to Jenny. Pointed out her window. "Them horse trails run right through there. Hard to see from way up here, but they run along that hogback ridge. Split off in a dozen different directions. One goes to those beaver ponds. Couple head up to tree line. Got a drop camp on that plateau, for elk hunting in the fall. One trail goes down to the Blue River. Take a lot of folks fly-fishing. I know the perfect spot where they're always biting."

He turned around and looked at Breck.

"You like fishing, don't you?"

"Oh yeah. The best fishing hole in the county is right by my place."

"That little algae pond?" Tibbs grinned. "If it's the best fishing hole in the county, then it must be chock-full of cutthroat trout. How many you pull out of there, on average?"

"Too many to count. Now, why don't you just worry about flying this plane, okay? There's an illegal grow field out here somewhere and I don't want to miss it because you're yapping my ear off."

Breck pressed his face to the glass. He didn't have as good a view from the backseat. The wings were attached to the fuselage beneath the side windows, and they blocked half the view.

"See anything yet, Jenny?" he asked, speaking into his headset mic.

"No, but the clouds are rolling in."

Tall rocky peaks rose up to their left. The plane was flying low, right at timberline. At that altitude, there was still a heavy layer of snow. Thick cornices curled over the cliff faces. Breck was glad he had worn a coat. The cabin was chilly. The thin mountain air seemed to seep right inside the plane.

A glimmer caught his eye.

"What's that down there? On the road?"

"Let's find out." Tibbs angled the plane downward, losing altitude. "That's Boreal Pass Road. Runs all the way into South Park."

"Yeah, I know," Breck said. "I've driven it a million times."

That was a bit of an exaggeration, but he had driven it maybe a dozen times. Breck liked hiking. He had summited all the local peaks and most of the trail access began along Boreal Pass Road or one of the four-wheel-drive roads close by.

Tibbs flew low enough they could see the white roof of a rectangular camper trailer, parked in a gully just off the road. It was in the trees, and maybe they wouldn't have even noticed it, but the sunlight hit the roof just right. Breck took out his binoculars. He could almost read some lettering painted on the front . . .

Raptor.

Their missing RV was a Raptor.

CHAPTER 66

Housefly

El Sangrador squinted into the rifle scope. He had the little airplane in his crosshairs. The buzz of its engine was like an obnoxious housefly that wouldn't go away. But timing was everything. Both in swatting houseflies, and shooting down airplanes.

Almost as obnoxious, the señora was blubbering again.

As soon as he first heard the plane's engine, the blood-letter instructed all the field laborers to hide in the trees. Quickly. Perhaps there was nothing to worry about, but it was best to err on the side of caution.

He did a headcount as they ran by, and all eleven were accounted for. But El Sangrador wasn't too concerned with runaways. The grow field was so far up on the hillside, so deep in the forest, that he would be surprised if any of them tried to escape. Where would they go? None of them even knew where they were. They had ridden in the back of a U-Haul truck for fifteen hundred miles.

"*Por favor*, señora." He kept his eye on the plane while he spoke. "Your wailing is annoying and I must concentrate."

The señora's husband, grave and fearful, tried to press his hand over her mouth but she bit him.

"My babies!" she cried. "My heart is broken for my *niños*, whom you have stolen from me. What have you done with them? You are a devil!"

"Hush, please," her husband begged and tried to cover her mouth again. His face hung like a whipped dog.

Every time the señora complained, her husband's face looked like that. A whipped dog. El Sangrador didn't even have to turn around to know it. But the husband's protests and desperate requests were no longer as effective as they once were. Despite repeated warnings, the señora's outbursts were getting more frequent.

Such things were expected, of course. But when there was a plane flying low, silence was required.

All along the southern border, small planes flew back and forth every day. They all sounded the same. Buzzing like houseflies. Immigration enforcers, patrolling the hot deserts and the mesquite thickets and all the rugged terrain along the Rio Grande, hoping to spot someone who they could run down and trap like a bunny rabbit.

An AR-15 was a good rifle. But it was not meant for airplanes, really. If he was lucky, with the right winds and distance, he might poke a hole in a wing. Shatter a window. While it would be satisfying to see fuel dripping into the sky, the plane would merely turn around and limp back from where it came. Worse, the pilot could simply radio the location of the gunman. Which was why El Sangrador hesitated to pull the trigger. He would not shoot unless the plane came real close, and he could get a nice clean headshot.

The sound of the buzzing grew louder.

Perhaps the pilot would not see them at all. Perhaps the plane would keep flying until it was out of sight. Once the danger passed the laborers could return to the field. There was still so much to do. So many seeds to plant. While the pizza man's cannabis was helpful, it was only a start. To be successful, to generate a massive amount of cash flow, there had to be a massive amount of product. And there would be soon. After all, they had a box of seeds that Zorrero had brought from Mexico. But it would take all summer to grow them tall and leafy.

A hasty bullet could ruin everything—if all it did was poke a little hole in the wing. What the blood-letter really needed was a .50 caliber. Such a gun would do more than just poke a little hole.

El Sangrador made a mental note to talk to the commander. Zorrero had a lot of clout, ranking so high in Los Equis. He could easily request one and have it shipped in the U-Haul truck, the next time the coyote came.

"Have you sold my babies?" The señora ripped free from her husband's grasp. "Only the devil would sell little babies!"

She rushed towards El Sangrador and clawed at him with her fingers. Using the butt of his rifle, he slammed her in the stomach and she buckled into a ball.

CHAPTER 67

Toothbrushes

By the time Matthews arrived at the Sheriff's Office, Breck already had the Jeep loaded with two shotguns, boxes of shells and pistol ammunition. The mayor had arrived just in the nick of time.

"You, sir, are a sad excuse for a sheriff." He slammed the BMW door.

"What did I do now?" Breck was using a bungee cord to attach a metal gas can to the side of the Jeep. "I really don't have time for this."

Hearing the commotion, Jenny appeared in the doorway. "What's going on?"

Matthews wagged two fingers in Breck's face.

"Twice! My daughter goes to the hospital twice, and you don't think it's important enough to call me. Either time! What kind of sick person are you, Dyer?"

The bungee cord snapped. Breck turned to Jenny and held it up like a dead snake.

"Can you find another one of these? We're not going to run out gas today."

Jenny disappeared back inside. She was wearing a black flak vest with SHERIFF printed on it. So was Breck. If Matthews had arrived just five minutes later, he would have missed them. They would be driving up Boreal Pass Road and Matthews couldn't let that happen.

"Hey! Did you hear what I just said?"

He tried to sound furious. Maybe fury would stop Breck from driving up there. What he was really feeling was apprehension. Apprehension at the thought of the whole enterprise getting thrown off the rails. A text had come in from Zorrero. A plane, flying low. Right over the grow field! It had to be the sheriff, sniffing around—too close for comfort. *Fix it, now.*

Jenny came back out with another bungee cord, and they got the gas can latched on tight.

Breck wiped his forehead. "Let's grab some water bottles and we're outta here."

Hearing that, Matthews raced to the door and blocked their path.

"You have a problem listening, don't you Breck? Always have. You can't stand authority and oversight, so you treat me like I don't have any. But I do."

"I did call you on both occasions." Coming real close, Breck pulled up just short of ramming into him but the mayor didn't budge. Breck looked him square in the eye. "I was right there digging her out of the snow with my own two hands. And I was right there when she was passed out in her own vomit. The question you should be asking is where were *you?*"

Jenny's eyes got big. "Uh, oh."

Pressing his hands against the door jambs, Matthews refused to let them pass.

"You bastard." His face went white with rage. Real fury now. "You have any idea what kind of trouble you're in? The crime rate in Quandary has skyrocketed since you took the badge. Break-ins, thefts, drugs, violence. Your own brother got shot in the chest by a drug cartel. Right here, on your watch. And that makes me wonder if the sheriff's own brother is working hand in hand with a foreign narcotics cartel, what does that say about the sheriff? It says he's in on it. And it's not just me. I've already called the governor on your ass. Get ready to have your world turned upside down."

That shut him up. The look on Breck's face was priceless. Matthews tried not to smile, even though he wanted to, bad. Fear was the sharpest tool in the toolbox. He didn't need proof. He didn't need truth. Those were the toothbrushes of weaponry—ineffective and soft.

"Whatever you think you're doing, forget it." Matthews held out his hand. "You resign right now, this all goes away. Just hand

me your badge and cooperate and things will go much easier on
you."

All he needed was a little more time. To pass the right legisla-
tion. To build the Clear Span. Then it would all be on the up and
up.

Jenny turned to Breck.

"Don't do it. None of that's true."

Pulling out a lime green package of American Spirit cigarettes,
Breck fished one out and put it in his mouth. He patted his jeans,
looking for a lighter.

"Anyone got a light?"

"Here, let me."

Jenny reached up and flicked it out of his mouth. The white
paper cigarette hit the asphalt and rolled away beneath the may-
or's BMW.

"You can't take my badge." Breck met Matthews' gaze. "I was
elected by the good citizens of Quandary County and you can say
what you want to the governor. Now, get out of my way or I'll arrest you for obstructing an investigation."

Not good. Not what he was hoping to hear. Matthews closed
his hand but didn't move.

"One of Johnny Tibbs' summer crew just about got killed."
Breck started to pull out another cigarette but didn't. "Whatever
you think you know, you don't know half of it. This is no joke."

What? Matthews was genuinely surprised. What was Breck
talking about? Did Zorrero shoot someone else? A sick feeling
started creeping through his stomach. The same feeling he had
when he was drinking Jack Daniels in the RV. But Zorrero had
assured him that there would be no violence. He said they didn't
do things like the other cartels did, south of the border. The old
ways were bad for business. Legitimate businessmen, leaders in
the industry. That's what they were. Right?

"Some cartel freak show tried to take out a poor college kid,"
Jenny said. "He was out alone, on horseback clearing trails. Barely escaped. Scared out of his mind."

"You sure about that?" Matthews asked. "You have proof it
wasn't some poacher hunting elk out of season? That sounds a
lot more likely."

She rolled her eyes.

"Put the cuffs on him, Breck. We need to get up there and
search that RV."

As soon as she said that, Matthews moved out of the way.

"Fine. Go make a fool of yourself. This isn't over." He strutted past them, got in the BMW and drove. But as soon as he was out of sight, he pulled over and texted a message on his phone.

They don't know about the grow field. But move the RV now!

CHAPTER 68

Pastrami

It had been heart-wrenching for Zorrero. Poor guy. Did his puppy just die? His firstborn child? That might as well have been the case, when El Sangrador drove away in the fancy Ford F350 pickup truck with the TorqShift six-speed, the oversized Raptor RV camper trailer in tow. And the further down the road he got, the more he began to understand why.

Adjusting the electronic side mirrors, the blood-letter could not lie to himself. It was a nice vehicle. The dirt road was nothing but washboards and erosion, miles and miles of teeth-jarring ruts, but the truck's suspension made it seem like he was floating on a cloud.

It took him hours to drive up and over Boreal Pass with that big heavy trailer. Around all the winding curves. He almost scraped the paint on a gritty boulder. But eventually the road evened out, the trees thinned, and he ended up in an old ghost town right by a busy highway.

A row of horses lined up along a barbed wire fence, watching him. Ears perked up.

It looked like the locals were doing what they could to bring the old place back to life. Several sagging homes were painted in unusually stark shades of blue and pink. Someone had even painted an outhouse lemon yellow.

El Sangrador drove past a railroad roundhouse from the olden days, made of river stone. A short stretch of train track petered out in the grass and led nowhere. Inside one of the bays, the blood-letter spotted a steam locomotive. Straight out of the movies! He took out his pistol and pretended to shoot at it. How much fun would it be to rob a train? Just like Jesse James.

The road teed into a lonely highway. This must be South Park. A wide grassy plain, many miles across, with mountains on all sides.

Once he was back on blacktop, El Sangrador was careful not to speed. There were many pickups with camper trailers and he did not want to draw unwanted attention to himself. The *policia* were surely looking for him, even way out here.

It was a good thing Zorrero's phone had worked as well as it did. The dude ranch cell tower was a good distance from the grow field, too far for clear phone calls but close enough to allow texts. And if the mayor had not sent a warning, the pesky sheriff would have found them.

The blood-letter regretted not shooting that tiny plane out of the sky when he had the chance.

Yet all was not lost. The Range Rover was four-wheel drive, and Zorrero drove it further up the gully to hide it better. The trailhead was unmarked. It looked exactly like a deer trail in an aspen grove. There were thousands of those all along the dirt road. Without the big RV sitting there, flagging the location, it would take great luck to find the right one.

Immense black storm clouds loomed in the distance. At a town called Fairplay, El Sangrador turned onto another paved road and started gaining elevation again. The mountains closed in around him again, and a green road sign indicated Alma was just a few miles ahead.

He was back in familiar territory.

By the time he pulled into the Almart parking lot, El Sangrador was getting hungry. He left the keys in the ignition, got out and stretched. The sky was gray. Those storm clouds were far away but perhaps they would be coming soon.

The parking lot was nearly empty. Just a dark green Toyota pickup with the paint flaking off the topper, and an Alma police car.

Stuffing the pearl-handled Colt .45 in his waistband, El Sangrador pulled on a rain jacket he found in the cab, in case it did start to rain, and headed inside the store.

Like last time, the same stock boy was standing in the cereal aisle, arranging boxes of Cheerios and Grape Nuts. The kid made eye contact with the blood-letter and froze. Like a chameleon, his skin color changed, and he vanished among the breakfast foods.

But El Sangrador was not there for dry cereal or Dinty Moore or yellow peas. He wanted something else. Something mouthwatering.

Walking past humming glass cases full of ice cream and frozen microwave meals, he paused and looked around. There! A refrigerated section with paper-wrapped deli sandwiches. Roast beef. Ham. Chicken. There were so many to choose from. Plus a metal rack full of potato chips. El Sangrador had been craving a sandwich and chips for quite some time. His hopes for a Subway visit had been stifled once Zorrero spotted the RV campground and diverted their plans from buying sandwiches to stealing a camper.

"You can't go wrong with the pastrami and Cheetos. That's what I always get."

It was the Alma police chief.

El Sangrador stared at him, sizing him up. The man was carrying a frozen pizza and a two-liter of Mountain Dew. He had a puffy belly and did not look either lithe or threatening.

As if to prove he was not threatening, Chief Waters even smiled—a forced and unnatural expression. He waited for a reply, some small talk perhaps. But El Sangrador offered no conversation in return.

"Well I guess that's not entirely true, I don't *always* get the pastrami." Waters held up the frozen pizza. "There's an oven back at the office, you see. Now and then, when we're not in the mood for sandwiches, me and Rhodes split a pie for lunch. So if you're not in the mood to get a sandwich, I highly recommend one of these bad boys."

El Sangrador tilted his head to look at the package. It was a taco pizza. Suddenly, Chief Waters' over-friendly smile faltered as he thought about what he was holding in his hands.

"I didn't mean to imply tacos were bad, or lawless, or negative in any way. Or even male." His face turned red. "Know what? I better go with the supreme. I forgot Rhodes likes supreme. Besides, we got no right to be eating something that might be disrespectful to your culture. As an officer of the law and a representative of our local government, I would never presume to eat a taco pizza. That would be cultural appropriation, and I apologize if I've offended you in any way."

He hastened towards the freezer aisle to put it back.

"There is a cultural sensitivity training workshop in Denver in a few weeks. I assure you, my whole department will be attending. Me and Rhodes, the both of us."

Then Chief Maxwell Waters hustled out the door without buying a thing.

CHAPTER 69

No Spine

Stealing the stock boy's Toyota pickup had been easy. The keys were sitting on the cash register and the kid was nowhere to be seen.

The cop was right—the pastrami was delicious. It was better than the roast beef and better than the ham. El Sangrador had stolen an armload of paper-wrapped sandwiches, plus a fist full of potato chip bags. The greatest challenge of the day was collecting the kid's car keys without dropping all the food on the floor. They were sitting by the register and the stock boy was nowhere to be seen.

On the drive to Quandary, El Sangrador ate one of each kind. A pastrami on the switchbacks, a roast beef in the canyon, and a ham parked outside Freddy's cabin.

Zorrero had mentioned the pizza man's broken faith. Freddy had made a solemn vow not to sell any more cannabis. Not a single joint. But after speaking with the mayor face to face in the RV, Zorrero learned the truth.

Freddy was dealing again. Not only had he sold marijuana to the ski resort manager, but he had also given him oxy and fentanyl pills. This was a serious offense.

When doing business with Los Equis, there were no second chances.

So when El Sangrador finished the last bite of his ham sandwich and licked the Cheetos dust from his fingers, he walked around to the back door, knocked out a pane of glass with the butt of his .45 and went inside to wait.

The Toyota pickup was out of sight, just in case Freddy might recognize it or grow suspicious of an unannounced visitor. El Sangrador parked it at the nearest neighbor's house, on the far side of a stand of pine trees. It had been such a disappointment to drive after spending all day cruising around in the brand new F350. The little clunker was built in the 1990s. Cloth seats stained and torn. Shattered dome light. The engine light was on and the seatbelt didn't click. The odometer was tipping 300,000 miles, but to his surprise, it drove smooth the entire way.

To his disgust, El Sangrador discovered a vape pen in the cup holder. The Almart stock boy's. Sniffing it—a sickening sweet strawberry odor. He flung it out the window immediately. The blood-letter was not interested in huffing flavored steam.

However, there were more interesting things to smoke in Freddy's cabin. The kitchen table had a stack of rolling papers, a pile of tobacco and some hash cakes. The living room was littered with burnt roaches and bongs with blackened flues. Dried cannabis leaves had been measured out in two and four-ounce bags, sealed and stacked beneath the television.

Yes, this was a serious offense indeed.

What a foolish thing to do. Did the pizza man not realize the stakes of the game? They had gunned down his distribution partner. Gunshot to the chest. That was as clear a signal as anything. Then they tracked Freddy down to the Sheriff's Office and marched right inside despite the presence of an armed deputy. Seeing him weasel beneath the jail cell cot was shameful. On top of that, he had wet himself while he was cowering.

Give him a scare. That's what the mayor told Zorrero. *The guy has no spine, and he's in way over his head.*

El Sangrador returned to the kitchen. The trash can was overflowing. Dirty dishes filled the sink. Greasy pizza boxes littered the counter. If it weren't for the prominent scent of cannabis, the smell of garbage and rotting food would have been unbearable.

Beside a pile of unwashed cups, there was a wood block with steak knives. El Sangrador pulled one out and examined the serrated blade.

Freddy had returned to his ways, despite a promise not to. A scare? They had already gone to the trouble of giving him a scare in the sheriff's jail. In the very place where he should have been the safest. There was no safe place to escape to, the message could not have been clearer. And yet the truth was undeniable. The evidence was plain. The pizza man was dealing pot again.

The blood-letter ran his finger over the blade. No spine? Perhaps he would see for himself whether it was in there or not.

CHAPTER 70

The Five Stages of Defeat

It was almost as embarrassing as running out of gas. Breck and Jenny drove up and down Boreal Pass Road all day long but turned up nothing. Where was the RV they spotted from the airplane? It had to be there, right? With each passing hour, the tension grew. The disbelief. More than once, they spotted a footpath and slammed on the brakes. Guns out, spider sense tingling. Every tree, every bush, a blind for a bad guy with a high caliber rifle.

All for nothing.

The evening dusk swallowed the forest, forcing them to give up the chase. What else could they do but turn back and head home? They drove the whole way in silence.

Breck went through a spectrum of emotions as the sense of failure set in. It was like the five stages of grief—except it was the five stages of defeat. Confusion, frustration, self-doubt, self-reproach, and finally embarrassment.

It was pitch black when they pulled into the office parking lot, next to the snowmobile. He should have left it alone. Not only did the solenoid not work, now the fuel injector was jacked up. Never touch a wrench.

They headed inside. Jenny tore off her sweat-soaked flak vest. Flinging it on the floor, she marched over to the refrigerator and glowered at the empty shelves. There were some more water bottles in there, but that's all they had been drinking all day.

"I need a beer." She slammed the door. "Too bad Danny's not out of the hospital yet. That brewery is a community service."

Breck sank into his chair and laid his head on the desktop.

"Why do I always feel like I'm always two steps behind?"

Jenny opened the fridge again and reluctantly pulled out two cold waters. She dropped one on his desk.

"You absolutely sure it said Raptor?"

Of course, it said Raptor . . . didn't it? Stage three, self-doubt. All over again. Someone should write a book about it. Maybe he would. Self-help was a bestselling genre, right? *The Five Stages of Defeat—Life Sucks and There's Nothing You Can Do About It.*

"The feds." Last resort. He hated working with federal agents on anything because they always claimed authority. Sidelined him on his own investigations. "They can do a satellite grid search of the area. That grow field is out there. It's just too big a project for you and me."

"And our crap budget," Jenny added, unnecessarily.

Breck took a gulp of water. He was exhausted. Mentally and emotionally, he had spent a lot of energy on Boreal Pass Road. Only to come up empty-handed. A Mexican drug cartel was running an illegal marijuana operation on a mountain slope above his town, but he just couldn't find it. Maybe it was time to hand this off to another agency. An agency with unlimited funding.

"City council meets tomorrow night." He shook his head thinking about it. "You want to give the Sheriff's Report this time?"

"I've already got plans. A bottle of red wine asked me out to dinner."

Breck smiled. That was funny.

"Johnny Tibbs gonna be jealous."

The office telephone rang. They both looked at it, but neither moved. Breck just wanted to go home and sit on the deck. Listen to the crickets.

On the fourth ring, Jenny creaked out of her chair and picked it up.

"Sheriff's Office. O'Hara speaking."

She cringed and mouthed *Waters*.

Breck put his head back on the desk.

"Say what now?" Genuine surprise in her voice. "And it says Raptor, right? Can you bring it down here? . . . Why not? . . . Okay, whatever. We'll meet you there tomorrow morning."

Hanging up the phone with a delicate *click*, she threw a pencil at Breck's head. He didn't stir.

"They found our RV. In the Almart parking lot. Of course, Waters won't drive it down here. We have to drive up there to get it."

Breck lifted his head. Eyes half open.

"I am so tired of that guy. What a waste of a day."

He eyes sealed and he went back down, face flat on the desktop.

The phone rang again and Jenny snatched it back up.

"I said we'd be there—what part of that didn't you understand, douche?" Then her face scrunched up. "Sorry, governor. This is Deputy O'Hara. How can I help you this lovely evening?"

She pressed the hold button and threw another pencil at him. "Governor on line one."

Any guess what this was about? Matthews had already threatened to get him fired. Go over his head, straight to the governor. Breck wished he was on a date with a bottle of red wine. But he wasn't. And it was better to get it over with, so he picked up the phone.

"This is Sheriff Dyer. Governor, how are you?"

"I am not happy and you shouldn't be either."

"We're on the same page, then. No worries there."

Breck instantly regretted the joke. When was he going to learn? Don't make jokes. Ever.

"You better be worried, sheriff. I got a call from Mayor Matthews expressing concern that the Quandary County sheriff is colluding with a Mexican drug cartel to distribute marijuana illegally. Corruption charges are serious, Breck. As the governor of Colorado, I am compelled to look into this."

Breck wasn't feeling like a fight at the moment. What could he say, except the truth?

"I can assure you that isn't true, governor."

Silence.

"Breck, I'm going to refer this to the District Attorney. He will be contacting you before the end of the week."

The governor disconnected. The dial tone hummed in Breck's ear. He stared off in space. Something about this was off. The mayor getting in his face, accusing him of heading up a crime ring. Where did that even come from? Why would he think that?

"Matthews told the governor that I'm corrupt. That I'm working with a drug cartel from Mexico." He eyes came back into focus. On Jenny. She was watching, waiting. Those five stages of defeat started swirling around in his mind again. "You know what? How did Matthews know about the cartel? When he asked for my badge. I never told him any of the details about what was going on. I never said anything about a Mexican drug cartel. Did I?"

Did he let it slip? Did someone else?

"I never told him squat," Jenny said. "You gonna hang that up?"

The dial tone was still ringing in his ear. As soon as he set the phone down, it rang again.

"Oh, come on! I'm done with phones. You take it."

But Jenny held her hands up in the air. "Not it."

"Mature. Professional. Make sure I'm at the top of your reference list next time you apply for a job." He picked it up again. "Hello? This is Sheriff Dyer."

It was Cash. Ski resort Cash. Opioids overdose Cash.

He mouthed his name to Jenny.

She shook her fist at the sky. "Wine, God. Wine!"

"You gotta get over here." The guy was whispering. "Please get over here . . . he's dead . . . oh holy damn, dude! He's dead."

"Who's dead?"

"Freddy."

CHAPTER 71

Short Enough

Jaundice yellow beams. The Jeep headlights. Every time Breck drove through the canyon at night it was a game of Russian roulette with the yawning abyss. Even the white line painted on the edge of the road was worn off. The black asphalt simply vanished into black sky.

Jenny had her eyes closed. "Tell me when it's over."

"I finally got an email from the Road and Bridge Department." Breck dropped the transmission into second gear. "Guardrails go up late September. Theoretically."

He didn't know what to say. Small talk felt wrong. None of it felt real. Was Freddy really dead? Maybe he was okay. Maybe Cash got into some bad ditch weed and was hallucinating, but they wouldn't know until they got there.

Since there weren't any oncoming vehicles, Breck crossed into the other lane to get further away from the drop-off. The speedometer glowed just as dully as the headlights. Fifteen miles-per-hour was the speed limit but he kept gunning the engine on the straightaways, then mashing the brake around the curves.

Jenny groaned and folded her hands over her stomach. Breck knew she was getting car sick with her eyes closed and the way he was driving. He felt sick, too, but it wasn't the road. What were they going to find at Freddy's cabin?

Cash hadn't said much. He was either high or in a state of shock. It was hard to tell with that guy. But Breck phoned the hospital regardless, and an ambulance was on its way.

Racing around the final canyon bend, the road entered the forest and the trees closed in around them. Just another mile or so. Breck felt his stomach flutter. Freddy was just a pothead. The best job he could get was delivering pizza. He liked a good pint of Ten Mile Milk Stout and skiing in the winter like everybody else. He thought Jenny was a foxy lady cop and told her so. He drove an old beater car because he couldn't afford anything better. He wasn't a threat. To anyone.

But Breck knew the rules were different when it came to drugs.

Jenny's eyes flicked open when he slammed on the brakes, skidding in the gravel. She pushed open her door and threw up in a wild raspberry bush.

"You all right?" Breck opened the rear hatch, got the shotgun and started feeding in shells.

She spit a long string of saliva.

"Don't worry about me."

He gave her the shotgun, and they both jogged up Freddy's driveway. His Honda Civic was parked there, in the dark, and so was a motorcycle. It was Cash's. And Cash was there too, sitting in the dirt, leaning against the garage. Feet splayed, eyes glazed.

"Are you okay?" Breck had his revolver out and up. "Anyone else inside?"

No response. The bottoms of Cash's tennis shoes were wet. Blood.

Aspen trees surrounded the cabin, silent sentinels in the gloom. Ancient pallbearers, waiting for their moment. And the moment had come.

The front door was wide open. The kitchen light was on. The hallway tunneled through the darkness like a gateway to another dimension of reality. A trail of red footprints. It had to be Cash? Just one set. Maybe the cartel men were still in there? They liked to hide in the shadows and sneak up in the darkness, there was no doubt about that.

At the end of the hallway, peering into the kitchen, Breck's heart stopped beating.

"Jenny, don't come in here."

But she did. He heard her step close. Her warm breath on his shoulder. She was right behind him.

"Good Lord . . ." Jenny gasped.

A siren. The ambulance was in the canyon. It would arrive soon. Breck tried not to step in the blood to check Freddy's pulse, but it was impossible to avoid. He pressed his fingers against cold skin and paused. Hoping against hope the guy might open his eyes.

"Come on, wake up."

But he did not wake up. Freddy was gone.

"We need to clear the house before the paramedics get here. Those cartel men may still be here." Breck looked at Jenny. She was shading her eyes with her hand. "Jenny?"

She spun around and headed back down the hallway. Breck heard her kicking open doors and flipping on lights.

He looked around the kitchen. Drugs on the table. Trash on the counters. Another set of bloody footprints leading out the back door. A pane of glass was broken. That was how they got in.

"All clear." Jenny's voice. She was down the hallway. She wasn't coming back. "Ambulance just got here."

The cartel was moving in and Freddy got in the way. Territory. Money. That's what this was all about. And that's all they cared about. Human life meant nothing to these men. Nothing.

Breck hung his head.

Life was short enough as it was.

CHAPTER 72

Long Metal Spoon

Jenny was numb. She couldn't fall asleep or even doze off, not even for a few minutes.

She turned on Netflix but every show she tried felt hollow. Trite. Meaningless. But it was good to hear voices so she found one she had never seen before. A reality show. Movie actor Ewan McGregor was riding a motorcycle across Europe and Asia with a film crew trailing along. He wasn't a very good rider. Across Mongolia, he kept laying the bike down in the dirt. There was nothing out there but grasslands and dirt roads and people living in yurts. Then something broke, and even though he had all the right tools he didn't know how to fix the bike, but some Mongolian local with two teeth knew exactly what to do.

It was just like Breck and the snowmobile. Maybe they could get that Mongolian guy with two teeth to come to fix the solenoid.

The jail cell cot. Freddy with his wet jeans. He sat down on Breck's sleeping bag while Jenny lectured him.

Get smart, Freddy. Can't you see what's going on? She had been pretty tough on him. *Look at me. Is this what you want your life to be? Shot to death by some cartel hit men who drove all the way up here from Mexico?*

Jenny felt cold and clammy. It was hard to concentrate on the television.

Every time a car drove by her little rental cottage, or a door slammed, she chambered a shell in the shotgun and pointed it at the door.

Crap, Freddy. And for what? So people can get stoned stupid? Where there's drugs, there's violence. End of story. Get it?

There was a bottle of red wine on top of the microwave, but she didn't touch it. One glass would make her sleepy, and it was tempting for just that reason. But she didn't dare risk it.

Jenny picked up her phone. How many times had she wanted to call Breck? But she didn't want to look weak. She was a deputy sheriff, not a cashier at Almart. Putting her life in danger was the job.

Carrying the shotgun to the kitchen, Jenny got a carton of coconut water and a Power Bar she had found in the Jeep. The clock on the microwave said 4 A.M.

Oh yeah. They were supposed to meet Chief Waters at the county line bright and early. Just above the switchbacks. Pick up the stolen RV. After what happened with Freddy, Jenny wondered if Breck was even going to remember. The plan was to meet at the office at 7 o'clock, drive up together. Jenny would bring the Jeep back and Breck would drive the stolen rig.

There was no time to waste now. They had to find those cartel men before anyone else got hurt. Or murdered.

"Those evil pricks."

Maybe there was a clue inside the camper. A misplaced cellphone. They could run the fingerprints through the federal ICE database. Put a name with a freak. Running drugs across the border, chances were they got caught before. Probably released immediately, too. Catch and release. Nice one, Obama. Hell, the cartel probably got their guns from the Fast and Furious program anyhow. Thank God that was all in the rearview.

They still needed to search Freddy's cabin, once the sun came up. Knock on neighbors' doors. Interview Cash again. It was obvious he went there to buy weed, and he probably wouldn't admit it, but maybe he saw something.

"I better see what's what."

Jenny pulled out her phone and typed a text.

Still meeting at 7?

Breck came right back. *Yeah, we need to.*

They were on the same page. Jenny smiled softly. He wasn't getting any sleep either.

She took the Power Bar, the coconut water and the shotgun of course, and went back to the couch. Ewan McGregor was in a yurt in Mongolia, seated around a big black kettle of steaming testicles. Cow balls, goat balls, sheep balls. Someone mentioned they were fresh cut that very day. An old lady with a long metal spoon dipped one out of the boiling water and offered it to him.

Jenny unwrapped the Power Bar and chewed off a corner.

"Things could be worse, I suppose."

CHAPTER 73

Life Went On

As they crested the last switchback on the road to Alma, Breck and Jenny saw the Raptor RV and pickup parked at the scenic overlook. Chief Maxwell Waters and Officer Rhodes were eating powdered sugar donuts, plucked from a blue paper bag resting on the hood of their police car.

"For a guy concerned with stereotypes . . ." Jenny didn't even need to finish the thought. "Leave the engine running, cuz I'm outta here."

"You don't want to talk shop with these fine gentlemen?"

"Waters has gonorrhea of the mouth. So, no."

Breck smiled.

"You mean diarrhea of the mouth?"

"Ain't gonna get close enough to find out."

Breck parked the Jeep by the overlook sign. Red Mountain Pass. Elevation 11,539 feet. Continental Divide. It was a dirt parking lot with a decent view. They were at eye level with a few windswept mountain peaks that rose above timberline, nothing but stony ridges and snow banks on top.

"Do me a fav," Breck said. "Swing by Freddy's. Walk the area, knock on some doors. Then meet me back at the office and we'll pull this RV apart."

He got out of the Jeep, but Jenny stayed inside and crawled over the gear shift into the driver's seat. It would have been easier to get out and walk around, but the risk of a chit chat grudge fest with the Alma chowder-heads wasn't worth it.

Grinding it into first, she let the clutch go a little too quick. The Corvette engine roared like a lion and the Jeep leaped forward but she got it under control, kicking up dust, and headed back down the switchbacks.

A glance at the gas gauge. Full. That's good, she didn't want to get stranded. Just as quickly, Jenny recalled it didn't work and that was the whole problem with this decrepit ol' wildebeest.

The hum of the road, the sun coming up. Jenny yawned. Zero sleep. It was starting to hit her.

The General Merchandise and More had both gasoline and coffee. Bad coffee. Really bad. Worse than the Folgers at the Sheriff's Office. But it was the only option between Alma and Quandary and she certainly wasn't going to Alma anytime soon.

Jenny pulled in and topped off the tank. Going inside to pay, she had to walk past the hot dog rollers to get to the coffee. The smell . . . smelled good. *Don't do it. Don't take the bait.* But whoa now, little doggie. Maybe this batch was okay? All she had eaten in the past twelve hours was that Power Bar.

Cheese infused. Pepperjack. Just one bite wouldn't hurt. She squirted some mustard all over it and walked up front to pay.

The guy at the register gave her a thumbs up.

"It's only 8 A.M. Bold move."

"A girl needs to eat."

There were blue bags full of powdered sugar donuts right there on the counter. She could have bought one of those. She might have if she wasn't wearing a badge clipped to her belt. And if she hadn't just seen Waters and Rhodes with white powdered sugar all over their smug little faces like a couple of coke whores.

Sitting on the hood, she worked the dog down and sipped hot coffee and watched the sunrise. The General Merchandise was high enough in elevation she could see the sun poking up between the peaks. It was nice. Down in Quandary, the sun never made it above the ridge before 10 o'clock and by then the day was in full swing.

Life went on, didn't it?

Freddy would never see the sunrise again. Or eat a gas station hot dog, or drink a cup of bad coffee ever again. Jenny's vision blurred. The napkins there were worse than sandpaper, but it was all she had to blot her eyes with.

"Get it together, Jen Jen."

That's what Breck called her when he was in nickname mode.

Just then, the Raptor passed by on the highway. Breck behind the wheel of the fancy F350. He was heading back to town. She better get moving, too.

There was a garbage can between the gas pumps. Tossing the mustardy cardboard tray, Jenny climbed back in the Jeep and looked around for a place to set her cup, but there was no cup holder. The coffee was scalding hot. Balancing it between her knees was not going to happen, not in a stick shift. Breck always had a ceramic *Ski Quandary!* mug in one hand. How did he do it? Using her jacket, Jenny made a nest on the passenger seat and balanced the Styrofoam cup in the middle. At least it had a lid. Maybe it wouldn't spill if she went easy on the clutch. Easy on the clutch? Who was she trying to fool? Driving the Jeep was like wrestling an alligator.

Breck had been flying downhill. By the time she was back on the road, he was long gone.

Turning onto Freddy's road, Jenny parked on the dirt road by his cabin. Crime scene tape was strung around the driveway and front door. Did they do that? Her memory was foggy in some places, crystal clear in others. Freddy on the kitchen floor—crystal clear. She would never forget that.

A pudgy magpie was in the driveway, hopping around Freddy's car. It cocked its head when Jenny got out of the Jeep. Beady black eyes. It chattered and nickered as she approached.

"Hungry, little fella? Got a little pepperoni gut going there, huh? Sorry. I don't have anything for you."

The cabin. The Civic. The yellow tape. She couldn't go in there. Not yet. Not alone.

Sighing, Jenny looked around the neighborhood. She could do that, she could check with neighbors. The closest cabin was just a short way up the road. If somebody had seen anything suspicious, they probably would have called 9-1-1. But maybe not. Taking her coffee along, Jenny started walking. The magpie on her heels like a puppy.

CHAPTER 74

Devil in the Details

Dusting for fingerprints was a chore. But the devil was in the details and Breck was determined to find him.

Where were Tom and Phyllis Nickles staying? The motel? Hopefully, they hadn't hopped a Greyhound for Kansas, or wherever they were from. Breck would need to get their prints since most of the prints in the RV would belong to them. And who knows who else. Kids, grandkids, bridge partners, BBQ buddies. Tom and Phyllis were going to be happy when they heard their truck and trailer were safe, but not so happy to hear it was part of an active investigation. They couldn't have it back just yet. Breck expected a royal stink to ensue but that was how it worked.

Already, he had lifted several sets from the door jambs, door knobs, cabinets, cups and dishes, and tabletop. Next step, scan them into the computer and upload to the FBI database, the ICE database, and even the DMV. It was a longshot, but who knew? Fingers crossed, so to speak.

Breck heard the Jeep pull into the parking lot. Jenny stuck her head in the RV door, looking apologetic.

"I spilled some coffee on the passenger seat. Sorry."

Without waiting for a response, she disappeared back outside.

The cartel men didn't leave anything obvious behind. Fingerprints were all he found. No notes, computers, iPads or cell phones. No drug paraphernalia. There was a pile of empty Jack Daniels bottles on the floor, and some empty cans of Dinty Moore stew. Maybe a better forensic team could find DNA samples, a hair on the pillow, but Breck couldn't afford a forensic team. It was up to him.

He put the fingerprint samples into a folder and brought it outside, to the sound of splattering. Jenny was wringing out her jacket on the asphalt.

"How do you drink and drive in that thing?" She gave the jacket an extra twist. "You know what I mean."

"Magicians never tell their secrets."

"Dry cleaners don't either."

Breck headed inside the old church building and went straight to the copy machine. Jenny followed and hung her damp jacket on the coat rack.

"This thing faxes, too. Right?" He leaned close to decipher the emblems on the keys. The thing was old and half the buttons were too scratched to read.

"Yeah. You push *fax*."

Sure enough, there was a button with the word *fax* on it. Barely legible, but it was there. How about that. He took the fingerprints out and started sorting them. He had written numbers and lift locations next to each print, not that it mattered much. He just hoped they could learn the identities of the two cartel men. If they knew who they were dealing with, they might learn something helpful.

"Got a dozen good prints here."

Jenny walked over to see what he had. Breck used graphite powder in the RV since most of the surfaces were white or light colored. Most of the whorls and lines were fairly clear.

"You can rule out the ones that have powdered sugar on them," she said.

Breck put the first page in the fax machine and hit the go button. The machine lit up and hummed. He had no idea how long it would take to get a match. But he had a couple of contacts at the FBI who might help move things along.

At least they had the screenshot from the Almart security video. That was something.

"So our cartel boys ditched the RV at Almart, then they stole the stock boy's truck out of the parking lot. Waters claims no one saw it happen." Breck wagged his finger. "And just because a nondescript Hispanic male with a pearl-grip pistol in his belt grabbed the kid's car keys off the cash register, *on video*, there is nothing to indicate he was the one who actually stole the vehicle. Who's to say? Someone else entirely could have hot-wired the pickup and drove off. It could have been anybody under the sun, so let's not jump to conclusions. Waters was very clear about that."

"Speaking of car keys." Jenny pulled the Jeep keys out of her pocket and handed them to Breck. "Let me guess. The stock boy drives a dark green 1990-something Toyota pickup with a topper."

"That's the one."

"Freddy's neighbor. Saw it parked by his mailbox and he had no idea whose it was. But let's not jump to conclusions."

Breck fed another sheet of fingerprints into the fax machine.

What next? They could look up the kid's license plate number and put out another BOLO. At least they knew what the latest stolen vehicle looked like. The cartel men were pretty good at disappearing, but they were going to make a mistake at some point.

With Freddy's murder, Breck was feeling a new sense of urgency. These men were very dangerous and one thing was clear—they weren't afraid to break any laws, legal or moral or otherwise.

"Almost forgot," he said. "I talked to Cash on the phone a little while ago. He claims he went over to Freddy's to play video games. Freddy was dead when Cash got there and he didn't see the killer."

"Maybe we should go back up in Tibbs' airplane." Jenny shrugged. "Look for that grow field again. It's got to be out there."

That was true. If they flew up on a clear day, there was a good chance they could find it. That RV had been parked on Boreal Pass Road for a reason—it was their base camp. Breck was tempted to call in the feds and hand it off to them. After all, it was in the National Forest. That was federally managed public land, technically speaking. Cultivating a secret grow field was still a violation of federal law.

"Sure you don't want to give the Sheriff's Report tonight?" Breck asked.

"Sorry. That bottle of red wine already made dinner reservations. I don't want to hurt its feelings."

CHAPTER 75

Horses and Whiskey

Standing outside City Hall, Matthews greeted the council members as they entered the building. There were only four of them. Besides Johnny Tibbs and Mike Jameson, there was Becca Butterfield who owned the Butterfield Bakery on Main, and Tya Tordenskjold—she and her husband Sven owned the ski resort.

Matthews pulled Tibbs aside before they went into the council chambers.

"Hey there amigo, before we head in there I wanted to touch base with you."

Up close, Tibbs smelled like horses and whiskey. Matthews put on an easy smile, but the clock was ticking. He needed things to happen and he needed to know how the chips were going to fall. When it came to getting his Clear Span "riding arena," no one was going to deny him the building permit. But legalizing marijuana was going to be tough. Jameson was on board, as long as he got his Subway. Matthews knew the two women, Becca and Tya, would vote against it without question. They were both mothers and mothers tended to be overprotective. Set up unnecessary boundaries for their children. Johnny Tibbs was the swing vote. If he got Johnny, it was three to two in favor.

"You get a chance to think about all that tax money? I hear Canada just made cannabis legal, the whole damn country. We're behind the times, Johnny. Let's catch up quick. Right here, right now."

Tibbs' face was cold, unreadable.

"You hear about the guy who delivers pizzas? He just got his throat slit and his guts strung out."

Matthews started to say something, a deflection. But he hadn't heard. What was Tibbs talking about? Was he drunk on whiskey? If this was a cowboy joke of some kind, it was a little macabre.

"I don't follow."

"Breck just called me," Tibbs said. "Wants me to take him up in my plane again. Look for a field of marijuana. Says there's a drug cartel growing weed up on the slopes somewhere, and the same sick bastards killed that poor pizza guy deader than dead."

This had to be a strategic fabrication. No one had been murdered—Matthews would have heard about it. The governor must have called Breck and told him he was under investigation for corruption, now Breck was fighting back any way he could. Trying to make his life miserable. Sabotage the city council. Poison Tibbs against him any way he could.

"Breck tell you that?"

"Yes, he did."

Maybe Sheriff Breckenridge Dyer was craftier than Matthews thought. Here was Johnny Tibbs, acting like everything Breck said was gospel truth. Zorrero wouldn't kill Freddy. Matthews told him specifically to give the guy a scare. That was it. Whatever he really did do to Freddy, Breck was spinning quite a tale out of it to shut down the city council's progress. It was a scare tactic, and Tibbs was dumb enough to bite.

"You know what else he said? Says wherever there's drugs there's violence." Tibbs tipped his hat. "That's my vote right there."

Matthews nodded, trying to walk the line between logic and lies.

"Even if that was true, think about the statistics. So many people are smoking pot these days, it's like over fifty percent of the country. That's a majority. That translates to sales and sales translates to taxes. Quandary gets rich overnight with just one vote. Think of everything we can finally do, as a city council. Hell, I bet we could even get the Tibbs Ranch an expansion parcel. Rezone that neighborhood next door. A little eminent domain for the city. Lease it to you cheap."

Tibbs recoiled. "Didn't your own daughter just OD on pills?"

Matthews felt the blood drain from his face. That was unfair—and a very personal dig. If that was how Johnny Tibbs wanted to play this, Matthews could punch back just as hard.

"You know half this town gets such patchy cell service. Putting that tower on the hill above your ranch might have been a mistake. Too far out. Maybe we should put it on the other side of town, right above Jameson's bike shop. Everyone in town would get a nice clear signal, wouldn't they?" He shrugged. "Except you, of course."

Tibbs shook his head and walked into the council chambers.

Matthews' mind reeled. If they didn't legalize cannabis, the Clear Span greenhouse would be a bust. He certainly couldn't make money off a therapeutic riding program. Those things were non-profit organizations, deadweight money pits, and "non-profit" was just what it sounded like. But he had already paid for the building—the Clear Span was scheduled for construction in a matter of days. Paid in full with a bank loan, and the bank loan was leveraged on Valerie's home in Frisco.

Maybe Tya or Becca would surprise him. Maybe he could get one of them to change their mind. All he needed was one more vote to greenlight weed. He needed to make a speech just before the vote. And it had to be a good one.

CHAPTER 76

Open Forum

The council chambers was a fancy name for an empty back-room at City Hall.

Nameplates indicated where everyone sat—Mayor Matthews sat in the middle, surrounded by council members Jameson, Tibbs, Tordenskjold, and Butterfield.

Matthews tapped his microphone. "Please stand for the Pledge of Allegiance."

He cast a side glance at Tibbs when he said allegiance.

Most every time the city council met, the rows of folding chairs were empty. It was always open to the public but no one ever showed up. Adrenaline surged through Matthews as he watched the seats fill up. *Of all nights.* The room was packed.

And taking up the whole front row—the avalanche protest group. Valerie and a very miserable looking Aspen, Mr. and Mrs. Chisolm and a very please-don't-fire-me looking Brittany.

Sitting behind them, it was the fire chief, city attorney, the ever-moody sheriff, and his redheaded lackey. There to give their departmental reports. Matthews wanted to laugh out loud at Breck. There wasn't much of a department left to report on, was there? How could he even afford to keep that girl on the payroll, anyhow?

The rest of the room was full of concerned citizens, undoubtedly. After Danny Dyer got shot and the stink about the avalanche, it was no surprise the squeaky wheels were coming out of the woodwork.

Matthews tapped his mic again. "We'll begin with the open forum. If anyone would care to speak, now is the time."

As expected, Valerie marched to the podium. Within spitting distance. Knowing her serpentine temperament, she would, too.

"As everyone knows, an avalanche nearly took the lives of our babies. Aspen and Brittany. The only reason they're alive today is that they were wearing avalanche beacons. How come avalanche beacons aren't required for every single skier on those slopes? Well, they ought to be. We have a petition signed by fifty people. And another thing. When there *is* avalanche danger, would it be so hard to shut the slopes down for a few days?"

Valerie handed the petition directly to Tya Tordenskjold, whose smile was both sympathetic and strained. Matthews knew her and her husband Sven. They were filthy rich. Their home was the biggest in town, a mansion on its own private driveway on its own private mountainside. They also had a second home in Norway and lived there half the time, half a world away.

Fifty names on a petition were embarrassing. If the slopes got shut down even for a day, that was a huge loss. To both the resort and the city. Matthews would talk with Tya later. Over white wine, hopefully. Tya was a cutie and Sven was out of town. Matthews could casually explain how his ex-wife was being irrational, emotional. Valerie didn't understand big business. Skiing was a risk, everyone knew it. Stay off the slopes if you were worried about danger. *You drank that down fast, Tya. Another glass of wine?*

Aspen lifted her head and caught his eye.

A feeling in his gut. Metallic. An acidic twist. Was that . . . guilt? What did he have to feel guilty about? So this was what it felt like to be irrational and emotional. Touché, Valerie. An emotional appeal was the strongest argument. Truth only went so far, didn't it?

"Anyone else for the open forum?" Matthews surveyed the audience. "Right now. Anybody?"

"I'm not finished, Seneca." Valerie went back to the podium. "What everyone may not know, is that my daughter nearly lost her life a second time—to illegal opioid prescription grade pills. There is a drug dealer on the streets of Quandary. I want everyone to be wary of this monster. And I expect the city council to take a strong stance against drugs in our community."

Valerie went back to her seat and put her arm around Aspen's shoulder. The Chisolms leaned over and silently congratulated Valerie on such a triumphant monologue.

At least she's done yammering. Matthews shuffled through a paper packet, pretending to scan the agenda. That little speech wasn't going to make the marijuana legalization vote any easier.

"My name is Bellevue J. Bolton." A thin, wilty looking man in a pinstriped suit appeared at the podium. "Proprietor of the Summit House Art Gallery on Main Street, across from the Blue Moose café. You'll have to pardon my shaky nerves. I just lost my brother last night, a victim of a heinous crime. Murdered. Frederick Bolton was the youngest in our family. A free spirit in his own way. A lover of Italian foods and partaker of Gaia's fragrant salves. But tell me this—what can the city do to prevent violent crimes like this from ever happening again?"

It was true then? Freddy *was* killed. Matthews glared at Breck. The mayor should not be blindsided with information like this at a city council meeting. What a blatant transgression! And the slight would not go unanswered.

"The city council will be discussing the matter with Sheriff Dyer, I can assure you of that Mr. Bolton."

Tibbs had been telling the truth. So who did it? The cartel men? Killing a rival went way beyond an intended scare. This was not good. Perhaps something else happened. Something completely unrelated. Matthews would get to the bottom of it. Talk to Zorrero, face to face.

But the thought of a face to face with Zorrero suddenly sounded . . . unsafe?

"Moving on," Matthews announced. "Building permit. I am seeking the council's approval for a building permit for an indoor horseback riding arena. To serve members of our community with special needs."

Mike Jameson perked up. "Motion to approve the building permit."

Tibbs nodded. "I second. Let's vote. All in favor?"

All five of them raised their hands.

That was better. Matthews needed a small victory to get the ball rolling. All that drug and death talk almost spoiled the momentum. *From now on, the open forum happens last.*

CHAPTER 77

Cats in Trees

The fire chief came to the podium and gave his department report. No city fires, no forest fires. But there would be smoke on the horizon next week, a controlled backburn to destroy the undergrowth along the highway. Nothing to worry about, if anyone calls 9-1-1.

The city attorney went next. Legal talk, blah, blah, blah.

Matthews shooed him away. It was time for the Sheriff's Report. This ought to be good. No matter what he had to say, Matthews would find a good excuse to cut Breck's budget again. That mouthy little carrot top better start sending out resumés.

Breck got up to speak.

"How many cats in trees this month, Dyer?" Matthews leaned forward to catch Mike Jameson's attention and held his fingers up like they were frantic kitty claws.

In response, Jameson held his own hands up like he was eating an imaginary sandwich. *Yeah, yeah, Mikey. Message received.*

"Things have been a little more . . . involved . . . than that."

Breck apparently was not amused with their pantomime.

Matthews waved his hand like a Roman emperor. *You may continue.*

"In addition to last night's homicide involving Freddy Bolton, there have been an unusual number of crimes in the past weeks. One of Johnny Tibbs' rental cabins was broken into, and one of his wranglers was fired upon with intent to kill. His horse was shot but the boy escaped unharmed. A pickup truck with an RV camper trailer was stolen from the Continental Divide Motel and

Campground—it has since been recovered. The General Merchandise and More was broken into. Items stolen, items not recovered. Daniel Dyer was shot in the chest at the Quandary Brewery by suspected drug cartel hit men. The drug cartel hit men, I believe, are still in the area. The Sheriff's Office is still investigating the matter."

The room swelled with murmuring voices.

Hearing the words *drug cartel,* Valerie's face sunk in horror. She seized Aspen's hand and Matthews could hear his ex-wife interrogating the girl as if she had El Chapo on speed dial.

"Quiet down please." Matthews banged his fist on the desk since he didn't have a gavel. "Is that the extent of your report, sheriff? Because we have a full agenda and it's time to move on."

Staring at the mayor, Breck drummed his fingers on the podium. "If this Sheriff's Office had proper funding, we could address all of these problems effectively. I am formally requesting a budget increase. A significant one. I need a full team of deputies, patrol cars and . . ."

"And a full-time assistant whose sole job it is to bring you a spare can of gasoline." Matthews thumped the table again. "Duly noted. Now take a seat, Dyer. Let's move on . . ."

But Johnny Tibbs' booming cowboy twang rattled the loudspeakers.

"Somebody took a shot at one of my wranglers. Killed one of my horses. I can't let that stand."

More concerned murmurs from the townspeople. So easy to elicit, with their Play-Doh naiveté. Ridiculous. It didn't take much to bait them into outrage, shock, and dismay. Matthews would have rolled his eyes, except things weren't going his way.

Even Mike Jameson *hmm'd* and *mmm'd* his solidarity, and Becca Butterfield whispered in Tya's ear. Matthews caught the gist—it was typical mother talk. How was she going to feel safe dropping her kids off at school now? In this day and age?

Then Becca hovered over her own mic, in her soft moth-flap voice. "Council member Tibbs. What do you propose we do?"

"I'll tell you what we do," Tibbs said. "Give the sheriff what he wants so he can do his damn job."

Okay, enough was enough. Things were spinning off the rails. Matthews had to do something or it was all over before it even began.

"Hold on . . . just hold on now. Throwing money at a problem doesn't solve anything. That's what's wrong with government. Just look at our national debt. What is it? Over twenty trillion dollars? Let's be reasonable and ask ourselves, what's the *real* problem here? Danny Dyer got shot. Freddy Bolton got shot. Tibbs' wrangler got shot—almost. The problem is pretty obvious, and so is the solution. I motion we institute a citywide gun ban. All guns. Illegal. Effective immediately."

Breck stood up and tried to speak, but Matthews waved him down. "You're out of order, sheriff. Everybody wait your turn. Tell me this isn't a good idea. Mike? Tya? Becca, aren't you worried about your kids at school? Kindergarten should be a safe space. But as it is, some crazy gunman could be parked out front with a loaded machine gun."

That worked. It was like he slapped her in the face. Becca nodded and mumbled something but Matthews couldn't hear her this time.

"Nope, that ain't gonna happen." Tibbs again. Rattling the speakers. "We're a Second Amendment kind of town. Guns don't kill. People do. So we need to kill *those* people with guns."

Despite Johnny Tibbs predictable objection, it was working. Tya and Becca were whispering again. Breck and Jenny were huddled in outrage, but that only made Matthews want to laugh out loud. He nodded at Jameson and held his hands like he was eating a sandwich.

"I second the motion." Mike winked at Matthews.

Breck jumped up and shouted something about how bad guys don't follow laws, and banning guns only meant the good guys couldn't protect themselves. Matthews ignored him.

"Let's vote on it. All in favor say aye. And I say aye."

CHAPTER 78

Hamster Wheel

Tya put her hand on Becca's forearm. A soft word in the ear. Then she tucked back a stray lock of blonde hair and spoke very distinctly. "I vote nay."

Becca nodded solemnly. "I vote nay, as well."

Nays? Matthews was stunned. What were these two ladies thinking? Didn't they value the lives of their offspring?

Besides, Tya's husband was Norwegian. All those socialists wanted to ban guns! He would talk to her later. See what was going on. Over that glass of white white, hopefully.

Between Johnny Tibbs and Becca and Tya, the gun ban was blocked. And down in the audience, in the second row, peering between Valerie and Aspen's shoulders like a gloating gargoyle—Sheriff Breckenridge Dyer.

Adjusting his suit coat, Matthews feigned disinterest.

"Fine by me. My kids are out of school anyhow." Becca gasped, but he didn't care. Wait, maybe he shouldn't have said that. The next thing on the agenda was cannabis legalization. Matthews glanced at her. "I apologize, that was just a joke gone awry."

If that mollified the woman, Matthews wasn't sure. She was dainty and introverted and shy as hell. The gun ban was just political posturing anyhow. Sleight of hand. The real magic show was about to begin.

"The next item on our agenda is the one that's going to change everything. We've been talking for years how Quandary is struggling financially from a lack of tax revenue. We've tried luring tech companies, startups, developers of all kinds. It's just not enough." Matthews let that sink in for just a second. Money—the universal love language. "As everyone knows, the state of Colorado legalized cannabis use several years ago. Distribution and sales are only legal according to each city and county's approval. Denver and Pueblo prove it is a successful taxation stance. Along with two dozen other cities across the state. Telluride, Aspen, Boulder, Pagosa. It's time to get out of the Dark Ages. I hereby make a motion to accept both recreational and medical cannabis sales in the city limits of Quandary."

It was a solid start to a solid sales pitch, and Matthews had a lot more under the hood. But Tibbs cut him off.

"Nope."

Matthews stuttered. Glared. He wasn't finished talking yet. That Johnny Tibbs was a complete and utter narcissist.

"Who will second this vital motion?" Forget the speech. Time to go for the kill before Johnny said anything worse. "Upon which our economy depends."

Breck was half out of his seat with desperation. But he was out of turn and he knew it. His deputy girl looked like she just got sucker-punched by a drag queen. It was hysterical. And Matthews would have plenty of time to laugh about it later.

Matthews turned his attention to Mike Jameson. They had a deal. He voted Matthews' way, and Matthews would vote Jameson's way.

But Mike's eyes were down. His wedding ring must have become too tight in the last thirty seconds because the guy was working it around furiously. It must have been quite bothersome because he didn't second the motion.

"Sheriff told me something," Tibbs said. "Told me, before you tear down a fence you should ask yourself why it was put up in the first place."

Since he was seated right next to Jameson, Matthews leaned in for a terse whisper. "Remember what we talked about."

Jameson kept his eyes on his ring but whispered back. "I thought you said Breck was on board with all this?"

"He's a flip-flopper. Another reason we need a new sheriff. One we can trust."

But Mikey didn't buy it. Even though Matthews was inches away, staring at him, willing him to make eye contact, the guy didn't even yield a glance. Or second the motion.

Tibbs was watching. Did he hear?

"I'm gonna make a motion myself," the cowboy announced. "That we never bring this subject up again."

At that, Becca found her voice. "Second."

Tibbs, Becca, and Tya raised their hands. And so did Mike.

Matthews felt stung. Betrayed in his hour of need. His ears were ringing and his face flushed. Cannabis? Never bring it up again? The Clear Span was going up in a matter of *days*. The plan was already in motion. It was the eleventh hour. How was he going to pay for that building now? The therapeutic riding program was an absolute ploy and his bluff just got called. What about the grow field on the mountainside? What would happen once the October snows fell, with no place to transfer the delicate plants? Zorrero would not be pleased with this turn of events, that was for sure. Everything hinged on this. Here and now. What could he do without the votes?

"What's next on the ol' agenda?" Tibbs asked. He flipped through the pages of the printout to find out. "How about we move on to the budget."

That was it? Matthews was scrambling, his thoughts on a hamster wheel—around and around but going nowhere. Was it over? He scoured the audience to gauge his support. No one was clamoring for a re-vote. Not Breck or Jenny. Not Valerie or Aspen. Not Freddy's brother in the pinstripe suit, Bellevue J. Bolton.

The room was strangely silent. Did the clock on the wall run out of juice? Did the battery just die? Because the seconds hand was stuck, it wasn't moving at all.

Matthews cleared his throat. Adjusted his suit coat again.

"Okay, let's talk the budget." His lips were dry. Did Brittany forget to put out water bottles for the city council members? That was her responsibility. But not one water bottle in sight. That girl was gone. Tomorrow morning. Fired.

Matthews' eyes fell on that wretched gargoyle again—Breck.

"That big list of crimes you mentioned? You forgot to point out that the sheriff of Quandary County is under investigation for corruption by the district attorney." Matthews had lost a battle. A major battle. But there was yet a war to be won. "I cannot, in good conscience, approve additional funding of the Sheriff's Office in this context. And add to that, the city's overall budget is strained enough as it is. With the rejection of cannabis, there will be no extra funding available. In fact, . . . we shall need to discuss whether the current funds available are enough to renew the current law enforcement contract with the Sheriff's Office, period."

Tibbs was scratching his chin, his mouth half open. "If we cut Breck loose, who's gonna keep the peace?"

Matthews shrugged.

"Hire private security to patrol the streets. The hospital uses one that is very reasonable in price. We can contract with them."

At that, Breck stood up and left the room. Jenny followed.

It was just a matter of time before they left Quandary altogether. And permanently. Matthews would make sure of that.

"I'd like to make a motion if I can." Mike Jameson's wedding ring was no longer bothering him, it seemed. "I say we call up the Subway headquarters and see about getting a franchise opened up in town here. Talk about big business? A popular restaurant will be a huge source of tax revenue. What do you say?"

But no one said anything.

CHAPTER 79

Tough Love

It was past visiting hours at the hospital, but Breck went inside anyway. Melinda was behind the front desk jotting notes on a clipboard.

"Is Michelle working tonight?"

"It's her day off." Melinda gave him a pathetic poor-puppy face. "She's on a dinner date. At a proper restaurant. Candlelight. Napkins made of cloth. Not a cold cut on the menu."

Melinda. Doling out some tough love. Was she mad he never got her name right?

Breck ginned up a faux smile. "Funny."

Everyone at the hospital knew Breck and Michelle had dated. That one time. It was so ironic Mike Jameson was pushing for a Subway sandwich shop in Quandary. It would be a daily reminder if it ever got built. The site of the epic crash and burn. Breck's own private Chernobyl. Like all things evil, this all circled back to Matthews, the great budget buster.

"I know it's a little late but can I check on Danny? I'd like to see how he's doing."

Melinda frowned at the clock.

Was she really going to tell him to come back tomorrow? It was barely sundown.

He waited for the verdict but there was no way Danny was asleep. Besides, it wasn't like the hospital was overflowing with patients. It only had a half dozen rooms, and now that Aspen had checked out Danny was the only one there. Who was he going to disturb? The security guard?

Speaking of which. Looking around, Breck spotted the guy. In the waiting area watching a cooking show on the big screen. The Pioneer Woman was whipping up her famous Chicken Enchilasagna.

"Holy smokes," Breck muttered.

Griffin, his goatee, and a can of pepper spray. Keeping Quandary safe. Well, he would be if Matthews could talk the city council into terminating the Sheriff's Office contract.

"Don't slip." Melinda went back to her clipboard. "I just mopped the hallway."

Sure enough, a yellow mop bucket was parked just outside Danny's door and in the fluorescent lighting, the water streaks were easy to see.

A tap on the door frame. Breck stepped inside and Danny was there in bed, staring out the window at the forested slopes. A television was hanging on metal brackets up in the far corner. It was off. So was Danny's cell phone—there it was, lying on the nightstand. Within easy reach. Breck had tried calling several times but it kept going to voicemail.

"Your phone's off, man."

Danny's eyes were vacant and swollen and it looked like he had been crying. There was a food tray on his lap. A plate of cold vegetables and a bumpy slice of meatloaf, or something like that, concealed in congealed gravy. A little box of apple juice with a mini straw jabbed in the top.

Breck picked up the juice box. "I bet you're wishing this was a Ten Mile Milk Stout right about now."

Danny didn't look. Breck followed his gaze out the window. Pine trees. Couple clouds above the ridge. Everything was sunset orange.

"I've got some bad news," Breck said.

"I heard."

It was a small relief. Breck didn't want to be the one to tell him Freddy was dead.

Danny finally turned, his face lined with tension.

"Those *narcos* from Mexico?"

Breck nodded. "Yeah."

Danny's eyes watered. He pointed at the doorway. At Aspen's room, just across the hall.

"Is that poor girl okay?"

The pills Aspen OD'd on. Cash bought them from Freddy. Danny must have figured that out. How much did he know? How much was he involved?

"She's okay."

Danny wasn't okay—that was obvious. Breck picked up a plastic fork and prodded the meatloaf. "Want me to bring you something to eat? I can run over to the 7-Eleven. I wish the Blue Moose was open. Maybe tomorrow morning we can . . ."

But Danny was lost out the window again. They laughed, they joked, they fought, but Breck had never seen his brother cry before. Except once.

When they were in high school, the family lived in a suburb near Denver called Golden. It was tucked up near the foothills and separated from the big city by the plateaus of North Table Mountain where Breck learned to rock climb.

Danny got a job at Pizza Hut and saved every dollar until he could buy a 1965 Ford Mustang. He was so proud of that car. Every waking moment, he was in the garage pulling the engine apart and putting it back together again. Carburetor, distributor, starter. He was so good at it.

Breck never got into cars. He was into mountaineering. Hiking all the big peaks in the summer, skiing them all in the winter. He didn't know anything about socket wrenches, but Breck knew exactly how to use a carabiner.

Their mother died on the way home from King Soopers. It was Danny's seventeenth birthday and she had been buying cake mix and ice cream and candles and Danny told her not to go, he was too old for birthday celebrations. But she went.

"Well, I'm starving." Breck paused at the door. "They've got those microwave burritos we like. I'll get two. Maybe Belinda can set us up with free apple juice."

That made Danny look up. "Melinda. Chick's name is Melinda."

CHAPTER 80

Unplugged

Sure enough. A utility truck with a cherry picker bucket and a six-man crew was parked on the access road. Dismantling the cell tower.

Johnny Tibbs' gut reaction was to draw his pistol and shoot a few times in the air, but that might be misinterpreted by a judge as menacing, in legal terms. In Tibbs' mind, it was called safeguarding one's property. No worse than chasing off coyotes from a chicken pen.

What kept him from pulling the trigger was a technicality—the tower wasn't his property. The property was, sort of. It was an easement between the Tibbs Ranch and the National Forest and he leased it to the city of Quandary. It was a blurry line, and maybe Tibbs could find a lawyer who could back him up but even so, a judge might not appreciate the finer delineations of cowboy justice.

Tibbs was riding his most reliable trail horse, a sorrel with a white star on his forehead—Peacemaker. He didn't spook no matter what. Rattlesnake on the trail. Lightning bolt in the sky. Gunshot from the saddle.

The men were all wearing hardhats and harnesses and dark sunglasses. One was sitting in a fabric camp chair scrolling on an iPad. Tibbs rode right up to him.

"I always know which one's the head honcho on a road crew." Tibbs pointed at the tower. "My phone went dark, the ranch WIFI skunked out, and now I know why. You wanna tell me who authorized this?"

"Above my pay grade." The crew boss didn't even get out of his chair.

Tibbs knew the answer already. Mayor Seneca Matthews. This was punishment for the cannabis vote.

"You just unplugged this whole town, you know that?" Tibbs twisted in the saddle and pointed through the treetops. Down in the valley, cars and buildings glittered in the sunlight.

The city of Quandary relied on one cell tower. Every single person down there had the same problem now. Even Matthews at City Hall. Didn't he realize that would happen? All because the vote didn't go the way he planned. The man governed by spite.

"Not my concern."

"It will be when you ain't got a job no more."

All that talk about helping the community was bull. If Tibbs even had a sliver of doubt about that, it was gone now. Just like his interest in Matthews' therapeutic riding program. What was that guy thinking? Tearing down the cell tower was declaring war. Working together now was impossible.

Tibbs shifted his weight and Peacemaker knew what to do. The horse turned around and started heading back down the access road. But they hadn't gone far when Peacemaker's ears went up, and he stopped to listen.

Another horse whinnied. Somewhere in the forest. Not too far away.

Tibbs watched and waited and before long, several riders filed out of the trees from one of the side trails. They were all carrying rifles and revolvers like a posse chasing bandits. All were Tibbs Ranch wranglers.

"We found Laramie's horse," one said.

"Where?"

"Far end of the hogback on the old trail to Inspiration Point." The one speaking was one of Tibbs' most seasoned wranglers. But he looked nervous. "Mr. Tibbs? We heard some voices out there."

"Voices?" Tibbs frowned.

"Yes, sir. Sounded like they were down the slope quite a ways. Heard 'em clear as day but didn't understand a word. They were speaking Spanish."

CHAPTER 81

Crap Weasel

The Sheriff's office felt like a graveyard. All the empty desks were tombstones on Boot Hill, the wastebaskets tumbleweeds wedged in place by the desert wind, and Breck—last man standing in a gunfight between the good, bad and the ugly. He was the good, and Matthews was both bad and ugly.

The laptop on Jenny's desk was buried beneath a scattering of papers, pencils and some napkins with the General Merchandise and More logo. What if he had no choice? Had to let her go? A meager severance package and a glowing recommendation would be the best he could do.

"Nap time's over, I'm back." Jenny strolled through the door with a case of coconut water cartons, and a Safeway bag. She took them to the fridge and stacked them inside to chill. "And I'm throwing the Folgers away. How old is that can? Tastes like you bought it in 1980."

Breck shrugged. "I don't recollect."

"This isn't a lie detector test."

True to her word, Jenny pulled the coffee can out of the fridge and tossed it. From the Safeway bag, she put a bag of fresh coffee beans in the cabinet. Along with honey roasted almonds, Sun Chips, saltines, a jar of peanut butter, and some key lime flavor yogurt cups.

"If my paycheck is getting slashed, I'm moving in. I spend ninety percent of my time in this office anyhow. Why pay rent?"

On the way to her desk, she paused at the jail cell. Breck's mummy bag was still on the cot, wadded up in a heap.

"I feel bad even asking . . . can you run that through the wash again? Hate to say it, but Freddy was the last person to crawl inside and I bet it stinks like pepperoni and pizzle."

Breck nodded. He could do that. The way things were going, he might need to move into the office, too.

"I want to wring the mayor's neck. Is there a law against that? Or can we just take a vote? Cuz apparently right and wrong mean nothing, as long as you have the votes." The city council depressed Breck, but Jenny looked like she was ready to fight it out. "Thinks he can mess with our game?"

She threw a couple of angry air punches, then cracked into a giddy psycho chuckle.

"Did you see the look on his face when Tya and Becca voted his gun ban down? I've been giving Tya shooting lessons at the gun range on Boreal Pass Road. She can hit a Diet Coke can at fifty feet. Remember when a bear tore through the screen in her kitchen? Last Halloween?"

"I read the report. That was the weekend I spent down in the San Juans. Trying to hike the Wilson-El Diente traverse. I got snowed out and ate pizza at the Brown Dog in Telluride instead."

"Well, Sven was off in Oslo, and it freaked her out. But she's a fighter, not a whiner. Even got her concealed carry permit. That chick is a badass."

Jenny snapped her fingers, hustled over to her desk and fired up the laptop.

"Speaking of Boreal Pass. Let's buy a drone. We can fly a camera over the whole area and look for that grow field ourselves. I found some online last night. There's one that's not too expensive. The problem is, the cheapies can only stay in the air for ten minutes and then the batteries need to be recharged. So that kind of sucks."

The computer screen came up blank. Something wasn't working.

"What the frick?" She tapped the keys and wiggled the mouse. "The WIFI isn't working. Our signal's down."

Breck got up and went over to examine the router. Sure enough, the little green lights had turned red. No data.

The landline rang and Jenny grabbed it. "Sheriff's Office? . . . Hi, Johnny . . . Matthews did *what?*" She gave the router a frowny thumbs down.

Quandary didn't have a cable provider, and the phone company was way behind the times. It couldn't afford to install fiber-optic lines, so everyone relied on hotspot routers pinging off the cell tower.

"What a crap weasel." She held her hand over the mouthpiece to whisper to Breck. "Get this. Matthews is ripping the cell tower down."

Another day, another fiasco. Breck went over to the kitchenette and opened the cabinet to see what kind of coffee Jenny had bought. It was Starbucks Breakfast Blend. Well, well, well. The day was looking brighter already.

"Can you saddle up a couple of extra horses and lead us up there? Today, right now . . . No, this isn't a *date*." She pointed a finger to her temple like a fake pistol and pretended to blow her brains out. "We'll be there in half an hour."

She hung up and pulled out her real pistol to check the loads.

"What was that?" Breck asked.

"Johnny Tibbs said his wranglers found the horse carcass. The one the cartel shot. It's in the backcountry on some old trail no one ever uses. And they heard people talking . . . in Spanish."

Breck put the Breakfast Blend back on the shelf and headed for the tac closet. The grow field. They found it. One thing was for sure. He certainly wasn't going up there without a long gun and a sniper scope. The cartel had shot that kid's horse with an AR-15.

"This all ends today." Breck slung a Colt M4 Carbine rifle over his shoulder, then paused. "Wait a minute. Did Johnny Tibbs ask you out on a date? Maybe I better stay here, I don't want to be a third wheel."

The phone jingled again, and Jenny picked it up.

"It's not a date and we're not going to kiss, so get that out of your mind." Then her face scrunched up. "District Attorney Brownton . . . I apologize. This is Deputy O'Hara, please hold for Sheriff Dyer."

She pressed the hold button and then keeled over, holding her hands over her mouth. A silent scream.

Breck went to his desk, cleared his throat, picked up the phone and pressed line one.

"Sheriff Dyer, how can I help you?"

CHAPTER 82

Death Shine

By the time Breck and Jenny arrived at the ranch, Tibbs already had three horses saddled.

"I thought it was just you and me, Jennifer."

Jenny pulled a blue rain jacket out of the Jeep and looked up at the sky.

"Get over yourself," she said. "Do I need this? Is it going to rain?"

"Probably."

Carrying his rifle and a Nalgene water bottle, Breck gave the hitching post a wide berth. One horse swished its tail. He nearly dropped both the gun and the bottle hustling out of kicking range. Tibbs watched it all with a slow grin.

"The look on your face. They call that a death shine."

"What are you talking about?"

"There you go, that's the right attitude, amigo. Fake it till you make it." Tibbs was decked out in full cowboy gear. Chaps, vest, spurs. Bending beside a dark brown horse, he picked up each hoof and brushed the sole with his fingers. "This one's yours, sheriff. Solid. Gentle. Rides as smooth as glass."

The animal had one brown eye and one blue eye. Much like the devil, Breck imagined. He reached out and tried to pet its nose but the horse pulled back, ears going flat.

"What's his name?"

"Ain't got one. He just got off the trailer. I bought him at a wild horse auction up in Cheyenne."

Breck looked confused.

"Then how do you know he's solid or gentle, or how he rides at all?"

Jenny snorted. "He's messing with you, Breck."

She went over to a tall narrow appaloosa. Standing next to it, the top of Jenny's head was even with the saddle. Tibbs moseyed over to give her a boost, but Jenny handed him her shotgun instead. "Hold that for a second."

She led the horse next to the corral fence, climbed it like a ladder, and slid onto its back without any problem.

"This one can look after herself. An attractive trait." Then Tibbs glanced at Breck. "What about you? Got any attractive traits?"

Breck wasn't in the mood to be the butt of any jokes. The prospect of being thrown or struck or stomped or bit to the bone was too preoccupying. He had never actually ridden a horse, but he'd seen enough Clint Eastwood movies to know what to do. Hopefully.

Gripping the horn and the pommel, Breck stuck a toe in the stirrup, bounced *one-two-three*, and clawed his way up like a monkey going after a banana. The horse's giant head swung around. That steel blue eye! Boring a hole in his soul like the Eye of Sauron.

"You really being investigated for corruption?"

Tibbs unlooped the bridle reins from the hitching post and handed them up. As soon as he was loose from the post, the horse whirled around and tap-danced in the dirt. Breck strangled the saddle horn with both hands but after a few jostles and twists, the horse settled down again.

"Holy hell." Breck could feel sweat beading up on his forehead. It wasn't even stress sweat. It was terror sweat.

Coming close again, Tibbs grabbed his foot and jerked it out of the stirrup, throwing him off balance. Breck seized the saddle horn again.

"What are you doing?"

"Gotta adjust the stirrups. They're too high. You're going to have sore knees if I don't drop 'em down a notch or two."

"How about, warn me next time?"

After Tibbs fixed the length, he walked around to make sure both sides were even. After dropping the other stirrup to match, and clipping it in place, he smiled pleasantly.

"Warning ya."

He tugged on the cinch strap, causing the whole saddle to rock.

Tibbs was chuckling under his breath. He was doing all this on purpose. Probably chose the worst horse out of the whole herd, too. Maybe they should have just called in the feds. Breck could be sitting at his desk, back at the office, sipping Breakfast Blend out of a *Ski Quandary!* mug. Zero saddle time. Maybe steal a bag of Sun Chips from Jenny's snack stash.

From a vest pocket, Tibbs produced his tin of Copenhagen and popped the lid long enough to pull a pinch of tobacco.

Jenny was riding around the dirt parking lot, starting and stopping and getting used to how the horse handled. She looked like a seasoned equestrian. Maybe she was. Breck had no idea. Either way, seeing how easy she made it look made him feel like a complete hack.

"Good boy. I bet you're thirsty." She walked her horse over to a big aluminum water tank. The appaloosa lowered his head and drank.

Breck gave Tibbs a bleak look.

"Matthews is sicking the DA on me."

"He ain't got much use for you, does he?"

"Not really."

"Well, he ain't got much use for me anymore, either."

Tibbs started checking over his firearms. A long leather rifle scabbard was tied to the side of his saddle, with a Winchester tucked inside. He also had a leather holster on his hip with a nickel-plated .45 revolver, laser-etched with floral patterns. He looked every inch the Man with No Name, clicking open the chambers and peering down the sights.

Breck had his assault rifle and .44 Special handgun, but he didn't want to let go of the saddle horn just to show off for the Second Amendment poster boy. His main goal was not to fall off and it took every ounce of concentration not to.

A squirt of tobacco juice shot from the corner of Tibbs' mouth.

"You sure you don't want none of my boys to come along?"

"No, I don't want to put anyone in the line of fire. In fact, once we get up there, I'll need you to stay back with the horses."

"Alright. But if things go south, just give me a holler."

Tibbs spun his pistol around by the trigger guard like a trick shooter. Jenny's appaloosa raised his head to watch the shiny silver metal spin in the sunlight. Water dripped from his mouth and splattered in the dirt.

But Jenny didn't look impressed with his gunplay. She looked impatient.

"What's the hold-up? Let's go."

"The lady says it's time, it's time." Tibbs holstered his pistol, mounted Peacemaker and swung around next to Breck. He lowered his voice for a moment. "Whatever's going on, I can tell you one thing—Matthews don't play fair."

"Hey, Johnny. How's your date going so far?" Jenny called.

"Terrible. He ain't as pretty as you are. And only half as fun to talk to."

Clucking his tongue, Tibbs angled Peacemaker towards the water tank. Breck's blue-eyed devil horse immediately fell in line, nose to tail. Breck hadn't even tapped his heels. The beast didn't care what he did, obviously. It was a sour trail horse, and it was going to do what it was going to do.

Breck tried some deep breathing exercises. It was going to be a long afternoon.

CHAPTER 83

Topo Chico

There was some verse from the Holy Bible about how God made man a little lower than the angels. For some reason, it stuck in El Sangrador's mind all these years. He first heard it when he was a youngster, during mass. A priest read it aloud, and as a child, it had captured his imagination. What was he, six years old? Holding his arms up like angel wings, he darted in and out of the tiny shack his family lived in. It was a hovel, dirty and full of clutter. His father built it with his own hands out of pallet wood, pieces of plywood and planks. White butcher paper was stapled over the walls to keep the hot winds from whistling through the cracks. And it kept the sand from blowing in, too.

"Topo Chico! Come inside!" his mother called. "Even angels get too hot to fly."

She was always worried he would overheat. Topo Chico meant *little mole*. It was his nickname, and it was also the name of the gently rounded mountain that rose up over Escobedo, right above their neighborhood.

Escobedo was a big city with much poverty, on the north side of Monterrey. Street after street, in every direction, many people lived in hand-built shanties like El Sangrador's family lived in.

But as a boy, his eyes were drawn to the heights. What it would be like to fly to the top of the mountain? To feel the air beneath his outstretched arms? To soar through the blue sky and the white clouds and see the whole world from on high? Like an angel.

Perched on top of Inspiration Point, the tall granite outcrop above the grow field, El Sangrador had just such a view. He could see a great distance, over the mountain ridges and snowy peaks. The round horizon encircled him. Boreal Pass Road looked like a winding brown snake from where he was. He could even see the little town of Quandary, down in the valley at the base of the slopes.

There were no hovels in Quandary. Everyone lived in condos and fancy homes with hot tubs and wooden decks with lawn chairs where they could sip craft beer with colorful labels and funny names and they all drove around in SUVs with big tires, tires that cost more money than El Sangrador's father made in a year working in the hot dusty quarries near Escobedo.

But that was another life, wasn't it? El Sangrador had risen like an angel through the ranks of Los Equis. He was no longer a poor child running around a sandy shanty while his mother boiled pinto beans on an old Coleman propane camp stove. Now, he was the one who got to drive around in a fancy SUV with thousand-dollar tires. And a craft beer with a funny label sounded pretty good at the moment. He would get one next time he drove to town.

The laborers were harvesting the pizza man's plants. Bathed in afternoon rains and warmed in the healthy sunshine, they had grown tall enough that they were ready to be cut, dried and baled.

The box of seeds had been planted and was already sprouting. Row after row of sprouts.

The blue plastic tarp was easy to spot from El Sangrador's rocky perch. Zorrero was in there, lying on a cot. He had been in a funk ever since they had to ditch the Raptor trailer and the expensive Ford F350 pickup truck. Now, instead of sleeping comfortably in the RV and eating meals at the little table inside, he had to sleep beneath the leaky tarp again. On those stiff folding cots.

Even from up on Inspiration Point, El Sangrador could see the glitter of Jack Daniels bottles. Zorrero had consumed most of them all by himself, but the blood-letter managed to sneak a couple up to Inspiration Point, for himself. It was better than nothing, and the days could get long sitting on top of the outcrop. The old folks had stocked the RV with a surprising amount of liquor. They must have been full-time drunks.

El Sangrador was a little drunk himself. On this lonesome rocky perch. With only the clouds for company.

But it was a worthy place. A watchtower. Not only did it provide a good vantage of the laborers, where he could keep an eye on them, but he could watch the skies for search planes, and the horse trails on the ridge for intruders. And sure enough, El Sangrador spotted three horses coming up the trail at that very moment.

He swished a Jack Daniels bottle around and took a quick sip before he trained his rifle on the horses.

Through the sniper scope, he could easily see who the riders were. The sheriff, his redheaded deputy, and the cowboy who ran the dude ranch. Only three of them? He aimed the scope up and down the trail but that was it. There was no one else. No horde of police, no SWAT team or *federales*.

How foolish.

Other cartel hitmen liked to take out the most dangerous enemy first if there was only time for one clean shot. It was a sound strategy, for it made good sense. In this case, it was the sheriff. One shot to the head and the others would rush off in terror and confusion. And there would only be time for one shot, at this distance, with his targets riding horses. As soon as he pulled the trigger, the horses would surely spook and he would not get an opportunity to shoot the others as easily.

But El Sangrador had noticed something, over the years. When the strongest was killed, other lieutenants would be emboldened to seek glory for themselves. They would rise up, with gusto. But when the weakest was shot, especially a child or an old person or a woman, it demoralized the strong men. For it robbed the protectors of that which they sought to protect.

So the blood-letter aimed at the redheaded deputy and pulled the trigger.

Sure enough, the force of the impact knocked her out of the saddle and spooked her horse, which in turn caused the other horses to lunge and caper about.

There would not be much time now. The two men would soon vanish in the leafy forest. El Sangrador knew he had to get off the granite outcrop and stalk them in the trees. While the outcrop was a good sniper position, it was also a bad place to get trapped. There was only one way up and one way down. He needed to get down right away, before he got pinned, and keep the advantage.

Taking another quick swig of bad whiskey, the blood-letter dashed across the gritty rocks. His bad shin gave out in a blast of white hot pain. In the same spot where he got boogered in the ladder, hanging heat lamps at the A-frame cabin.

Wheeling his arms, the blood-letter went over the edge. He tumbled through the air. His gun went flying and all he saw was a whirling blur of green trees and blue sky and then he hit the ground.

CHAPTER 84

Lying in the Kinnikinnick

One moment they were walking their horses along the quiet trail—then suddenly Jenny's whole body flew backward like a leaf swept by the wind. A loud gunshot thundered at the moment, and all three horses jumped. Even Johnny Tibbs' gelding, Peacemaker.

"Jenny!" Breck felt his blood turn to ice.

Tibbs had been jabbering the whole ride, ever since they left the ranch. He was non-stop chatter. Self-hype. Self-congratulations. He was pouring it on thick, trying to impress Jenny any which way he could. Even when praising his horse for being unflappable, Tibbs was actually praising himself. What a great job he did training Peacemaker. Not just anyone can train a horse right. Some horses blow up when they see a plastic grocery bag. Some horses shy when you snap your gum. Some horses refuse to cross a creek or step over a lead line. Not Peacemaker. Not Johnny Tibbs' personally trained horse.

But Peacemaker bolted like a rabbit. Seeing a rider rocket out of the saddle was a brand-new experience. He hadn't been trained for that.

Not to be outdone, Breck's blue-eyed devil horse bolted off the trail, right between two aspens. One of Breck's knees knocked a tree trunk and the next thing he knew he was lying in the kinnikinnick.

Rolling over, he looked back. Tibbs was still in the saddle, to his credit, but Peacemaker was not having any of it. He was heading straight back to the barn. Breck could hear Tibbs' shouting:

whoa, whoa, whoa! The sound of hoofbeats faded and he was gone.

Breck jumped up and ran towards Jenny but she was lying in the open and there was a shooter waiting for him to come back into sight. He paused and looked around wildly.

"Screw it." Breck double checked his vest was in place and raced over to her anyhow. He cringed, expecting another gunshot at any moment.

Jenny was on her back staring at the sky. Mouth working, gasping. Tac vest shredded. The round had hit her square in the chest. But it hadn't gone through.

"It's okay, you're okay." He grabbed her vest with both hands and dragged her like a rag doll. She was much lighter than he was expecting. Or his adrenaline was pumping too hard to care. He didn't stop until they were in a thick stand of pine.

"Breck . . ." she gasped.

"Just breathe."

His rifle was gone. Where was it? Breck looked towards the aspen trees. There—in the kinnikinnick. That devil horse was long gone, and so was Jenny's Appaloosa. Everything was silent. The birds weren't chirping anymore. The squirrels had cut their chatter. It felt like the forest itself was holding its breath.

"Breck . . ."

Where was the shooter? He looked around and spotted a rocky pinnacle through the treetops. That must be Inspiration Point. And that was where the shooter was.

Jenny gripped him by the sleeve.

Feeling her hand, Breck snapped his attention back to her. How bad was she? He leaned close and checked her over again, closer this time. She was scraped up from hitting the dirt, covered in pine needles from being dragged, but there was no bleeding. He cradled her head in his hands, checking to see if she banged it when she hit the ground. She flinched. Her hair was full of gravel, but no blood. Maybe a concussion. She needed to see a doctor. An MRI. She needed to be off this mountain somewhere safe.

"You've been shot but it didn't penetrate your vest. It knocked the wind out of you. Relax and breathe, okay?"

"Hurts . . . to . . . breathe."

"I know."

It was obvious she was in serious pain. Not only had she been shot in the chest with a high caliber weapon, but she had also been thrown from a horse onto a rocky trail. It had been a hard landing. She was lucky she didn't break her neck.

Breck looked up the trail again, at the rocky pinnacle. It was the obvious sniper nest. No movement. Was it the cartel *sicario* with the silver sunglasses? Of course, it was. It had to be.

"Shooter's up on that bluff."

Jenny tried to sit up but couldn't. She gave him a curt nod. "Go . . ."

Breck frowned.

"I'm not gonna *leave* you."

She released her grip on his forearm and pushed it away.

"Go . . . dammit."

Breck looked back down the ridge, the direction of the ranch. Where was Tibbs? Peacemaker had been running full blast. How far was that thing going to go before Tibbs got him under control? After all that talk about a bombproof horse.

Then he saw the man, still in the saddle, off the trail and angling back through the trees. His cowboy hat was gone and his face was scratched and bleeding. He must have gone for a wild ride through a blue spruce or two. No hat? It was strange to see Johnny Tibbs without it. Like he was missing an arm or a leg or something.

Breck waved to flag him over.

"Johnny's coming. He's going to stay here with you." Breck drew his .44 Special. "I'm going hunting."

"Where's . . . rifle?" Jenny was still gasping her words. A tear leaked across her face.

Breck stroked her hair.

"It's over there, where I fell. Don't worry, I'm not going anywhere without it."

She gave him a strained smile.

"Go get that freak."

CHAPTER 85

Ángel

Voices shouting. Spanish words and phrases. It was all coming from downslope, somewhere below Inspiration Point.

Breck paused and spotted some movement through the trees. Frantic running, back and forth. He had finally found the grow field, but he wasn't going down there. Not yet. He kept heading for the rocky pinnacle—Inspiration Point. He had to get up there. It was tall, maybe seventy-five or a hundred feet. Nothing but a sheer cliff. How did the shooter get on top? There had to be a way to climb up, an easier angle, probably on the far side.

But Breck didn't need to find it.

Twisted among the stones at the foot of the bluff was El Sangrador.

Breck approached slowly, rifle trained on his skull. Blood was everywhere. The silver aviator sunglasses were lying there, too, shattered. The AR-15 was nowhere to be seen, and neither was the Colt .45 with the pearl grips. Both weapons were probably nearby, in the trees or brush or boulders.

"Ángel . . ."

"No," Breck replied. "I'm not an angel."

He glanced up the cliff face. What happened? The *sicario* obviously fell. He must have slipped trying to get down.

"Next time take the stairs, amigo."

Quaking, El Sangrador raised his hand to his chest and reached inside his shirt. He took out a gold necklace and gripped it tight.

"¡Oh! Malverde milagroso . . . concédeme este favor . . ."

Then his grip waned, eyes went unfocused, and he slipped away.

Breck lowered his gun and wiped the sweat from his face. It was like a big weight had just lifted off his shoulders. But the danger wasn't over yet. There was much more to do. The cartel commander was still around somewhere, probably right down the slope. Not to mention the field workers. They could all be dangerous. They could all have guns. He could be walking into a haze of gunfire.

"Get a grip."

He took a couple of deep breaths. Checked the magazine on the Colt M4 Carbine. It had a single fire and an automatic mode, and he almost flipped it onto auto but until he understood the situation better, he didn't want to get trigger happy. In the heat of the moment, it would be easy to shoot first and ask questions later. But that wasn't how he operated.

"Alright, here we go."

Breck moved downhill, in and out among the pine and fir. Every few steps he paused to survey the area. There was no way they didn't hear the gunshot, the AR-15. It might as well have been an alarm bell. They all knew he was coming at this point. They had to.

But the cartel workers must certainly be expecting a full-scale raid. How would they react once they saw it was only one guy? Breck had to make the most of their assumptions. He cautiously approached the tree line and peered across the grow field. He spotted a group of people huddled around a blue tarp. Voices raised, nervous arguing. They were pleading with someone.

Breck wished he'd paid more attention in high school Spanish class.

"Sheriff's Office! Everyone lie down on the ground!"

He might as well have tossed a grenade. The workers scattered. But they weren't armed—that was good news. They were just average people, he could tell. Not an army of battle-seasoned commandos. So Breck risked it. He charged through the rows of cannabis plants, circling towards the blue tarp.

"Sheriff's Office!"

A woman screamed, desperate for help. Breck got closer to the tarp and saw her. A man was behind her, holding her by the hair. It was the other cartel man, the one with the trimmed mustache and slicked-down hair. Last time Breck was this close, it was Freddy's kitchen. But the fellow who snuck up and knocked his lights out was busy at the moment, signing up for the Lake of Fire jacuzzi package, so Breck wasn't worried about a repeat head-thunk.

"You are trespassing, sheriff. Once again. This is becoming a bad habit."

"Cut her loose and we'll talk."

"I don't think I will do that."

Zorrero smiled.

But it was not an easy smile. Not like in Freddy's kitchen. Back then, he had the advantage and he knew it. But now? Breck took a step closer. Zorrero drew his Glock and put it to the woman's head. She began weeping and quivering.

"Mi niños! Quiero verlos, por favor!"

"Sheriff, you pretty sneaky," Zorrero said. "You remember what happened last time? Better watch your back."

"You talking about your gunman? He won't be joining us."

Zorrero's smile faltered.

"Did you get Sangre? You arrest him?"

"Something like that."

Zorrero clucked his tongue like he was scolding a child. "I find that hard to believe."

He looked past Breck, searching the trees, then glanced up at Inspiration Point.

The rest of the field workers had vanished in the forest. Except for one young man, who was hovering nearby, just past the blue tarp, staring at the woman. His eyes were full of angst. Breck could tell he was worried about her. These poor people were not there by choice, were they?

"Let her go, and we can talk. What's your name?"

Zorrero ignored Breck and called for the blood-letter as loud as he could. "Sangre!"

"You'll have to yell louder than that."

"Did you kill him?"

"I didn't have to." Breck took a step closer. "Now put the gun down. This is all over, and you know it."

Zorrero shook his head, his face turning hard. But he lowered the Glock. "You a lawman. Don't shoot me in the back, lawman."

Then he whacked the woman with the butt of the pistol, pushed her towards Breck, and ran down the access trail.

CHAPTER 86

Bad Feeling

The señora collapsed. Her husband rushed forward, crying out hysterically. Breck lowered his rifle and knelt by them. She was conscious. A little lump on her scalp, but nothing too serious. Zorrero had hit her as a distraction, just to slow Breck down. And of course, it worked.

"She's going to have a headache, but that's all." He squeezed the man on the shoulder. "I'll be back as soon as I can."

It was hard to tell if the couple understood English, but Breck figured they understood enough of what he said. Now if they would be there when he got back was anybody's guess.

Looking down the mountainside, he spotted Zorrero jogging down the trail. He had a good head start. And he was right about one thing—Breck wasn't going to shoot him in the back. The cartel commander had even dumped the Glock. It was lying on the trail in plain sight. Now he wasn't armed.

"Dude is playing my conscience against me."

Breck slung the rifle over his shoulder and began running down the trail, too. The rifle was heavy and slowed him down a bit, but there was nothing he could do about it.

Where did this trail wind up? Breck could guess. It was going to pop out on Boreal Pass Road. If the cell tower hadn't been disconnected, he could try and get a text out. Ask for some help. But even if he did, who was going to come? Chief Waters in Alma? The State Patrol in Frisco certainly would—if he could get through. But the tower wasn't operational. Although, tower or no tower, even on a clear day, Breck never got a reliable signal in the backcountry. It was a moot point, of course. No one was getting cell service. Not the good guys or the bad guys.

On top of everything, Breck's knee was sore. From that stupid horse raking him against the aspen tree. Between his knee and the M4 Carbine, he was having trouble catching up. But Zorrero was having trouble, too. He wasn't used to living at high altitude, let alone trail running at high altitude. He was only a few hundred feet ahead but had to stop and catch his breath. Breck could hear him wheezing.

"Where are you going?" Breck called. "You're busted, pal. It's over. Let's just wrap this thing up."

"You kill *mi hermano?*" he called back. "I'm gonna kill yours."

Breck sprinted towards him, but Zorrero leaped off the trail and cut through the trees, slipping and sliding into a steep gully. Two vehicles were parked down there. Breck recognized them both. The black Range Rover and the stock boy's green Toyota pickup.

Zorrero pointed a key fob at the Range Rover. The tail lights flashed and the engine auto-started. He yanked open the driver's door, disappeared for a second, and came back out with another Glock. Breck ducked behind a tree, but Zorrero wasn't aiming at him. He shot out the tires on the Toyota, pumped a couple of rounds into the radiator, jumped into the SUV and sped off down the gully.

Sliding the rest of the way down the steep slope, Breck leveled his rifle, hoping to shoot out his tires, but it was too late. Zorrero got out on Boreal Pass Road and raced away.

Limping the rest of the distance, Breck made it to the dirt road and looked around. There was a cloud of dust hanging in the air. He coughed a couple of times and sat down on a fallen log to massage his knee. The Tibbs Ranch was straight down the road about a half hour drive. Zorrero would be driving right by it on his way into Quandary. But it would take ten times as long to walk. There was no way Breck could catch up on foot.

He looked up and down the road, hoping to spot another vehicle. But there wasn't one. Boreal Pass Road was pretty much untraveled. Except for a little weekend traffic. Hikers and hunters. But it wasn't a weekend.

"Breck!" It was Jenny. She was on the appaloosa. "Did you take out the trash?"

Tibbs emerged from the trees, too, trailing Breck's devil horse by the reins. He still looked weird without his cowboy hat.

"No, he got away. He's in that Range Rover. It was hidden in the gully."

"We're not too far behind—if we run these horses." Tibbs rode close and handed Breck the devil horse's reins. "Saddle up."

The Jeep was parked at the Tibbs Ranch corral. If they could get there quick, they still had a chance. But Breck dreaded the thought of riding a horse at a walk, let alone at a full-blown run. Why didn't they make seatbelts for saddles?

"What's the rush, really?" Jenny asked. She was sitting awkwardly, hunched to ease her chest pain. "He's heading straight to Mexico. We might as well call the staties and let them pop his tires on the interstate. Call it a day and go get some dinner."

But Breck had a bad feeling.

"He's not going to Mexico. He's going after Danny. He told me that to my face."

"The hospital?" Jenny coughed and winced and closed her eyes for a second. "So what are we waiting for?"

"As soon as we reach the ranch, we need to call Michelle from a landline. They need to lock the whole building down." Breck took a step closer to his horse. Its ears went flat. "All they have is that security guy, Griffin. And all that dude carries is pepper spray."

Was Zorrero really going after Danny? Or was it just a threat to mess with his mind? Breck didn't know for certain. There was just no time to waste thinking about it. Riding horses was his own private hell, but what choice did he have? He grabbed the stirrup and clawed his way on board, clinging to the saddle horn like Danny's life depended on it.

Four-Legged
Fright Fest

Breck swallowed. His horse's eyes were half-closed like he was napping. But he wasn't, was he?

"Pat him on the neck, tell him he's a good boy." Tibbs gave him a wink, but it wasn't a friendly wink. "Then snap those reins, kick him in the side, and hang on for the ride."

"You sure?" Breck asked. That didn't sound like good advice.

He looked around one last time. But Boreal Pass Road was still empty. Surely an ATV would be racing by any moment. Breck squinted, listening, hoping for the rumble of an engine, any vehicle at all, coming down the road. But the only sound was the afternoon breeze.

"No more chit chat," Jenny said. "We've gotta roll."

"Jennifer says we roll, we roll."

With a tap of his boot heels, Johnny Tibbs put Peacemaker into an instantaneous comet launch. Jenny's appaloosa shot after him, and the blue-eyed devil horse didn't want to be left behind. He bolted after them. Breck just dropped the reins and grabbed the saddle horn. Why even pretend he was a rider? He was baggage. A barnacle. A tick on a dog. But it didn't matter at this point. What mattered was getting to the Tibbs Ranch as quick as possible.

Racing along Boreal Pass Road on a wild horse was a four-legged fright fest. Breck felt his stomach flutter away. He was terrified his feet were going to slide out of the stirrups, they were flopping around so bad. Tibbs had set them too long—probably on purpose.

Breck's knuckles were white he was holding on so tight.

Danny's life was in danger. His own brother, so deep in the illegal drug trade that a Mexican drug cartel commander announced he was going to murder him—how did this happen? How did everything get so far off the rails? It was strange. How things turned out. How the world worked. Weren't they just kids a couple of seconds ago? Sitting at a picnic table, eating cold fried chicken and potato salad and pretzels, stomping empty cans of Coke into flat metal discs and throwing them like Frisbees at the chipmunks while their mother warned them not to litter or she would cancel their family hike to see Buffalo Bill's grave, which was right up a winding mountain road on a hilltop above Golden, hardly ten minutes from their home, but it felt like another world, a gateway into another era, the Old West, and Breck was Captain Woodrow Call and Danny was Captain Augustus McCrae, former Texas Rangers turned cattle drovers taking a herd north to Montana, and Blue Duck was out there in the deep dark pine, hiding and watching their every move, and so was Kicking Wolf, hoping to steal their horses, and there was never a question who the bad guys were.

Tibbs' pace was relentless. They kept riding and riding. The road curved left and right and up and down then started losing elevation and winding into the lower forest. Finally, they crossed a short wooden bridge over a narrow trickling creek, where the dirt road turned into pavement. There it was. The Tibbs Ranch. They rode past the A-frames and turned at the wagon wheel sign, and trotted straight to the corral.

Johnny Tibbs jumped down and shouted at a couple of wranglers to help with the horses. He led Breck and Jenny inside the main lodge, reached over the welcome desk in the lobby and picked up a telephone.

"There you go, partner."

Breck dialed the hospital. *Come on, Michelle. Pick up.* But she didn't.

"No one is answering."

Several staff members, all college kids in their twenties, were standing in the lobby, watching, but said nothing. They could tell something serious was going on.

"We gotta go." Jenny pointed at Tibbs. "Keep calling until you get through."

"Yes, ma'am."

Breck and Jenny ran back outside and jumped in the Jeep. The Corvette engine under the hood roared to life. Breck threw it into gear, kicking up dirt. Jenny gripped the dashboard handle with both hands, eyes wide. Breck smiled grimly. It might have a broken gas gauge. The soft top might leak and the headlights were dull. But this was an animal he could control. This was his kind of steed.

Unwinding the CB from the gear shift, Breck handed it to Jenny.

"Try channel nine. Maybe it's a busy day and all the phone lines are lit up."

"Okay." Jenny let go of the dash handle with one hand and grabbed the mic. "This is Deputy O'Hara calling Quandary Medical Center, come in. Come in, please, this is an emergency."

Static.

Breck felt a sick twitch in his gut.

"Quandary Medical, come in please." Jenny adjusted the squelch. "Do we even have a signal?"

They had a signal. Breck knew it. "Try the State Patrol. Maybe they've got a unit near the hospital and can get there first."

He downshifted and braked as they exited the forest, popping out onto Main Street right next to the brewery. Danny's brewery. Silent as a tomb. The whole Jeep rocked on its chassis with the centrifugal force of the turn and Breck gunned it, tires squealing.

"Oh, shiza!" Jenny dropped the mic and seized the handlebar with both hands again. "Don't kill us, Breck! That's your only job at the moment."

CHAPTER 88

Niña Tonta

The phone rang again. And again.

Covering her mouth with both hands, Michelle tried not to make any noise. She had never crawled beneath the reception desk before. It was a mess under there. Cables and cords, pieces of popcorn, hair bands, rubber bands. An old ballpoint pen.

It was hard to control her breathing. It was coming in huffs and her pulse was pounding in her temples. From where she was hiding, she could see the can of pepper spray. It had rolled near the reception desk. There were beads of blood on it. Griffin's blood.

The phone rang some more. It wouldn't stop. Somebody was trying to get through but Michelle didn't dare go for it. The man with the gun. Where was he? Did he leave? From beneath the desk, she couldn't see much. Maybe it was worth sneaking a peek. Grab the phone. Call for help.

The ringing continued. Until someone picked it up and yanked the phone line out. Her heart raced. Hands trembling, she pressed them tighter over her mouth.

Footsteps. Soft, measured.

Then shoes. He found her.

"You hiding from me?" Zorrero grabbed a handful of Michelle's hair and dragged her out.

She began hyperventilating. It was hard not to. The man was not much taller than she was, but his grip was vicious. He shook her and she collapsed on her knees and he began dragging her into the hallway. Right past Griffin, the security guard, who was sprawled near the lounge couch. He had been shot several times in the chest and once in the cheek. Blood was all over his shirt and face and all over the floor. She knew he was dead. Michelle closed her eyes. She couldn't look.

"Let's go find him." Zorrero gave her another shake. "Where is he?"

"Wh . . . who?"

"The brother. The sheriff's brother. I know he is here."

The hospital was small. There were only a half dozen rooms. Three rooms on each side of the hall. But there were also other doors. Doors that led to the operating rooms, prep rooms, pre-op and post-op, storage and staff lounge. He clearly had no idea which went where, and Michelle had no intention of giving him good directions. What could she say?

Zorrero's grip got tighter, pulling the roots. She yelped and gasped. "Ow, ow, please, don't!"

This man was a killer. He had an aura of destruction about him. She could sense it. She risked a glance up at his face. He was pleased that she was begging. Fearful. It was an ugly look.

"He . . . he checked out. He went home. You just missed him."

Zorrero's smug face turned dark.

"That sounds like a lie. You don't want to lie to me, *niña tonta*."

He dragged her through the hallway, studying all the doors, and randomly chose the room where Aspen Matthews had been staying.

"Danny boy. You in here, Danny boy?"

It was empty.

Michelle hoped Dr. Heller and Melinda heard the shots. Where were they? In the lab? Surely they heard the gunfire. *Please don't come out in the hallway*, she thought. She wanted to yell at the top of her lungs. *Call Breck!* But she didn't. There were phones in the lab. If they were in there, they would have called for help by now.

"I see you!" Zorrero laughed and pointed his Glock across the hall at Danny's room.

The door slammed. Danny had peered out of his room. Why did he do that?

"Oh, *niña tonta*." He looked down at Michelle, his face hard again. "You told me a white lie. I know that for certain now."

He put the barrel of the handgun against her forehead. It was cold and hard and he pressed it into her flesh.

"Aw, I guess I have told white lies myself, a time or two."

He dropped her. Michelle collapsed. She laid very still on the cold tile, unmoving. She heard his footsteps as he went to Danny's door and rattled the knob. But it was blocked. Danny had blockaded the door.

Ramming his shoulder into it, Zorrero got the door open a couple of inches. There was a scraping sound as he pressed harder. Michelle knew that sound. It was one of the corner chairs. How many times had she moved those chairs to pick up a dropped syringe that rolled back there on accident? Or a cup of Jell-O that an angry patient threw.

"Open up, Danny boy. I just want to say hello." Then Zorrero turned and winked at Michelle, and whispered. "A little white lie."

Then he rammed the door again and again until he could slip inside. Michelle jumped to her feet, looking up and down the hallway, feeling her head spin with fear and adrenaline and a frantic desire to run away. But she tried to focus. The phone at the reception desk. No, it was broken. The cord had been torn out.

She heard Zorrero pound the butt of his gun on the bathroom door in Danny's room.

"Danny boy. You taking a big shit in there? Better unlock this door, Danny boy."

There was a phone in the lab, but that was all the way up the hallway. There was one in the staff lounge, too. There wasn't much time! But both rooms were so far away and Michelle would have to run past Danny's doorway. What if the gunman saw her rush by? She had to try.

Michelle tensed up, ready to run.

Until she heard the Glock firing inside Danny's room. Loud, percussive. *Bang. Bang. Bang. Bang.* Michelle covered her ears.

The fire alarm. The little red pull handle was right there on the wall. Michelle grabbed it and pulled. Instantly the hallway began flashing with a white strobe light and the fire alarm went off. It was as loud as the gunshots.

That was the best she could do. She definitely needed to run now. So she did. The closest escape was the lobby door. But she only got a few steps before she heard another gunshot and felt a fierce punch in her back, like getting hit with a baseball bat.

Michelle crashed on the floor. Right next to Griffin. His face was white and blue. The blood had stopped pumping beneath his skin. Was that how she was going to look? She could feel her back was wet, and it felt hot and cold and numb and painful, all at once. She had been shot. *Play dead. Play dead. Don't move. Lay still.*

"Bad, *niña tonta.*" Zorrero had to shout to be heard.

She could feel his presence. He was standing directly over her. He even tapped her with the tip of his shoe. Was this it?

She felt the air change. He was gone. She opened her eyes. From where she was laying, she watched as a vehicle pulled up in front of the hospital. She could see it through the lobby windows. It was the Jeep. It was Breck.

CHAPTER 89

Swiss Cheese

The automatic doors swished open. Breck had his Rossi .44 Special revolver drawn, finger on the trigger guard. People were outside in the parking lot hiding behind cars fumbling with cell phones that didn't work, but inside the lobby was empty. No one was at the reception desk. Strobe lights pulsed. Fire alarm blared.

Two bodies were on the floor by the desk. Near the entrance to the hallway. Griffin. And Michelle! His first impulse was to rush right over. But what if Zorrero hadn't left the scene? Maybe he was right there, somewhere, waiting. Hiding by the vending machine? Or inside the janitor's closet? Maybe the bodies were bait.

Breck grit his teeth. He hated seeing Michelle like this. Quickly, he checked behind the desk and the couch. The nook by the vending machine and the restrooms were clear. The hallway was empty, too. It only took a matter of seconds to clear the area but it felt like forever because every second wasted was critical to her survival.

He knelt by Michelle. The security guard was lifeless but she was still awake.

"Breck?" She rolled on her side. Looked at him with those dark brown eyes, normally so unreadable. He could read them now.

"I'm here, Michelle. I've got you."

Her back was slick with blood. It was coming from a bullet hole. The fabric of her shirt was soaked.

"I tried, Breck. I tried . . . Danny? Is he . . .?"

"Don't move. We need to stop the bleeding."

"Dr. Heller. He's in the lab, he can help. Don't waste time on me. Go check on Danny." Her face was tight with pain. She blinked as the reality of what happened washed over her. "The gunman. Did you stop him?"

Breck squeezed her hand.

"I'll get the doc."

He raced down the hallway. Conflicting priorities. Michelle was bleeding out. She needed surgery now or she was going to die. But a cartel killer was lurking behind one of these doors. And Danny—what happened to him? Was he shot or dying or dead?

Breck paused at his brother's room and looked in. The corner chair was in the middle of the room, knocked on its side. The bed was empty. The bathroom door had bullet holes in it and scuff marks where Zorrero must have kicked at it but the door held. Breck rattled the handle. It was locked.

"Danny! Danny!"

It was hard to think with the fire alarm going. Someone needed to shut it off. The Quandary Fire Department was only a couple of miles away. They should be here any second. And the State Patrol. Where were they?

"Breck? Is that you?" The door clicked and opened. Danny was unharmed. Terrified but unharmed. "Dude tried to swiss cheese me, man. But I laid flat in the tub. Bullets whizzing over like crazy. Holy hell, man. Look at me, I'm shaking like a leaf."

"Where did he go?"

Danny's face fell. "You haven't . . . you don't got him?"

"Lock the door. Wait till I come to get you."

Breck went out in the hall again, gun up and wary. Michelle was still lying where she fell. Her eyes were closed now and her back was arched funny. The clock was ticking.

He couldn't count how many times he'd been in this hospital. He had been in all the rooms at one time or another. The lab was at the far end by post-op and he went right to it and banged on the door.

"Dr. Heller. This is Sheriff Dyer."

The door swung open and the doctor peered out cautiously. Melinda was in there, too, kneeling behind a cabinet.

"Michelle needs your help. She's been shot. You gotta hurry."

Breck kept an eye on the other doors in the hall while he spoke. Most of the rooms were closed. The cartel man could be hiding behind any one of them. Which one was it?

"Did you see the shooter?" Breck asked.

"No. But we locked the door as soon as we heard the first gunshots."

"Grab a med kit. She's bleeding bad."

CHAPTER 90

Governing the Darkness

At the rear of the building, Jenny spotted the emergency exit door. It was probably locked, of course. How was she going to get in there? Suddenly it burst open and she was face to face with the cartel commander. Just like that night in the Sheriff's Office, with Freddy in the jail cell and fresh spring snow piled in the parking lot out front. It felt like a million years ago, so much had happened.

Jenny yanked out her 9mm Luger and Zorrero raised his Glock and they pointed their weapons at each other.

"Drop the gun, douchebag!" she shouted.

But he didn't. He smiled instead. A slow, easy smile. Absolute confidence.

The door swung back into place, clicking shut, muting the sound of the fire alarm. The sun was hanging above the west ridge, just about to drop out of sight. It was a warm sunny summer day, late in the afternoon. What was it? Wednesday? Thursday? Jenny couldn't even remember. She should be back at the office, fighting the fax machine. Or choking down a bad cup of coffee. Things like this never happened in Quandary. Ever since she took the job, the worst thing she saw was a fender bender on Main Street. The only reason she ever drew her sidearm was to oil it and put it away again.

"You pretty sneaky, waiting out here."

Zorrero took a step closer.

Jenny was already tense but she tensed up even more.

"Are you deaf? I said drop it."

He chuckled, a little playful. "Why don't you put that little pea shooter away?"

"Why don't you lay down in the grass and put your hands behind your back?"

But Zorrero took another step towards her. Jenny backed away, her feet shuffling. He was trying to intimidate her. Just like last time. She felt her gut knot up.

"You know who I am, yes?"

"I know you're a sick ass cartel freak who is leaving here in handcuffs."

He chuckled. "I am Commander Zorrero of Los Equis, in Monterrey. The deadliest narco-cartel in the entire free and sovereign state of Nuevo León. Now I am here. In this sleepy little mountain town. College girls on skis. Condos and hot tubs. Eggs sunny-side up at the Blue Moose café. I think I like it here."

Mind games. That was his style. But there was still something about him that made her feel very insecure. Even though she knew what he was trying to do. It was something about his manner. The look in his eyes.

"Yeah? Well, don't get used to it." Where was Breck? Jenny's fingers and arms were getting sore, she was gripping the Luger so tight. "They'll probably put you in the Supermax. That's down near Cañon City and let me be the first one to tell you . . . it's gonna suck."

Zorrero shrugged.

"I would not count on such a thing. Nothing can stop me from doing what I please. Not your laws. Your border walls. Your American *policía*. They're like the ants in the dirt. But I am the moon, governing the darkness. I have my own path across the night sky. The constellations are mine to command and there is nothing you can do about it. Except pray for the sunrise."

The fire alarm was still going off inside the building. Jenny could hear sirens somewhere up the road. The fire department, probably.

"One last chance." Her mouth was so dry. "I will shoot to kill."

The words did not affect him. He wasn't threatened by her. Not even a little bit. How many headlines had she read, in the last year alone? About the dark underbelly of Mexico. The death toll from the massive amount of cartel violence. Politicians murdered. Journalists murdered. A whole busload of college students simply vanished—killed and incinerated. Ashes and bone scattered in a river. Rival gang members tortured each other all the time. Hung by the neck. Dismembered. Set on fire with gasoline. And here was Jenny. A girl deputy in a small ski town in the middle of the Colorado mountains, five feet tall with fire-red hair, pointing a 9mm Luger like she was the one in control. No wonder he thought this all was a joke.

"Where are you from?" Zorrero asked. "Not from around here, huh? All by yourself in that tiny ol' rental cottage, eating peanut butter and yogurt. I don't know how you can drink that coconut water all the time. Tastes pretty sour to me."

Jenny's heart stopped.

"No husband. No boyfriend. Watching TV all night long." He shook his head like it was the saddest thing. "Who's that in the photograph? On your dresser? Your papa and mama? I bet they're so proud. Maybe I'll go to meet them. You think they like pizza?"

Chills ran through her. The cartel man had been *watching her*. Studying her for weakness. Even though she had both hands on the Luger the whole thing was trembling. No matter how hard she concentrated.

"Put your little pea shooter down," Zorrero said, with that soft smile and those dark cold eyes. *His* hands weren't trembling. The Glock was pointed right at her face. Who was the cat and who was the mouse?

With a bang, the emergency exit flew open. Breck raced out, and hearing the door Zorrero spun and swung the Glock around, firing, and Breck staggered, and Jenny pulled the trigger and she saw the cartel commander's head snap to one side and dark blots of blood spray up from his hair.

CHAPTER 91

The Dragon's Den

There was a light knock on Matthews' office door. Brittany. She leaned in the doorway, peering into the dragon's den and she was about to be vaporized in a whoosh of fire.

"What is it?"

"Your wife is here to see you, Mayor Matthews, sir. Should I let her in?"

Brittany was chewing gum, snapping it. Her little jaw flapped like hummingbird wings. The girl grated on his nerves. Why didn't he just fire her already? Matthews slammed his pen on the desk.

"*Ex*-wife. How many times do I have to tell you? It's called a divorce. And get rid of that gum. I don't want to see you chewing gum in this office ever again. It's unprofessional. Do you under-stand me?"

Whoosh. Vaporized. Brittany was gone. But Valerie Matthews appeared in the doorway, waving an envelope in the air—and she was ticked off.

"*Foreclosure?* The bank is taking my house, Seneca! What have you done this time?"

What was he going to say? I'm sorry. I mortgaged your home so I could buy a big building, turn it into a greenhouse, and grow an industrial amount of pot. But my business partners shot up the town and got shot to death themselves. The grow field was raided, the product seized. City council voted no anyhow, so I'm starting to think this might not be the best timing for an entrepre-neurial endeavor, after all.

"It's okay Val, just listen to me." He tried smiling. It didn't work. "I'm having a little legal dispute with Clear Span, but I called my lawyer and he's all over it. The fine print in their contract is completely misleading. They think sub-soil shouldn't be covered in the footing costs? Well, any reasonable person knows it is. They're in for a fight, let me tell you what. It may take a few days but I'll get every penny back. And more. I'm suing for false representation of contract."

He picked up a stainless-steel travel mug with the Clear Span logo on it. He held it out to her.

"They sent this to me when I first signed the deal. Why don't you take it? Pour your mimosas in here."

Valerie snatched it out of his hand and slammed it in the wastebasket.

"Unbelievable."

"I get it. You're upset." It wasn't going over as well as he hoped. Time for a magnanimous gesture. "Listen, it's not as bad as you think. That's just a Notice of Default. They're not foreclosing, or kicking you out, just because we missed a payment or two. Why don't you give me that envelope? I'll take care of it. And then, I am going to take you and Aspen shopping. Where is she? Is that her in your car?"

He tapped on the window.

"Hi, ptarmigan!"

Aspen was sitting in the passenger seat with a stack of Tupperware containers in her lap. Texting someone. Matthews tapped on the glass again but Aspen didn't look up. Someone needed to pry that cell phone out of her hand.

"We'll drive down to the shops in Dillon. I'll pay for everything."

He reached for the bank notice, but Valerie spun away and tucked it in her purse. "I'm showing this to *my* lawyer."

She stormed out of the office. Matthews watched her through the window. Stomp up the sidewalk, get in the car and slam the door. Race off down the street.

Sinking back into his chair, Matthews rubbed his eyes. That didn't go over very well. The Blue River Bank. What a bunch of incompetents. They were supposed to mail everything to his home, not hers. What was the name of that loan agent? Guy was gonna be out of a job.

CHAPTER 92

Meatballs and Mashed Potatoes

"Honey?" Valerie glanced over at her daughter. "You didn't want to go in and say hello to Brittany? Not even real quick?"

Aspen held up her phone.

"I did already."

Putting on the blinker, Valerie got into the turn lane. Waited for the traffic to pass. She stared at the big sign on the corner. *Quandary County Medical Center* was etched into a big slab of white Dakota sandstone. It was carefully landscaped. Ruby red Indian Paintbrush and yucca plants in a bed of river stones.

All this violence. And in a hospital! Churches. Schools. Hospitals. Places like that were supposed to be safe. Malls. Like the shops in Dillon. Maybe that would have been a good idea. Go shopping. Let Seneca pay for everything out of his dirty little pocket. He was caught up in all this, she could feel it. All he did was lie anymore.

What about the dark-colored SUV? Parked on the street across from her home. How many nights had it sat there? A man inside, just watching. Smoking cigarettes. She thought he might be a private investigator at first. Wouldn't be the first time Seneca had pulled that stunt. Well, she could watch, too. On the top shelf in the hall closet, there was a pair of binoculars she took to football games in Denver. Magnified, he looked foreign to Valerie. Suspicious. Certainly suspicious. He was no PI. She kept the curtains drawn just to keep the man's prying eyes out and then he stopped coming.

Then what about everything the sheriff said at the city council? His brother getting shot by suspected drug cartel men. Right there in Quandary County! Now, with the hospital shooting, everyone was talking. A man walked right inside the lobby in the middle of the day and shot the security guard and shot the receptionist and when Sheriff Dyer tried to stop him, he even got winged. And what about the pizza delivery man? Was that all about drugs, too?

"Mom?"

Valerie snapped out of it. The oncoming lane was empty and clear as far as the eye could see. Taking her foot off the brake, Valerie drove into the hospital parking lot and found an empty space.

Together, they both carried the Tupperware trays inside the lobby. Everything had been cleaned up. It looked like nothing had happened but Valerie still looked for evidence. Bullet holes in the wall, or broken windows, or blood stains on the floor. But there was nothing.

"Hi, Val. Can I help you?" Melinda was at the front desk this time. She smiled warmly. "So good to see you up and about, Aspen."

"We're here to see Michelle. And Dr. Heller, too." Valerie held up the Tupperware. "Home cooked meal for all the staff. You, too."

Melinda came around the reception desk and led the way down the hall, straight into Aspen's old hospital room. Michelle was in the bed, looking pale but she smiled when they came in.

"Hey, it's my gal pals."

"Hey girl," Valerie said. "Brought you all some real food. My daughter and I spent many nights right here in this very room, so I know exactly what you serve patients. I've got meatballs and mashed potatoes and asparagus."

It was a strange role reversal. To see Michelle in the bed. To be the visitor. But Michelle and Dr. Heller and Melinda had been a huge support after Aspen was brought in. Both times. The avalanche and the opioids.

Michelle brightened up considerably.

"This looks delicious. Thank you."

"I'll go see if Dr. Heller is free," said Melinda, and she headed up the hallway.

Aspen opened a big bag with silverware, plates, and napkins, while Valerie started to dish out the food. At that moment, there was a tap on the door frame. It was Sheriff Breck and Deputy Jenny. They must have had the same idea because they were carrying paper-wrapped Subway sandwiches.

"Sorry to interrupt," Jenny said. Then she sniffed the air. "What the . . .? Are those meatballs? Is that real food? Can I have some?"

Valerie passed her a plate. "I made a ton of this stuff."

Breck went over to the bed and held up a Subway sandwich. "You can't pass this up. It's a hero sandwich."

Michelle smiled. "You keep it."

"Can I speak with you for a moment, sheriff?" Valerie gave the serving spoon to Aspen, who began dipping meatballs onto Jenny's plate, and they stepped out in the hall.

"I understand you were wounded?"

Breck pulled his collar back far enough to reveal a white bandage beneath his shirt. "I've had bee stings that were worse."

How was she going to say this? Part of her hated her ex-husband. And part of her felt like he was a good man, deep down. Was she wrong about him? Wrong to think he was caught up in something shady? Or was she wrong about him being a good man?

"You okay, Valerie?"

She felt a lump in her throat. Breck had been the one to dig her daughter out of the snow slide. He had been the one to resuscitate her after the overdose. And he wasn't afraid to run into the hospital with an active shooter inside. There was no question who he was, what kind of man Breck was.

"I think Seneca is involved somehow," she whispered.

Breck raised an eyebrow. Waiting for more. Valerie shifted, looking around to make sure her daughter wasn't close enough to hear anything.

"I can't say for sure or point to any one thing. But something's off. This whole time something's been off. I think he had something to do with the drugs. Those cartel people."

"Why do you think that?"

"I'm not sure, but Seneca . . ."

She sighed. That was all she could say. Maybe she shouldn't have even said that much. What did she know for certain, anyhow? That Seneca wanted to legalize cannabis? That he seemed distant and disengaged when his own daughter overdosed on drugs? That he used her home for collateral, without her knowledge, so he could build some kind of big empty facility, and only God knows why? Or that a strange car was parked across the street? With a strange man. Watching . . .

"Mom?" It was Aspen. "I dipped you out some dinner and it's getting cold."

"Here I come, honey."

Valerie followed her daughter back inside.

CHAPTER 93

Bad Fuel Pump

Jenny unzipped the passenger window to let in the fresh summer air. They were in Breck's Jeep, driving to the shops in Dillon, and they stopped at a McDonald's drive-through. Some middle-aged lady leaned out, listening.

The engine had a distinct whir.

"I've had that problem before." She spoke in a sage tone. "It's a bad fuel pump."

Breck pulled twenty dollars out of his wallet and handed it to her.

"Can I get two cream in my coffee?" he asked.

Jenny leaned over the gear shift so she could get her attention. "Don't put any in mine, please. I like mine black as death."

The lady leaned back in the window.

"It's the racing gears," Breck said. "That's what she's hearing."

"My coffee better be black."

"Just taste it before we drive away."

The Jeep had that old car smell. What was it? The original vinyl seats? They were cracked and split and yellow foam was seeping through. Jenny sank back and gazed outside. Cars were driving by on the highway and pulling in and out of the gas station next to the McDonald's. A group of bicyclists passed by in the bike lane. Jenny could hear their voices as they glided past, one guy was talking about his daughter. She was in the third grade now.

"Life goes on, doesn't it?"

Breck was half-heartedly trying to unwind the CB cord from the gear shift, but he didn't say anything.

Black as death. Jenny cringed at her own word choice. She shouldn't have said that. The whole reason they were in Dillon was so Breck could buy a suit jacket and tie. He didn't have anything decent to wear to Freddy's funeral. There were several high-end outlet stores that sold suits. Tommy Hilfiger. Calvin Klein. Ralph Lauren. There were a lot of good options and if it was her she'd spend an hour trying on a dozen just to find the right one, but she already knew what would happen. Breck would go in the first shop and go straight to the clearance rack and buy the first one that fit. Then he would head into the camping store and look at headlamps.

Back at the Sheriff's Office, the latest copy of *Rock & Ice* magazine was waiting in the mailbox, and in the product reviews, there was a whole article on headlamps. Breck was obsessed with them and there were two at the top of the editor's recommendation list. Which brand should he get? The Petzl or Black Diamond? The Petzl headlamp was retina-scalding bright. Rated at 600 lumens, it would light up a trail at midnight like it was noon. But it ran off four AAA batteries so how much did that thing weigh? It must be heavy. How long before it started chafing his forehead? The Black Diamond was only rated at 350 lumens but it was super lightweight. Plus, it had a red-light setting for a soft glow. Much easier on the eyes when he was setting up a tent or reading a map. Which one was better? Bright or lightweight? What did Jenny think? Jenny couldn't care less and she told him so, but that didn't stop him from talking about it.

But all she could think about was Freddy. The funeral was in a couple of hours and they had to buy Breck a suit coat and tie and drive back to the Quandary cemetery, and Jenny still needed to go home and take a shower and dig through her closet. She had a dress, but she hadn't worn it for a long time. When was the last time she'd gone out to some nice restaurant? Or dancing? All she did anymore was work, work, work. Or stay home and watch Netflix. Johnny Tibbs had asked her out on a date again. *I don't know too many women who can get shot off a horse and then go shoot a drug lord in the skull.* He was alternately charming and annoying. Maybe she should go ahead and let him buy her a steak. No one else was asking. What, were they intimidated by the badge? Probably. Whatever it was, it was getting old. And life was short.

"You might want to get that fuel pump looked at."

The drive-through lady handed Breck a paper sack and then carefully passed him two cups of hot coffee.

"Thanks, I will."

He pulled around the building and parked in the shade of a big spruce tree. As soon as he cut the engine, the whirring sound of the racing gears stopped. It wasn't a bad fuel pump, but Jenny could understand why someone would think that. Why put racing gears in anything except race cars? It was a unique sound, and if you hadn't heard it before . . .

"Dang it, Breck." Jenny leaned out the window and poured her coffee onto the asphalt.

"Hold on." He popped the lid off his cup. It was black. "This one is yours."

"Oops."

"Not a big deal. Give it to me. I'll run back inside."

She traded him coffee cups. Breck got out of the Jeep and headed inside the McDonald's.

Just before they left Quandary that morning, District Attorney Brownton had called. At 8 o'clock on the nose. Jenny barely got the front door unlocked when the phone started ringing. The man was officially opening an investigation into corruption charges. It was ridiculous. Breck wasn't corrupt. He had just busted a drug cartel commander, and shut down an entire grow field! Who could possibly think he was working with the cartel?

The legality of it all was confusing. Breck was an elected official. No one could fire him, could they? Maybe the governor? But at the very least, a corruption investigation would be bad press and Breck was up for re-election next year. He would be campaigning under a cloud of suspicion, so the timing was terrible. If the newspaper got hold of the story, it would land on everyone's doorstep. Even worse, what if the Denver news stations showed up at the Sheriff's Office with cameras? That didn't sound like fun.

Who the hell called the governor in the first place? This was going to be ugly. And the DA was a pit bull. It was like someone was trying to sabotage his campaign for re-election before it even got started. Maybe somebody was.

"Mayor Matthews. That douche."

The sack crinkled when she opened it. Two Egg McMuffins. Classic. Cheap. Good. Better than the gas station hot dogs from the General Merchandise and More, that was for sure.

Jenny started to unwrap her sandwich but decided to wait. Breck would be back soon.

About the Author

MARK MITTEN an American author whose work is primarily set in the Old West or contemporary Colorado. His novels *Sipping Whiskey in a Shallow Grave* and *Hard To Quit* were both nominated for Peacemaker Awards. Mitten is a member of the Western Writers of America. He resides in Winsted, Minnesota, with his wife Mary.

Made in the USA
Monee, IL
05 May 2021